D1238314

MY BIG,
FAT DESI
WEDDING

PAGE STREET YA

A YA ROMANCE ANTHOLOGY

MY BIG, FAT DESI WEDDING

EDITED BY
PRERNA PICKETT

PAGE STREET YA

Contents

The Season Begins
AN AUNTIE'S PERSPECTIVE

The cottage smelled like cardamom and sugar. Potted plants with leaves of green crawled along the corners of the room, hung from the ceiling, stretched across the mantel above the fireplace in the cozy living room. Light from the small window above the sink streamed onto the invitations strewn across the round kitchen table. Envelopes colored in whites, reds, and one even in black.

A breeze shifted through the room as the invitee strolled across the kitchen, a cup of chai in hand. She pulled out a chair and stared at all the envelopes, placing the cup on a rainbow-hued coaster.

Which ones would she attend this season? There were so many choices, so many places to visit. California, India, New York . . . So many love stories to unfold and promises to be made.

The romantic in her shivered with excitement. Weddings were her favorite. Big declarations of love, gold-spun dresses, glittering jewelry, dramatic interactions with family members, and the food. Oh, the food.

She moved the pile around, closed her eyes, and grabbed a handful. She'd used this same method every time during shaadi season. A season of her creation. Opening her eyes to the dusty blue-colored room, she stared at the invitations she'd chosen. The right ones always found her. The ones she needed to witness and perhaps the ones that needed her help.

A soft smile pulled at her mouth as she read the announcements. Oh, yes, these invitations held the promise of age-defying romances and love. It was going to be an incredible season.

The Disaster Wedding

PRERNA PICKETT

"This is going to be a disaster."

My heart lodged in my throat as soon as the words were out of my mouth. I swallowed, stared at the ten-mile-long traffic jam filling my view as I sat behind the wheel, and prayed like there was no tomorrow that no one heard me. Despite the sunny day, the fluffy white clouds dotting the periwinkle sky, doom settled into my belly.

"I can't believe you just said that," Dev piped up from the back seat where Priti had banished him.

And there went any hope of escaping.

No. No. I needed to keep a positive attitude. There was still a chance nothing would happen.

I glared at Dev in the rearview mirror, and he had the audacity to raise his brows as if to challenge me. Letting out a huff of air, I moved my head to the side, trying to see if the line had moved up at all since the last time I checked fifteen seconds ago. The LAX exit sign taunted me in response.

"No, seriously, you do realize what you just said, right?" Dev said, louder.

Of course he wasn't going to let it go.

"Yes, I know exactly what I said, and it is the perfect summation of the situation I currently find myself in. Nothing more." Please, nothing more.

"Words have consequences." He gave a quick shake of his head and went back to staring at his phone.

Words have consequences. A phrase our mother often muttered in our home. Careful what you say, because those words hold power, and they could come to pass. Consequences because the women in my family had a tendency to make things happen with those words, for better or for worse.

Better or worse. Funny that term came to mind. I had wedding on the brain. My sister's nuptials that would take place in three days. Laxmi, Mumma, and Papa were currently situated at Grant's family's beach house in Santa Barbara while I navigated the seventh circle of hell, also known as LA traffic.

And for what? Correction, for who?

The bane of my existence himself, Grant's half brother, Damian Bastian. His original flight had been delayed and he missed the connecting flight and got diverted to LA.

"Why can't you pick him up? You're not coming up until later today anyway," Mumma had asked earlier that morning.

I seriously regretted convincing my parents to let Dev and me stay behind so we wouldn't lose too much time at school for the wedding. My mom warned me it wasn't a good idea. She said I would regret it. And look at that. I did. Severely. Words had consequences.

In this case, I wished my mother's words didn't carry so much weight and weren't laughing their asses off at me.

"Finally," I said as the never-ending line in front of me started moving.

"What do you think is going to happen exactly?" Priti asked.

My brother looked up from his phone. "Oh, I'm sorry, are we talking now?"

I clenched my jaw. My best friend and brother dating didn't bother me that much anymore; honestly, they were made for each other. But there were times I wished the two of them had never fallen in love in the fifth grade. Like when they decided to get into a fight about college right before I had to drive us all the way up to Santa Barbara for the next couple of hours and get there in time for the Sagan ceremony, the opening event for the wedding weekend.

"You know what happens. You've seen it in action. She said it's a disaster and now everything will be."

"It's just a superstition. Our entire family is entirely too 'stitious if you ask me. Mumma has gotten all these weird things about magic and manifestation into our heads." But, who was I kidding? Our family wouldn't be so 'stitious if there wasn't truth behind the stories.

I gripped the steering wheel and took a long breath through my nose.

"And curses. Don't forget the curses," Priti chimed in.

I cast her a glance that said she so wasn't helping, and she mumbled an apology.

But she wasn't wrong. There had been talk of a curse. One placed on a distant aunt by a witch. This all took place in their village back in India well before I was born. It seemed so unfair that I had to deal with the consequences of an ancestor's actions. Cruel, even.

An unwelcome niggle pecked at my brain and a shiver ran down my spine. The air had shifted. Just a hint, like someone had sucked 10 percent of it out of the car.

"You feel that?" Dev asked, sitting forward until his head was in between my and Priti's seats.

"This is NOT going to be a disaster," I said, loudly this time. Maybe saying those words would erase the ones I said previously.

"You know that's not how it works," Dev said with that signature annoying smirk.

Pursing my lips, I pushed him back and started inching the car forward. The inch turned into feet, and before I knew it, we were pulling off the exit.

"Guess you were wrong," I said.

"Not the first time," Priti huffed.

Dev stuck his tongue out.

"Oh my gosh, what are you, five?" Priti hissed.

"Would you two stop? Dev, please text he who shall not be named that we're about to pull up, and he needs to be ready to go."

"Got it. Texting *Damian* now." Dev started texting before I could finish my sentence, naming the name I didn't want uttered with a pointed look and a smirk that made me want to reach back and smack the phone out of his hand.

Probably because he and Damian texted quite often. More often than I liked. The fact that my brother made friends everywhere he went while I only made enemies was a source of many of my irritations. It wasn't that I didn't like people, or didn't try, I just had resting bitch face and didn't care to fix it.

"He says he's good to go."

"He better be." I narrowed my eyes as the memory of my first encounter with Damian flashed across my mind.

The ice cream, his face, the smug smile, the ice cream on his face. The smug smile removed. That got me to smile.

Then I remembered the absolute berating I received from my parents and sister right after it happened. They grounded me for a month, and I had to write an apology text to Damian. That was the last time I had any correspondence with him. He texted back, but I deleted the message before reading it. Sure, we'd seen each other here and there since the incident, but we both made sure to pretend like the other didn't exist. It was an unspoken understanding between the two of us.

The only person who got a kick out of that ice cream event? Dev. Who was now best friends with my enemy. He'd laughed his butt off when it initially happened, but changed his tune after I got a tongue lashing from Mumma and Papa. I never mentioned that he was the one who told me to do it. That little secret I kept to myself and would reserve use for when I really needed it. I cast my older brother a look, but he wasn't paying attention. He was too busy smiling at whatever Damian had texted back.

Both Dev and I were seniors even though Dev was older than me. Not because he'd failed but because we'd always been in the same grade. Dev and I were Irish twins. Dev was born in June and then Mumma found out she was pregnant in August. I came along that May. We were also in the same grade because Mumma wanted us to have each other. Not that it did us any good after kindergarten. Dev and I always kind of resented the other, but such was life. We dealt with it in our own ways. He by dating my best friend, me by complaining about it.

Laxmi was six years older than us. Our parents had trouble having another kid until the two of us came along. Mumma said we were penance for her past mistakes. Not that we were all that awful. It was just, Laxmi had always been the perfect, dutiful daughter. And Dev and I were both hardheaded and . . . the opposite of dutiful.

We finally made it to the airport exit lane. LAX was an absolute nightmare to navigate. It made no sense whatsoever, and part of me thought it was built as a psychological testing facility. The test? To gauge human reactions to the absolute nonsense way they'd set up said airport. The one and only other time I'd driven there to pick up Laxmi, I ended up getting lost. It took almost an hour to figure out how to get to the baggage claim.

This time I felt much better prepared. Or at least that was what I told myself in order to keep the anxiety at bay. My gut clenched, and I immediately regretted eating that breakfast burrito we got from our favorite local 24-hour Mexican restaurant. The faint taste of chorizo and egg started to come back up. Grabbing my water bottle, I took a small sip to push the food back down where it belonged.

A few minutes later, I found the airline Damian used and pulled up in front of the baggage claim. Familiar puffy blond hair moved through the crowd as Damian appeared like an unwanted mirage in the middle of the sidewalk. He waved his hand like I hadn't already spotted him, making my irritation rub raw.

I pulled the car up to the curb and waited for him to get in. "See, not a complete disaster," I told my brother smugly.

Then Priti started unbuckling.

"What are you doing?" I asked, reaching out a hand to stop her.

"Sitting in the back so Damian can sit here." She pulled her signature curls into a messy bun before grabbing her purse from the ground.

"No. Why?"

"Dev and I have to figure our shit out before we get to the beach house, that's why."

"You're going to make me talk about my feelings, aren't you?" my brother asked with panic dripping through his words.

"Yes. And we're going to fix this before it blows up." She eyed my brother, her cheekbones turning even sharper with her serious gaze.

"Priti, please, don't do this." I reached for her arm as she pushed open the passenger side door. But it was too late, and I caught air.

Priti got out and gave Damian a hug before opening the back door. Damian bent over and looked at me.

"Hey, Jaanu," he said. "Mind if I take this seat?" The familiar green of his eyes flashed my way.

"Whatever."

The smile dropped. "So, it's going to be like that, huh?"

"Yup." I flared my nostrils and moved my gaze to the windshield.

Dozens of people walked out of the airport. Buses and cars filled the roadway, moving in and out like puzzle pieces clunkily coming together. It was a dangerous combination, the vehicles and the people.

Damian sighed and walked back to the trunk to put his suitcase away. I watched him heft it in, a weary expression on his brow.

"Be nice," Priti said, pinching my arm.

"Ow." I swatted her hand away and grumbled a "Leave me alone." I could be nice. I was perfectly nice. Okay, sometimes I was nice.

But where Damian was concerned? It would take practice. Maybe being nice wouldn't be all that hard. He'd spent yesterday and most of today in cramped airplanes to make it to his brother's wedding, after all. It would be fine.

Nothing was fine.

We made it to the beach house, yes, so that was all well and good, but the actual ride? What should have been an easy two-hour commute up to Santa Barbara turned into three and a half hours of torture.

Dev and Priti kept whispering and making out in between those whispered conversations. Disgusting. Which left Damian and me with nothing to do but . . . not talk. I was fine with not talking, more than happy not to acknowledge his existence, but he insisted on trying to bury the hatchet, as he called it. What seventeen-year-old even spoke like that? He sounded like my dad.

"The hatchet is perfectly fine where it is," I had told him, squeezing the steering wheel. It was my only form of therapy in the car at that moment.

"Look, we need to be on the same side for this weekend. After it's over, you can go back to hating me."

He'd made sense. I didn't want to ruin Laxmi's big weekend. She and Grant had been engaged for almost two years.

I reluctantly agreed. I thought that meant we could spend the rest of the car ride in silence, but no. Damian had to keep trying to engage me in conversations that didn't interest me. Then the traffic only got worse because of an accident. Not unusual, in fact I should have planned for it, but it felt like those words I'd spoken earlier were definitely coming to pass. Oh, and it started raining. Heavily. Perfect pre-wedding weather.

By the time I pulled up to the beach house, I was all talked out, and I needed space from Damian. ASAP. Which wasn't exactly possible given the fact that the Sagan and Chunni ceremony was supposed to already be underway and had to be delayed because we weren't there. Tomorrow was the Sangeet and mehndi party, and then Saturday was the official wedding.

After slamming the car door, I ran to the trunk to grab my things and get inside before I got soaked. Damian beat me to it of course and insisted on helping me.

"I've got it," I said, reaching for my bag.

"No, it's not a problem." He reached for it at the same time and our hands touched. I pulled mine back like it had been burned.

Damian furrowed his brows. "I don't have the cheese touch if that's what you're worried about."

I rolled my eyes as rain made my sweatshirt heavier. Priti let out a laugh as she joined us.

"The cheese touch! I haven't heard of that since elementary school."

I glared at my best friend for laughing at Damian's ridiculous attempt at comedy. Priti shrugged and grabbed her own bag without giving me another thought. I pulled my bag out of Damian's hand and rushed inside, using my purse as an umbrella.

The house smelled like a mixture of sunscreen and spice. The sound of chattering uncles, aunties, and cousins blended with the crashing waves.

A calm stirred beneath my breastbone. I loved coming to the beach house. Grant invited us up often, and our family took full advantage every time we visited. Only family members were allowed to stay at the house that week, and the wedding was taking place at a nearby ranch.

The calm quickly disappeared when Mumma came rushing over to greet us, her face set in fury, her bright blue sari flashing beneath the fluorescent lighting.

"Finally! We have been waiting forever." Her dark eyes grew big, her thick brows lowered in annoyance, with the bright lipstick she wore pulled thin.

I shook my head. "Sorry, Mumma. The traffic was insane."

"This is what happens when you don't listen to your mother. I told you that you should have come up with us earlier in the week."

"I had a calc test! You know I couldn't miss that." Keeping my grades up was vitally important. Nothing was going to stop me from keeping my GPA at 4.2.

"Hurry. You need to get upstairs and get dressed so we can get started. Oh, hi Damian." Mumma's demeanor immediately changed when she spotted Damian at my back, putting on her million-dollar smile.

"Hi, Mrs. Atwal, it's good to see you again."

And there Damian went putting on his charm.

"Priti, let's get upstairs and change," I said over my shoulder, ready to get away from Damian.

Priti unglued herself from Dev's side. The two had been busy whispering and giggling behind me. Their fight was officially over. Thank goodness.

"That really wasn't so bad," declared Priti once we closed the door to our room behind us.

I gave her a pointed stare.

"Not a disaster, anyways," she added.

Throwing my suitcase on the bed, I quickly unpacked my things. Priti did have a point. All things considered, it wasn't a complete disaster. We were late for the Sagan, but nothing unmanageable.

"Not bad. Sure."

I browsed the three beds situated in the small room. Priti, Laxmi, and I were all sharing a room for the wedding week. The bed next to the window appeared to be Laxmi's. Her favorite stuffed animal, a worn white polar bear, sat on top of the perfectly made bed. Rain hit the window, creating a tinkling sound inside the room.

"Damian seems to have forgotten the whole fiasco from the first time you met. That must be a relief," Priti continued, prying with that little hint of a question to her words.

"Such a relief." What a lie. My entire body stood on edge, waiting for the moment Damian would finally address that elephant and take his revenge. I had to be prepared.

We both grabbed the garment bags with our lehengas hanging in the closet. Mumma absolutely refused to allow us to pack them on our own. They were much too precious and beautiful.

Priti used the bathroom in the bedroom first while I unpacked my makeup and hair products. I needed to get dressed and ready in less than fifteen minutes, which was next to impossible.

"Sister!" Laxmi burst through the door, her dark hair flying over her shoulders. "You're here!" She pulled me into a tight hug that left me out of breath and startled. "I'm so glad you made it." Laxmi pulled away and took my face in her hands. Her light brown eyes were bright, but bloodshot. She smelled bitter, like alcohol.

I made a face and pulled away from her. "Are you drunk?"

Laxmi walked past me and threw herself onto my bed, face to the ceiling. She wore a pink lehenga with woven golden threading, which she would most definitely wrinkle if I didn't get her to sit up immediately. Hurrying to the bed, I pulled her up and she wobbled a little.

"I'm not drunk. I don't drink. Remember? Mumma and Papa would be ever so disappointed in me if I did."

She was correct. She didn't drink and our parents would definitely have something to say about her behavior if they found out. Shit. The ceremony hadn't even started and my sister was plastered?

Laxmi sighed. "I'm getting married," she said to herself. I don't think she remembered that I was standing right next to her.

"Isn't that great?" She didn't respond. "Lax, what's wrong?"

"Mumma and Papa have been arguing with Kristin and Michael about the flower arrangements for hours."

Of course. My parents and Grant's parents didn't always see eye to eye on things. Our parents were much more traditional, and the Bastians? Well, they were rich and white. Their beliefs and lifestyle didn't always align with ours. But everyone had put aside their differences to make this wedding possible. Grant's parents adored Laxmi and everyone was excited those two were finally tying the knot.

"I'm sorry."

Laxmi sniffled. I froze. My sister did not cry. Ever. I grabbed the tissue box on the nightstand and blotted the tears before they could slip down her face and ruin her makeup.

"Then Vayla masi wouldn't stop complaining about the food we served while waiting for you guys, and someone else was making snide comments about the fact that I'm going to wear a white dress and do a western ceremony along with the Hindu ceremony, and then Grant's aunt Mabel, who's definitely a racist, started in on how she can't abide Indian food. It's just overwhelming. I don't know what to do. Everything has been so great lately, and then today it's like no one is happy. The last few hours have been a complete disaster."

Warning bells sounded in my head as my ears latched onto the word *disaster*. Oh no. No, no, no. I gulped. This had nothing to do with what I said earlier. It was simply a coincidence.

"Lax? Where are you?" The deep, booming voice of Grant Bastian carried down the hallway.

Laxmi covered her eyes with her hands. "Oof, why is the room spinning?"

Panicked, I quickly exited the room and shut the door behind me just as Grant appeared at the end of the hall with Damian at his heels. Wonderful.

"Hey, Jaanu, have you seen your sister?" Grant's blond brows furrowed with concern.

I once again marveled at how different he and Damian appeared. Grant had brown eyes, Damian had green eyes. Grant had a dimple on his chin, Damian did not. Grant also wore a stern look at all times, like anything and everything was of grave concern, whereas Damian had an open face and smiled freely. Why the hell was I standing there comparing the two brothers while my drunk sister cried in the bedroom?

It was strange to see Grant in a pink kurta that matched my sister's lehenga. He must really love her if he ditched his usual, boring button-downs and khakis for something so much more colorful.

"Um. She just needed to a minute to . . ." *Think, Jaanu!* "Fix her hair!" I exclaimed, making Grant jump back a little.

Grant's features smoothed over. "Oh good. Tell her one of your aunts was asking for her."

"Which one?" I had a few. My dad had two sisters and my mom had two of her own, and that didn't include their cousins, who were also considered our masis, as well as my parents' own aunts.

Grant frowned. "Uhhhh . . . the one who likes to talk about her son who goes to Harvard, I think?"

Tara masi. Or Terror masi, as I liked to call her.

"Okay, I'll let her know. You should go back downstairs and mingle. I'm sure everyone is so excited to finally meet your family." I grabbed Grant's arm, turned him around, and pushed him down the hall. Thankfully he didn't resist and gave me a quick wave before disappearing down the stairs.

I leaned back against the wall, relief slinking through me.

"What's going on?" Damian asked once Grant left.

I let out a surprised yelp. I totally forgot he was there. "What makes you think anything is wrong?"

"Jaanu!" Laxmi's cry echoed through the walls. "I think I'm going to puke!"

Damnit. I rushed into the room and quickly searched the premises for a puke bucket. A trash can sat in the corner next to my bed. I ran for it and shoved it beneath my sister's wobbling chin just as the first wave hit her. She clutched the sides of the trash can.

"Is she drunk?" Damian asked, face cringing.

Once Laxmi got done with all the puking, I laid her on my bed, grabbed the trash can, holding it out while suppressing a gag, and signaled for Damian to follow me. We headed to the bathroom down the hall since Priti was in the one in our room, where I flushed down the evidence of my sister's drunkenness.

"What's going on, Jaanu?" Damian asked once I washed my hands.

"Lax is . . . overwhelmed. There's been a lot of drama between family members."

"Did Aunt Mabel tell her she and my brother were going to make beautiful babies because mixed-raced babies are always beautiful?" Damian made a face like just saying the words made his insides cringe.

I shook my head. "No. Maybe. I don't know. It's mostly people being hangry and jealous and who knows what else."

And maybe I jinxed the wedding by saying it was going to be a disaster.

"Oh. That explains the knuckle cracking."

Grant only cracked his knuckles when he got anxious.

I thought of my sister getting drunk and feeling overwhelmed. She and Grant deserved an awesome wedding. And I had to fix what I had broken by speaking those words.

"I need to fix this."

Damian furrowed his brows. "What do you mean you have to fix it?"

I opened my mouth and closed it again. The last time I discussed my family's "gift" with Damian, he'd laughed, called me ridiculous, and I'd shoved my ice cream cone into his face.

He looked me up and down, eyes fixed on my clenched jaw. "Does this have something to do with . . ." His voice trailed off and he mimicked a wizard using a wand.

"It's not a spell," I hissed at him.

He threw his hands up in surrender. "You don't happen to have any ice cream on you by chance?"

I bared my teeth at him, and he laughed.

"This isn't funny."

He shook his head. "Look, I'm sorry for the way I acted when you and Laxmi told me about the whole words having power thing with the women in your family." I stiffened with surprise at this apology. "But you can't really think what's happening is your fault."

And the surprise melted to annoyance.

He still didn't get it. He probably never would until he ended up caught in the words-have-consequences web. Okay, I called my family too 'stitious, but only because I was trying to downplay just how badly I'd messed up. I'd seen what happened when women in our family said the wrong thing, when the intention behind our words didn't match the tone just right. Grant had even witnessed it in action and was a believer.

One of the reasons women in my family didn't drink? Because when they did, they said things that got them into a lot of trouble. Or other people into a lot of trouble.

"I said that today was going to be a disaster earlier, and now everything is falling apart for the first time since this whole wedding business started." I turned away from him and paced the hallway, trying to get him to understand the gravity of the situation. "My sister does not drink, Damian. Ever. Our parents have been trying to make this wedding go as smoothly as possible and now everything goes wrong? It's not a coincidence."

Damian leaned back and crossed his arms. I did not like the look he gave me down his nose. I didn't like that I had to look up at him at all. He was taller than six feet and towered over me. I instinctively found myself puffing up my chest, trying to make myself taller. Damian made a fist and coughed into it. He was definitely trying to cover a laugh. I narrowed my eyes at him.

"Don't you think you're being a little . . . dramatic?"

He. Did. Not. Just. Say. That.

He swallowed. "I'm sorry. That's not what I meant—I mean that wasn't the right thing to say."

"No, it wasn't."

He released a breath and ran his hand through his thick hair. "I don't know why I always say the wrong thing when I'm around you."

I loosened my defensive posture. Damian appeared defeated. And truly apologetic. "Let's just move on. And I'm sorry, too. For throwing that cone at your face."

The corner of his mouth turned up. "You're forgiven. Maybe I can help you 'undisaster' this wedding to make up for my wrongs."

I squinted at him, still a little suspicious of his sudden change in attitude.

"Um. Sure."

I'd let him help for now, but if he said or did anything to mock my family's curse, he would pay for it later.

Damian hurried downstairs to get Laxmi a cup of coffee. Sending him away while I figured out how to really fix things seemed like a way for both of us to win. Besides, we needed Laxmi to sober up immediately. Priti finished getting dressed, and I caught her up on everything.

"Oh no. Your brother is never going to let us live this one down."

I snorted. "He'll be insufferable." More than usual. If there was one thing Dev loved more than Priti in this world, it was being right.

Laxmi lay on the bed, clutching her stomach, mumbling something about Mabel and shoving teacakes up her homophobic butt? My guess was at some point Mabel made a comment about Grant and Damian's lesbian aunt. Very Mabel-like behavior.

I went to get dressed and texted Mumma that Laxmi's stomach was acting up because of the nerves (which was partially true—my sister's stomach tended to get upset when she was anxious), and that we would be down soon. Keeping suspicion at bay was our number one priority.

I got dressed and did my hair and my makeup in record time. My hair, though straight, was thick and difficult to manage, especially on humid days, so I just sprayed some water into it and put in some product to give it a wavy look. It didn't go exactly as planned. It only got poofier, messier, and my makeup looked way too shiny. More disastrous behavior sent to me by the universe.

"How is she?"

Priti stood by as Laxmi drank a steaming cup of coffee. Damian must have dropped it off. I shoved down the little niggle of surprise and suspicion. Damian's sudden change in behavior would take some getting used to.

"Better, I th—oh my gosh, what happened to your hair?" Priti said with an audible gasp.

"Are you wearing a wig?" Laxmi tilted her head and narrowed her eyes, peering closer.

"I know. It's awful, but I can't do anything about it right now. Lax, how are you feeling?"

Laxmi answered by taking another gulp of the coffee and then hissing in pain, because of the temperature. "Better. Dizzy, but better. I think I can make it through the ceremony."

"Good. Let's get this show on the road. Mumma is going to burst through that door if we don't get downstairs now."

Priti and I helped Laxmi stand up. I inspected her perfectly altered lehenga and makeup and hair to make sure nothing was out of place. Once that was done, we placed her in the middle, which allowed her to use us as crutches.

The beach house bustled with activity. The sweet scent of incense layered the air. The Sagan and Chunni event was more of a welcoming into each other's families with gift exchanges and a ceremony of sorts where the groom's mother or sisters placed red chunni on the bride's head.

I had only attended one other desi wedding, and that was when I was six, so I had very little memory other than being bored during the actual wedding and having a blast at the reception. You know, kid stuff.

"There you are!" Mumma bustled over to us, using her false cheerful tone. "Is everything okay?" she asked under her breath when she reached our sides.

"All good."

Priti and I helped Laxmi to the couch while the crowd of masis, masus, aunts, uncles, and cousins gathered. There were about thirty people total, but it felt like so much more. Tomorrow morning was the mehndi party, and then tomorrow night the sangeet, which would be a much bigger event, was being held at the country club.

Grant sat on the couch with Damian standing next to him. Mumma and Papa began the event by welcoming everyone. The caterers passed out refreshments, which helped quiet the room because everyone was too busy chewing to complain or gossip.

Laxmi appeared mostly recovered and even sent Grant a watery smile. He smiled back, although a frown wrinkled along his forehead. The caterers passed out glasses to everyone. Champagne for the adults and apple juice for everyone else.

"We're so grateful to the Bastians for hosting us today," Papa said, raising his champagne glass. "And are excited to finally join our families." Everyone else also raised their glasses, preparing to drink. "We are proud of our children for taking this step." Dad continued his speech, but my eyes were on my sister.

"I can't do this," Laxmi said under her breath, staring at the glass like it was poison.

My heart thudded in my chest. Damian grimaced while Priti exchanged a look of concern with me and leaned over to whisper in Dev's ear. Thinking quickly, I stepped in front of my sister, blocking her from view, squatted down so we were eye level, and pretended to fix her hair while exchanging our glasses.

"Thanks," she said, eyes glistening.

"Get it together, sis," I said, trying not to be too harsh.

She nodded and cleared her throat. I stepped away from her and stood up.

"To becoming family," Dad finished his speech and took a sip of his drink with everyone following his lead after repeating his words.

I schooled my face and took a sip of the champagne and pretended like it wasn't the most disgusting thing I had ever tasted. I'd had sips of alcohol here and there, but champagne? No thank you. It was the worst.

Everyone clapped and we proceeded to the next part of the ceremony. Gifts were exchanged by family members, Dad put a tikka on Grant's forehead, Grant's mom placed the veil, or chunni, over Laxmi's head, and it all went on without my sister puking.

It felt like it went by too slow, yet much more quickly than I anticipated.

"Congrats." Damian approached me out on the deck.

The rain hadn't let up, but we were sheltered beneath the gazebo-like structure.

I'd just finished catching up with a couple of my cousins on Papa's side of the family who had flown in from India. It was so good to see them in person. Sure, dealing with the gossiping masis annoyed me, but they were few and far between, and most everyone was excited to be there to celebrate the nuptials.

"Thanks," I said, brushing my hair back from my face. All I wanted was to put it up in a messy bun. I know it hadn't improved from earlier in the day.

Damian kept glancing at it and hiding a smile behind his hand every time our eyes met. It was my own fault. I'd cursed myself.

"I'm sorry, what are you congratulating me for?"

"For managing to get through that whole ordeal without anyone suspecting your sister was drunk."

"Grant knows something is up," I retorted. He'd kept an eye on Laxmi all afternoon.

"I told him she ate something that didn't sit well."

"Thanks, I appreciate that."

"So, what's the game plan?" he asked.

"Yeah, what's the game plan?"

Damian and I turned in time to catch Dev and Priti stepping out to join us. Priti made sure to close the sliding door behind them so we would have some privacy.

"I had to tell him," Priti explained with an apologetic squeeze to my arm.

"I swear if you say I told you so, I will kick you in the nuts."

Dev rolled his eyes. "Fine. Now, what are we going to do?"

"Can you take the words back?" Damian asked. It was strange to see him in the deep purple kurta. He pulled at the neckline and appeared uncomfortable. I momentarily thought about teasing him, but I knew he took the whole cultural appropriation thing seriously. Dev mentioned he'd texted and made sure it was okay for him to wear one.

"That's not how it works," I stated. "I actually don't really know how it works."

None of us did. Not really. We just said things with enough power behind them and they happened. But not all the time. Like I couldn't say "I won a million dollars" and magically get that money. Whoever placed that particular curse on our family would pay someday. It only seemed to happen when we believed. Like earlier. I fully believed the day would be a disaster, and now everything was. Wonderful.

Words have consequences.

I cast a glance at Damian to read his reaction.

He didn't scoff or roll his eyes. I let out a breath and relaxed my shoulders.

"We just need to watch out for anything that might be disaster-like," I suggested. "Disaster potential?" I frowned, playing with the words in my head.

I stared into the house, watching everyone mingle. Some family members were heading back to their hotels, a few still lingering. Laxmi and Grant stood in the corner of the room, hidden from everyone inside. Tension pressed against their faces.

"I'll go see what's up," Damian volunteered, his gaze glued to the same scene.

"We'll make sure no one sees them." Dev and Priti headed inside.

And I remained stuck where I was, feeling like the worst sister ever for ruining Laxmi's wedding weekend. What would the day have been like if I hadn't said those words? Probably filled with joy. Instead a dark smear hovered in the air, waiting to curl around any and all joyous moments. I refused to allow that to happen.

"This wedding is *not* going to be a disaster," I said out loud. "My sister deserves the best wedding ever."

Maybe I couldn't take back what I said, but I could speak something better into existence. The universe would not get the best of me or my sister's wedding weekend.

I awoke to the calming sound of the waves gently rolling in. A heavy sense of nostalgia caught hold of me. Saturdays spent at the beach with my family. Laxmi teaching me and Dev to not turn our backs to the water, digging in the sand with our shovels and buckets. The salt hardening on my skin and in my hair. Then the sound of the rain beating heavy against the room wiggled its way through and all calm washed away.

Laxmi's snoring drowned out the ocean waves. My sister only snored when she was stressed. I rolled over on my cot and faced her. Her mouth hung open, and I frowned at the way her brows wrinkled like even sleep didn't offer her relief from the insanity of the wedding.

Lifting my head to look at Priti's bed in the corner of the room, I found it empty. She probably snuck out to be with Dev. They said something about grabbing breakfast yesterday.

The knots in my stomach tightened when I remembered the day before. The curse. My words.

Laxmi mumbled under her breath and rolled over to her side. I checked my phone for the time. Only seven in the morning. Deciding to let her sleep in, I pushed away my blanket and quietly tiptoed out of the room into the bathroom.

After throwing off my pajamas, I slid on a pair of shorts, my bra, and a tank top, making sure to roll on some deodorant. I'd shower later.

Lax slept soundly, her snores quieting a bit, as I snuck out of the room and made my way downstairs.

"I just want to know what really happened yesterday. I know Jaanu wasn't being honest with me." I paused in the middle of the staircase, Grant's voice reaching me.

I was still hidden from the people below and stayed put, listening in.

"Nothing is happening, Grant. I promise. Don't worry so much. Right now, you just need to focus on today's event. The mehndi and rehearsal luncheon is happening in a few hours and then the sangeet is tonight, remember?"

My throat loosened as I let out a slow breath.

Tomorrow was the wedding. The real deal. Both a Western and Hindu ceremony were planned. My sister's dresses were perfect and gorgeous. I couldn't wait to see her in them.

Grant's parents were pretty understanding of Hindu traditions as long as they got to host the rehearsal luncheon. Kristin, Grant's mom and Mr. Bastian's first wife, looked forward to all the events because she got to wear traditional Indian clothes for each of them. Mr. Bastian went into it a bit more reluctantly, but I think that was mostly because he was pretty over weddings in general. He was on his third, after all. Damian's mom, Sandra, was his second wife. And his current wife, Laurie, kept to herself. In fact, I'd only seen her once yesterday at the sagan.

"Fine. But you'll come to me if anything goes awry, right?"

"Yes. I promise."

Some shuffling took place and a soft grunt echoed in the room. I quietly stepped down the last few steps and caught the brothers in a hug. Relief and gratitude slinked through me. The fact that Damian hadn't said anything to his brother about yesterday made some of my suspicion and guard drop a little.

Damian faced me and immediately pushed away from his brother when he saw me standing by the stairs.

"Morning," he said, clearing his throat.

Grant turned to me and offered me a wan smile. "Is Laxmi awake?"

I shook my head. "But Priti isn't in the room, which means she's all alone and you can go wake her up if you want."

Grant didn't wait for me to finish my sentence before making his way up the stairs.

Damian moved to the side of the counter and poured himself some orange juice. I grabbed a bowl from the cupboard and went searching for some breakfast. Spotting a box of chocolate cereal, I poured myself some, along with milk, and headed outside to eat.

"It could be worse," Damian said, following me.

The cool morning breeze wrapped around us. I held back a shiver as the rain thumped steadily against the canopy.

"True. And it shouldn't get any worse as long as we stay on top of things. Thanks, by the way, for helping." I tapped my spoon against the cereal, which started to turn to mush because I'd poured way too much milk.

Damian shrugged, shoving his hands into the pockets of his sweatpants. "It's the least I can do after mocking you when we first met."

I swallowed. "I probably overreacted. Shoving that ice cream into your face was a little extreme."

Damian smiled; It changed his whole face, lighting him up. "At least it was ice cream and not something less appetizing like pie."

"I can't believe you don't like pie. There's something wrong with you," I teased.

We sat down at the small mosaic-designed table set in the center of the back patio. Despite the rain (which had better be gone by tomorrow), the day felt still. A nice reprieve before the chaos set in. Desi weddings were always chaotic and dramatic.

Yesterday Ranveer masu got a little tipsy (much like my sister) and told everyone that he planned on getting a hair transplant.

"I really don't think you have anything to worry about," Damian commented, facing the ocean as a breeze ruffled his hair. "Yesterday didn't go exactly as planned, but nothing we couldn't handle."

"Please don't jinx the day before it's even begun." I glared at him, shoving a bite of cereal into my mouth.

A hearty laugh echoed around the quiet landscape. "I am not."

"How about we don't take any chances?" I said after swallowing my bite and placing my bowl on the table.

"I really think today will be much better."

Hurried steps bounced against the ground. Mumma rushed outside and closed the sliding glass door behind her.

"What do you mean the dress won't be here in time?" Mumma said in a harsh, panicked voice.

Damian and I exchanged a glance. I let out a groan.

And let the day begin.

The wedding shop owner's mom was in the hospital. Laxmi's white dress was supposed to arrive today, but since it was a family-owned business, everyone was flying out to be with the mother. We had until eleven o'clock tonight to pick up the dress, otherwise it wasn't going to make it on time. Why had I opened my big mouth yesterday? This all could have been avoided if I had just kept the words inside. I knew better.

At the age of five I had set off a chain of events that ended with Dev getting a broken arm and me with a huge bruise on my head. Mumma decided it was time I learned about the women in our family and how at times we caused . . . trouble with our words. Magic? Maybe. Curse? Most definitely.

"Is there anyone from the wedding party that's still in LA?" Damian asked.

Damian, Dev, Priti, and I were gathered in a small room at the country club. The day's festivities had already begun. My sister and Grant had done the haldi ceremony at the beach house before we all met at the country club for the mehndi party and luncheon. There would be a small break before we gathered again for the sangeet. The day was chock-full. Lots of opportunities for things to turn into disasters.

I bit down on my lip. "Maybe. Let me think."

"I can call my mom and ask," Priti volunteered.

"Great idea, babe." Dev leaned over and kissed her forehead.

I curled up my lip in disgust, but wiped it away before anyone noticed. Besides Damian, who coughed to hide his laugh.

"Thanks, Priti." I squeezed her arm.

Literally anything would help.

I adjusted the top of my salwar. It hung on my frame comfortably, but the golden design around the neck was a little itchy. Most traditional Indian clothing was. The color for today was aquamarine.

"Let's get out there and keep an eye on things," I said, opening the door.

The four of us walked down the hall, determination in our steps, like Laxmi's own personal wedding army, ready to protect her from any harm.

The ballroom smelled like lilies and roses with just a hint of warm bread. My stomach grumbled. Eating only a bowl of cereal earlier in the day wasn't my best move. But I also hadn't had much of an appetite. Priti and Dev headed for the buffet sitting on one side of the room, the trays filled with sandwiches, salads, and soups.

I glanced around the crowd and spotted Laxmi sitting on the little delicate French-style love seat with wooden legs while getting her mehndi done. The pants of her short-sleeved yellow salwar were rolled up as the henna artist created an intricate design on her foot.

There were a few more artists working on some of the masis.

"You getting one?" Damian sidled up to me, keeping his eyes trained on the room for any potential disasters.

"Definitely, but first, I just spotted my first battle."

"Huh?"

"Follow me."

Making my way around the guests, I made sure to also greet my family members. Ignoring anyone would be seen as a slight, and I so did not need the headache of an auntie or uncle guilt trip.

A couple of minutes later I arrived at my destination.

"Meena masi! You look lovely."

Meena masi stopped mid-sentence, the fury in her eyes soothing over. "Oh, beta, you look lovely!" Masi adjusted her purple dupatta and stepped away from my other aunt, Geeta masi.

Meena masi, Mom's sister, and Geeta masi, Dad's cousin, constantly bickered. Yesterday we got lucky they managed to stay on opposite sides of the room, but today? Not so much. I had no idea what the two of them were fighting about, but I needed to defuse the tension immediately.

I felt eyes on my back and spotted Laxmi watching us, her face scrunched in worry. She knew how ugly things could get between our masis. Last time they were together they got in a shouting match that could be heard all the way in India. Over a Bollywood movie of all things. Which, I understood, as my people take Bollywood movies very seriously, but during a funeral? Uncalled for!

"Geeta masi, I love that shade on you." The bright orange actually did look really great on Geeta masi. She'd styled her hair in a tight bun with flowers, and her round cheeks were dotted with blush.

Meena masi sniffed in disapproval.

"Have you met Grant's brother Damian, Meena masi?" I reached behind, grabbed Damian's hand, and pulled him forward. "He loves rugby. Doesn't Anmol play rugby?"

Meena masi ran a hand through her long hair, the dark locks straight and perfect. My hair wasn't much better than the day before, and I seriously envied her style.

"He does. He's on the varsity team and he's only a freshman," she said with pride.

When in doubt, compliment a masi's son to distract her. Then I asked Geeta masi about her latest houseplant, making sure to walk her over to the other side of the room while doing so.

Crisis averted.

For the next hour one issue or another popped up. Mr. Bastian loudly proclaiming that all Indian food tasted the same, which Damian took care of by telling his father just how intricate and diverse Indian food is all throughout the subcontinent, thus getting his father to apologize for his comment. Kristin definitely got a kick out of the way her ex turned red while his son put him in his place.

I think even Laurie, Mr. Bastian's current wife, enjoyed it. I spotted them whispering in a corner by the French doors that led outside. It was strange to see the two of them together. Kristin was a power-suit-wearing lawyer with a no-nonsense attitude and dirty blond hair she kept in a neat bob, whereas Laurie was in her early thirties, wore tight clothes, and kept her red hair long and her skin spray tanned. The two could not be more different, but they appeared to get along just fine.

"I think it's your turn," Damian said, approaching me after helping my dadi dish up her lunch. He'd escorted her to a table and fed her, since her hands were covered in mehndi. It was very endearing.

Which annoyed me. I did not need to find Damian endearing. Ever.

I flicked my gaze to one of the henna artists that finally freed up. Excitement flitted through me. I had been looking forward to getting mehndi all day. Damian didn't have to entice me over.

"Hi," I said to her. "You're doing an amazing job."

The young girl, probably college aged, managed a shy smile. Her dark hair was up in a bun and she wore shorts and a comfortable, green shirt. "Thanks," she said, brown eyes glittering. Mumma insisted on hiring South Asian henna artists for the day, which I thought was pretty cool.

"How long have you been doing this?" I asked, settling into the chair in front of her.

"Since forever. One hand or both?" she asked.

"Both, please."

The girl began working on me as I kept an eye on the room. My sister sat behind the long table reserved for immediate family members. Mumma had decided not to tell her about the dress until absolutely necessary. Laxmi did not need more problems on her plate. She appeared relaxed and laughed at something Grant said. He leaned in and gave her a quick kiss on the lips.

It took about twenty minutes for the henna artist to work on my design. She did an incredible job. After she finished, my stomach grumbled.

She let out a soft laugh. "You should probably go take care of that."

I thanked her and stood up, heading for the buffet. Which was when I realized my mistake. I had no hands to eat with. Staring at the delectable goodies spread out in front of me, my mouth watered.

"Need a hand?" Damian asked, laughing at his own lame joke. "Sorry, just figured I'd offer my services." He waved his empty hands. "Turns out I'm pretty good at it." He'd helped more than a few women who had gotten their henna done.

I scrunched my nose.

"Come on, Jaanu, let me help you out."

Side-eyeing him, I reluctantly agreed. "But you better not do that choo-choo thing I saw you doing with my cousin."

"She's only five," he said, rolling his eyes.

After dishing me up, we went to the table to sit by Laxmi and Grant.

"Everything's going great, right sis?" I leaned over and asked my sister.

Laxmi turned to me in her seat. "Yeah, it is." Her eyes shone with excitement.

I let out a breath. My plan was working.

Damian fed me a few bites of the salad I'd chosen, then held up the turkey sandwich I'd asked for, shoving it into my mouth.

"This is familiar," Damian said, holding the sandwich against my mouth as I took a bite. "Except we're in opposite positions."

I frowned until I realized he was referring to the ice cream incident.

"Ah. Yes. That's why it feels wrong."

He pulled back the sandwich just as I moved forward to take a bite. "It's kind of nice having all the power."

I grit my teeth and let out a low growl. "Do not get between me and my food unless you want it to end badly, Damian."

He laughed and lifted the sandwich back up for me. "I'm glad we're friends now."

"Are we?" I asked, raising my brows.

"Oh yeah, definitely. I'm helping you fix your magical-words thing."

I snorted. "That's a great way to describe our current situation. Look, you don't have to believe it; you just have to respect that it's something me and my family believe."

"And I do. Now. I think it's kind of cool, actually."

"So cool having your entire life controlled by a curse a witch placed on your family."

"Don't you think it's also kind of like a self-fulfilling prophecy? If you think what you say affects your entire life, then it will."

I tilted my head. "I've never really thought of it that way. But you've also never experienced it in action until now."

"Weddings are always tense and disastrous, Jaanu. A bunch of people who don't always get along are packed into one place and expected to be on their best behavior. That never ends well."

"Maybe," I said. But it was more than that, and I didn't know how to convince him otherwise.

Mumma sashayed over to us with a little pep in her step. She had been speaking with Nani and Nana, hands moving in exaggerated gestures.

"Beta, I need to discuss the sangeet with you and Damian. Where are Dev and Priti?" She searched the room for my brother and best friend. They stood by the buffet. She caught Dev's attention and waved him over.

"What's up, Mumma?" Warning bells rang in my head.

"Nani thinks the four of you should do a dance at the sangeet tonight."

My stomach dropped. No. No. No. "Are you serious?"

"I'm sorry, what does that mean? You want us to dance together?" Damian asked like it wasn't that big of a deal.

"A few of your cousins have their dances all coordinated and planned and it doesn't seem right that the sister of the bride doesn't. I'm sure you can figure it out. It doesn't have to be complicated."

Mumma made it sound so easy, but I had watched my cousins practice their routines yesterday evening and they were much more elaborate.

"You needed us?" Dev and Priti arrived.

"What's such a big deal about dancing?" Damian leaned in to whisper.

"She wants us to coordinate an entire routine to a Hindi song. Sangeets always have them."

Damian's brows rose as my words settled in.

"You know this wedding dress problem wouldn't have risen if Laxmi had chosen to wear my mother's dress," Kristin Bastian's voice rose above the rest of the crowd.

"Shhh, Kristin." Laurie tried to quiet her. But it was too late. Laxmi had heard.

"What are you guys talking about?"

Panic seeped into Mumma's face. "Nothing, beta."

"What's going on with my dress?" Laxmi started standing.

Kristin sighed. "They can't get it here in time. But it's really not that big of a deal. I brought my mother's wedding dress with me in case you changed your mind."

Laxmi's face turned green. "My dress isn't going to be here for the wedding?" Her voice pitched higher.

I exchanged a knowing look with Damian. The curse had struck again.

Trying to get anything done with mehndi on my hands proved to be tricky. But I did manage to calm my sister down and told her the dress issue was being taken care of. Okay, I lied, but Laxmi started breathing funny, a prequel to a full-on panic attack. I had to do something.

"My mom said she can get the dress," Priti told me a few hours later as we washed off our mehndi. The greenish brown color swirled down the sink.

"That's great news," I said, releasing a breath. I could have hugged her if not for the wet henna still covering my hands.

"She says she'll pick it up tonight and be here early tomorrow morning."

It took a few minutes, but after we were done, I admired the dark orange designs. The sangeet started in a half hour and we needed to hurry up and get dressed. Laxmi, Mumma, Papa, and the rest of the adults were already there.

We'd stayed behind to practice our dance routine. The four of us were clunky and the dance lacked imagination, but we had something down. We chose our song and sent it to Mumma who would let the DJ know. Dancing in front of pretty much the entire wedding party sounded like a nightmare, but it could have been worse—at least it wasn't a solo.

Priti and I met Damian and Dev at the car. We all looked hot. Damian wore a light blue button-down and some dark blue slacks, Dev had on a kurta with a floral design, Priti's rose-colored salwar blended beautifully with her skin tone, and my light blue kurta surprisingly matched Damian's shirt.

When we got to the ballroom at the country club, we found everyone lingering. Everyone minus the bride-to-be and my mother.

"Will you please check on your sister and Mumma? They were supposed to be here twenty minutes ago." Dad sidled up to me and whispered, making sure to keep a smile on his face. He knew not to show when something might not be right in front of our nosy family members, who were always looking for something to gossip about.

"Can do." I squeezed Papa's arm and rushed toward the hallway.

"Where are you going?" Damian joined me.

"Checking on my sister. Keep an eye on things for me."

Damian gave me a thumbs-up and headed back toward Grant, who watched us with a frown. He was probably wondering why Damian and I were suddenly so chummy. Since the ice cream incident, we learned to ignore each other, usually keeping to separate sides of the room. This was the first time in years we were being nice and getting along. And I was beginning to realize I could trust Damian, and he was more than making up for the past.

I knocked on the designated bridal room door and waited. A giggle followed by Mumma's shushing sounded from the other side before the door opened a smidge.

"What's wrong?" I asked as soon as I saw Mumma's face.

Her frown lines deepened and she grimaced. "Come in. Hurry." She pulled me into the room and quickly shut the door.

Laxmi sat on the edge of a wing-backed chair, holding up a bangle. The golden details of her salwar glimmered against the light when she moved. Her hair fell in gentle tendrils around her face, and her makeup, though subtle, highlighted all of her best features, including her cheekbones. She looked gorgeous. She looked like a bride-to-be.

Laxmi tilted her head and turned the bangle in her hand. "How did they make it so round?" she asked with a laugh. The laugh turned into a snort. She proceeded to throw the bangle up in the air and play catch with it.

"Is she high?" I asked in horror.

Mumma grimaced. "Possibly."

"What happened?" I hurried over to Laxmi and took her chin in my hands.

"Whoa, your eyes are so light right now, sister. Oh, you should definitely do something about those pores."

I jumped away and covered my nose. My pores were not that bad! Okay maybe I did a half-assed job removing my makeup last night, but she didn't have to point it out.

"I gave her something to help with her nerves." Mumma remained on the other side of the room, wringing her hands. "She hadn't calmed down after hearing about the dress."

Laxmi glided over to the window like she was a princess in a Disney movie and did a twirl. "Isn't the world just so magical?"

"What did you give her, Mumma?"

"Valium," she confessed, dropping her hands.

I let out a gasp. "Where did you get Valium?"

"Kristin. She gave it to me earlier in the week. Don't give me that look." She pointed her finger at me before stalking over to Laxmi and placing her back on the chair.

"This is my fault," I said with a groan, pacing the room. Things were going from bad to worse.

"No, it's not. You didn't drug your sister."

"No, I didn't, but I might as well have. I'm the reason this whole wedding is falling apart." Laxmi grew fascinated with the back of her hands.

"What did you say?" Mumma asked with a low, knowing tone.

Time to fess up. "I said that things would be a disaster and now they are."

Mumma sighed. "How many times have I told you to be careful what you speak into existence? But, beta, this isn't all your fault. You only give your words more power when you believe them to be true. The less you focus on them, the easier things will get."

Damian's own words echoed in my mind, about the words being a self-fulfilling prophecy. Maybe they were right, maybe I was giving them too much power. If I stopped agonizing and obsessing over them, maybe things would get better.

"What do we do about her?" I asked, biting my lip.

"We'll get her to her seat. All she and Grant have to do tonight is sit there and enjoy. The pill should wear off in a bit. Hopefully before her dance."

Laxmi was the dancer in the family, not me. She started taking Kathak lessons at five and taught a class on weekends and during the summer. That gene hadn't passed onto me. Or Dev for that matter, not that he seemed to notice or care.

I took Laxmi's hand in mine, Mumma took the other, and we helped her stand. The distinct sense of déjà vu hit me. At least when Lax got drunk we had coffee and water to help sober her up. I had my doubts about the Valium.

"You can do this, Lax. Just a couple of hours of sitting there and looking pretty. You can do that."

Laxmi snorted. "Like an ornament. I always liked the idea of being a trophy wife. Part of me wants Grant to work full time while I take Pilates classes and teach Kathak instead of becoming a lawyer."

"That would be a waste," Mumma chastised. "And you're better than that. You're my ambitious girl, remember?"

Lax sighed. "Yup. Ambitious. That's me."

Being the oldest definitely had its downsides, and in that moment I keenly felt the pressure Laxmi had on her shoulders. The last couple of days were the first time I'd seen her let go and relax, and it was only because she got drunk and high. That was unfair. Another reason I wanted to fix the wedding for her. She didn't need more stress in her life.

We made it to the ballroom and walked Laxmi over to the dais set with two plush chairs. Grant already sat in his with Damian by his side. They were whispering together.

"You've got this, sis, just act natural," I told Laxmi, giving her a kiss on the cheek after helping her sit.

Standing back up, I lifted a chin at Damian, gesturing for us to meet in the corner of the room. He followed after me as Papa and Mumma began the festivities by welcoming everyone.

"How are things out here?" I asked Damian once we were relatively alone.

"Not bad. People appear to be behaving well."

What a relief. Maybe the universe was cutting me a break. "That's good."

"Is Laxmi okay?"

I pulled my mouth to the side of my face. "For now. I'm just glad we figured out the wedding dress thing, otherwise we might not make it to the wedding."

Just as the words left my mouth, Priti ran up to us. "We have a problem," she said, concern filling her eyes.

"Oh no," I muttered.

"My mom went to the dress shop and it was closed. She couldn't get the dress in time."

My heart plummeted. "No. My sister isn't going to have a dress for her wedding?"

"She'll have her lehenga?" Priti offered.

But she didn't get it. The white dress had been a point of contention between the families for a while. Kristin insisted on Laxmi wearing her mother's dress, but Laxmi finally stood up and said she wanted her own. And now the dress she had chosen for herself wasn't going to be here.

"We can fix this," I said. But at the back of my mind, I knew it was too late. The shop owner had flown out of town, and breaking in wasn't a possibility.

"Let's just get through tonight and we'll figure out the dress thing later," Damian offered, squeezing my arm.

I sniffed and nodded.

"Hey, Jaanu, it's going to be okay," he said.

I shook my head. "I need a minute."

Making my way to the exit door, I let myself outside just as the tears began to fall.

The night was calm. Stars sparkled in the sky with clouds covering the moon. The rain had stopped. Finally. The scent of fresh-cut grass surrounded me.

This was all my fault. My sister wouldn't have her dress and it was my fault.

I wiped away the slow trickle of tears, slipped off my shoes, and walked onto the wet grass.

"Jaanu." Damian's voice carried over the dark. I turned to see him standing by the building, worry coating his eyes.

"I swear if you say this isn't my fault, I will throw something at you."

Damian's mouth twitched. "I believe you. And that's not what I was going to say."

I crossed my arms and waited for him to continue.

"This situation isn't ideal, but I really think it's going to work out the way it should."

"How?" My voice shook.

Damian took a few slow steps, closing the distance between us. I looked up at him. The night made his eyes appear darker, even prettier. Which was ridiculous.

"Grant and Laxmi love each other, they want to get married more than anything. A dress isn't going to change that. We need to stop hiding what's going on from the both of them. If we tell them the truth, I bet their desire to get married trumps a wedding dress."

"That sounds awfully romantic."

His mouth curled up. "It is. And it's true. You've seen them together. Nothing is going to stop the two of them."

Damian was right. Not that I was going to tell him that.

"Let's just get through our dance. After everyone leaves, we'll tell them."

"And after the pill wears off," I muttered.

"What?"

I laughed and shook my head. "Nothing. Okay, let's do this."

Damian took my hand and gave it a squeeze. "You look beautiful, by the way."

My cheeks burned with the compliment, and the way he looked at me. "Thanks. You look pretty great, too."

A pause settled between us. Time slowed for the first time in days. It didn't feel like it was rushing everywhere, forcing me to run to keep pace with it. I could breathe.

"The two of you coming? It's our turn!" Dev's voice carried over the sounds of the night.

Damian jumped away from me. "Yeah, let's do this."

We exchanged one last glance, one filled with a sensation nei-ther of us were ready to face, and headed inside.

"Did I interrupt?" my brother whispered as I walked past him.

I sent him a glare.

"Desi Girl" played overhead as my cousins Reena and Kriti finished their dance. No desi wedding would be complete without that song. The music ended and everyone clapped. They'd done a fantastic job.

Priti, Dev, Damian, and I took our places on the dance floor, preparing for our number.

"Hey, guys, let's just have fun, 'kay?" My brother's cheerful tone took me by surprise. He gave me a wink.

The four of us nodded as "Piya Piya" began. Our routine started off with a twirl and the four of us pairing off: me and Damian, and Priti and Dev. The dance had a mix of Western and classic Bolly-wood moves. A few times we forgot what we were supposed to do and improvised. At one point my mind went completely blank, and I started doing the sprinkler. Damian didn't miss a beat and followed my lead.

Laughter filled the air. An idea formed in my head partway through. I ran over to my sister, who smiled brightly, took her hand, then Grant's, and pulled them onto the dance floor to join us. Pretty soon a dozen or so other family members danced with us, too. The song ended with all of us showing off our goofiest moves. Damian, as it turned out, was a decent dancer.

Applause followed our performance, and my cheeks hurt from smiling and laughing. Laxmi squeezed me into a tight hug.

"Thanks, sis, that's just what I needed." She kissed my cheek before taking Grant's hand and giving him a kiss on the mouth.

The two of them took their seats again. Everyone emptied the dance floor as Mumma and Papa took their places for their dance.

"I'd say that was successful and not at all a disaster," Damian said, joining me in the corner of the room.

I fanned myself and nodded to the door. Damian got my drift. The night air was a relief from the heat inside. Neither of us spoke as we began to stroll around the side of the building toward the parking lot. My heartbeat regained a steady rhythm, calming after our dance routine. The music pounded through the walls of the building into the parking lot.

"Thanks for everything, Damian." I broke the silence. "Even if nothing has gone as planned, it was nice to have your help on this little . . . 'adventure.'" I used quotation marks.

Damian pocketed his hands. "Does that mean you finally forgive me?"

We stopped under one of the streetlights spread around the country club. Cars dotted the spots. I couldn't believe tomorrow was the wedding. The last couple of days felt like a disaster in some ways, but in others? Not so much. I wasn't looking forward to telling Laxmi about the dress.

Guilt wove through my limbs. There was nothing to be done. Not anymore, but I could still make it up to her. In some way. I promised myself I would.

"You more than earned my forgiveness. In fact, I think we might actually be friends."

A bright smile engulfed Damian's face. "Friends. Sounds ominous."

I shook my head. "You said it, not me." Thank goodness. I did not need to work any more magic with my words.

Damian took a step closer. The moment earlier, when the tension between us felt electrified, returned. He cleared his throat. I took in a breath. He smelled like the ocean, familiar and welcome. I swallowed as our eyes locked.

The sound of a car engine and tires turning into the parking lot pulled at our attention. A small white car drove into the parking lot, the headlights shining in our eyes. We both turned away as the driver parked up front and cut the engine.

"Who's that?" Damian asked as a slight woman in a green salwar stepped out of the car.

Her hair was in a sleek bob cut; the light highlighted the small mole above her mouth. As if sensing our stares, she turned to us.

"Oh, hello. I'm so sorry I'm late. But I was told that this belongs to someone." She pulled open the back door of the car and lifted a garment bag.

My heart skipped a beat.

"Is that . . ." Damian's voice trailed off.

No. It couldn't be. It was too good to be true.

"Are you Jaanu?" she asked, stepping forward with the bag.

I nodded, mouth hanging open, unable to speak.

The woman's face cleared. "Oh good. Your mumma mentioned that you needed this picked up. I was on my way to the wedding and figured I could do it. I hope you don't mind."

I lunged at the woman, wrapping my arms around her in a tight hug. "Thank you."

She laughed and patted my back. "It's not that big of a deal, honestly."

The relief felt momentarily dizzying.

Letting go of the woman, I took the garment bag in my hands. "You just saved the day. You have no idea."

She waved a hand. "Well, I hope I'm in time for the food."

"Oh, please go in and help yourself."

She squeezed my arm one last time and headed into the building.

"Wow, that was so perfectly timed it's almost like we're in a movie," Damian commented with a disbelieving laugh.

I unzipped the bag and inspected the dress. Yup, it was the right one. The one Laxmi had chosen for herself. The one she would get to wear during the wedding. We'd made it. Well, almost. There was still tomorrow.

The ceremony was perfect. Some would say suspiciously perfect. But for me? It was exactly what the doctor ordered. Aunties got along, so did the uncles. No one complained. Everyone ate, drank, danced, and had too much fun.

The wedding ceremonies could have been shorter, but that was the only complaint. Laxmi looked perfect in each of her dresses. The red wedding lehenga was classic and she looked like a Bollywood bride. The white off-the-shoulder ball gown she'd chosen for the Western ceremony had made her look like a true Disney princess. Gorgeous, happy, and completely sober. She didn't need a single drink or drug to get her through the day. It helped that everyone was on their best behavior.

A slow song played in the reception hall. Tables with white tablecloths and pink roses the same shade as my bridesmaid dress dotted them, a change from the lilac lehenga I'd worn for the Hindu ceremony. The day had been a perfect seventy degrees with a light breeze. The clouds had dispersed and the sun shone. I swayed to the song as Grant and Laxmi danced one more time.

Couples took the floor, including Dev and Priti. It was all so romantic and it didn't even make me sick. I was just so freaking happy it was all over and my sister got the day she so deserved.

"Will you honor me with this dance?" Damian appeared next to me.

We'd spent most of the day side by side but hadn't interacted much, too distracted by the festivities.

"Of course." I placed my hand in his as he led me to the dance floor.

He wrapped an arm around my waist. We were close. So close I wondered if he could hear my heart beating.

"We made it," he said, nodding around the room.

"We did." Relief clung to me, making my back curve in release.

"They look happy, don't they?" He lifted his chin to Laxmi and Grant.

My sister tilted her head back and let out a hearty laugh.

"They're so cute, it's gross." I wrinkled my nose. "It's the perfect day she deserves." A tingle went up my spine and a light breeze swept through the room.

"Did you feel that?" Damian asked.

I nodded. "Words have power."

His eyes widened a fraction. He'd finally felt the magic. The first time was always a little scary.

Hiding a smile, I took another glance around the room. I'd tried to find the auntie who had brought the wedding dress all day to thank her again. I'd caught glimpses of her here and there, but she disappeared every time I tried to approach her.

"You know what's weird," I said to Damian. "When I told my mom that her friend had picked up the wedding dress for us after she called her, she told me she hadn't spoken to anyone about it. She figured Priti's mom had it covered."

Damian frowned. "But then who was the woman from last night?"

I shrugged. "I don't know. Maybe a fairy godmother? Maybe my mom forgot she spoke to someone? Whatever the case, I'm just glad we survived."

"Me too. Not such a disaster, after all."

The music made the air vibrate as Damian smiled down at me.

"No, or maybe you were right; maybe giving the words power is what caused all of this to happen in the first place."

"You don't believe in magic anymore?"

"Curse, you mean?" I chortled.

"Whatever it is, I think it's kind of cool. And I also think you hold more power in how it all happens than you think. You just need to believe in yourself."

"Cool, huh? You're a believer now?" I nudged him lightly as the song stopped and we along with it.

"More a believer in the magic of Jaanu."

My cheeks bloomed with heat. The way he looked at me, it made my insides all squishy. I ducked my head and noticed we were still holding on to each other. I gently pulled myself away from him. We walked toward our table, where our families were already situated, chatting and laughing.

"What next?" Damian asked.

I shrugged. "Finals. And then summer."

"You know Laxmi and Grant are going to be in New York part of the summer. You and Dev should come, too. I'd love to show you around the city."

Pressing my lips together, I bit back a smile. "That actually sounds like fun. I'd love to."

"Then it's settled. New York this summer. And another adventure. Maybe not as chaotic this time."

"No, definitely not! It will not be a disaster, in fact it will be the best summer either of has ever experienced," I said loudly, tipping my head back and staring at the ceiling.

Damian raised his brows.

"Just in case," I said, lowering my voice. "I'm not taking any chances."

A Cynic at a Shaadi

AAMNA QURESHI

*W*hen you've just gotten your heart broken, the last thing you want to do is go to a wedding.

"Mama, please don't make me," I whine, lying on my bed as she takes out various accessories for my outfit. "I don't feel well."

"Tch, Sajal, stop complaining," Mama says, lightly smacking my leg with the gold dupatta in her hands. "It's Asif Bhai's dholki. You love Asif Bhai. You're always going on and on about how he's your favorite cousin, and Asif Bhai this, and Asif Bhai that. Now you don't want to go? Ajeeb larki."

"Ammaaaaa," I moan, burrowing into my pillows, my black hair strewn about me. "Bas, nahi jaana. I'm not in the mood."

"Why not in the mood?" she asks. She's unperturbed, pulling out shoes to go with the outfit she's chosen for me.

"Because love is a farce."

Mama rolls her eyes.

"You're seventeen."

"I'm going to die alone."

"Teek hai. Be ready in thirty minutes. I don't want to be late."

I can't tell her that the messenger of this recent epiphany came in the form of one Haris Ahmed, my secret boyfriend. Or at least he *was*, until about three weeks ago when he decided he was bored of me and consequently dumped me.

"Amma, please, don't make me go," I say, sitting up to give her my best pout. She fixes me with a glare, no longer indulgent.

"Thirty minutes," she repeats, voice stern. Then she's gone. I groan, collapsing back into my bed, and the chudiyan she's left out jingle around me from the movement.

I really do love Asif. He's my khala's son, the younger of two, and even though he lives on Long Island, about three hours away from where I am in New Jersey, my whole life he's always been such fun: taking me out go-karting and to Six Flags, eating ice cream together and watching scary movies. I can't abandon him on such a joyous occasion.

Today's just a dholki at his fiancée's place (she lives down the road from him), but I know he'll cause a fuss if Mama and Baba show up without me. So, begrudgingly, I get out of bed and change into the freshly pressed shalwar kameez suit. It's a rust kurta with a gold and orange patiala shalwar.

I do my makeup, trying to hype myself into the mood. I used to love weddings, truly. Declaring in front of the world *This is the person I love!* What could be better? But now I'm sullen and a cynic. Having your heart bulldozed will do that to a person.

After my makeup, I tie my hair up into a bun, then wrap a matching scarf around my face, careful of the teeka that rests on my forehead. Finally, I slip into my khussay and put the gold-edged dupatta on my shoulders, fanning myself from the effort. Summer weddings are cute, but the heat is not.

When I gaze at the mirror, I look great, but a frown mars the final image. Haris always said I looked good in warm colors. Once I wore an orange and yellow dress, and he had me stand in the sun for an hour, taking pictures of me on the beach. They're some of the best pictures I have of myself.

I sniffle. He was right, of course, I do look good in warm colors, but no matter how many warm colors I wore, he still dumped me.

I don't understand how he could have liked me so much and then, one day, just . . . stopped. How can people change so easily, so quickly?

It's why I've recently discovered love isn't real. It's an illusion that will inevitably fade.

As I bound down the stairs and into the car, my mood only grows worse. At least Mama and Baba spend the entire car ride lightheartedly bickering with one another, not trying to talk to me when they see I'm asleep (or pretending to be). We listen to music, old qawwalies my father loves and my mother hates.

"Change karo," Mama says, trying to turn the volume down. My father's hand closes over hers on the knob, turning it up. I can't look away. Then he starts singing to her, and Mama giggles.

"Can you guys stop?" I snap. Baba gives me an alarmed glance in the rearview mirror.

"Kya hua, Sajal beta?" he asks, concerned. "What's wrong?"

"Nothing," I say, feeling sorry for snapping at them. "I just have a headache."

It's not their fault my boyfriend left me, the entire saga of which they know nothing about because I'm not supposed to date, and Mama will just say, "Dekha, this is why."

When we pull into Asif's street, I feel more glum. The entire street is covered in lights, leading from Asif's house, on the end of the street, to his fiancée's place a few houses down. Both of their houses are also decorated with lights, just like they do in Pakistan, and in front of Naadia's house there's a sign in Urdu that says, *"Shaadi ka Ghar,"* the wedding house.

I used to love details like that, but now it just makes me ill.

"Mood teek karo," Mama says, elbowing me when we get out of the car. "Smile."

I attempt to, but it must resemble a grimace because Mama shakes her head. Baba wraps an arm around my shoulder, patting me lightly, and that gives me enough strength to push through the doors and enter the chaos of a shaadi ka ghar.

The party is fully underway, all set up in the backyard. Women's voices carry in from outside, singing along to the quick beat of the dhol and clapping hands and a clanging spoon. The music and singing is deafening when we go outside, and now I really do get a headache, even though we've been here for two seconds.

"Assalam u alaikum!" Mama says, greeting the hosts, Naadia's father and his younger sister, who's lived with them since Naadia's mom passed away.

I kiss the auntie's cheeks, though she's not that old, then greet Naadia's younger sister, Humaira, who's such an elegant lady, even though she's only a few years older than me. She just graduated college with honors.

I can't imagine her crying over a stupid boy.

We go around, greeting more people, kids running around us, bumping into our knees. Going to greet my mother's sister, I kiss my khala's cheeks, then finally make my way to the stage, where Asif and Naadia are sitting, both of them giggling.

The stage is decorated with orange, pink, purple, and white curtains, and flowers and hanging lights. In the center sits the happy couple: Asif in a white shalwar kameez with an orange waistcoat, Naadia in a matching orange and green outfit, radiant face framed with a lovely chiffon hijab.

"Sajal!" Asif calls upon seeing me. "You're late!"

"You live in the middle of nowhere, Asif Bhai, so obviously

it's gonna take us forever and a day to get here!" I say, having to shout because everything is so loud. I squeeze through the crowd to reach them.

He grins, holding his hand up for a fist-bump, and despite everything, I smile, too, touching my fist to his.

"Naadia Baji, you look incredible," I tell her, and she squeezes my hand, positively buzzing. "Everything looks great!"

"Ah, thank you! This was all Humaira," she tells me. "My only job is to show up and look cute."

"Which you're doing perfectly," Asif says to her. Naadia beams. Ugh.

"I'm gonna go sit," I tell them, and they wave me off, ebullient in their little bubble. Mama grabs me and sits me down with her and Khala. Absent-mindedly, I clap along with everyone, but even though I know the words to the songs, I can't bring myself to sing.

"I'm going to the bathroom," I tell Mama, standing and making my way through the ladies sitting cross-legged on the floor.

When I get inside the house, I close the door tight. Here, at least, it's a little quiet. Shutting my eyes, I take deep breaths.

What is wrong with me? He was just some guy! I shouldn't be this upset. I'm being too emotional; I'm being too much.

I breathe, trying to stay calm.

And then I feel someone crash into me. A thick, cold liquid falls all over my body.

"What the—" My eyes fly open. There's a tall guy with thick frame glasses standing in front of me, an empty tray in his hands, his mouth an open, shocked O.

"Ohmygod, I'm so sorry!" he says, moving into action. He's dropped an entire tray of dahi balle on me. My eyes flash murder at him. This was the last thing I needed.

I expect him to bashfully retreat after seeing the look on my face, but to my horror, he starts talking: "Auntie sent me inside to grab this tray to refill outside, but I wasn't paying attention because they're singing 'Bachna Ae Haseeno,' which is one of my favorites, and maybe I shouldn't have tried dancing while holding this tray, but let me help you clean up. I'm so sorry again. Who are you by the way? Are you from the guy's side or girl's? I'm Raza. I'm family friends with Asif Bhai, we live on Long Island, too. Oh, are you one of his cousins from Pakistan? He did say some of them were flying in, but I didn't think they were coming until the actual wedding . . ."

He keeps talking.

I stare at him, in total shock. By now, the yogurt from the dahi bhalle has soaked through my clothes and is sticking to my skin, along with the sweet imlee chutney. No, no, nooooo. This can't be happening.

"Sorry, are you deaf?" he asks, when I still say nothing. "Shit, I didn't know." He does some complicated gestures with his hands. "I haven't taken sign language in a long time, but that should mean *are you okay*. I'm pretty sure."

"No, not deaf," I manage to say.

The stress on his face melts into relief, his warm eyes crinkling behind those massive glasses.

"Oh, great! My sign language skills aren't very extensive, as you could tell." He laughs. "Anyway, let's get you cleaned up."

"It's okay," I say.

"Let me help!" He starts dabbing at my arms with paper towels, which only pushes the yogurt further into the fabric. Ugh. So gross. I squirm.

"Seriously. I'll be fine," I tell him, vision blurring. I didn't even want to come in the first place, and now look what's happened.

"White vinegar will help with the stains," he says. "I always get these awful grass stains while I'm out gardening, and Baba even got me some fancy gardening pants for Eid last year, but I always forget to wear them. I find it sort of comforting, you know? The feel of the soil on my knees."

I cannot believe this is happening. He reaches over with a fresh paper towel to wipe at my other arm. I give him a withering look that I hope conveys my irritation.

He holds his hands up in surrender, and I almost sigh in relief, thinking he'll leave now, but he just stands there.

"You should ask someone for a change of clothes," he says.

I stare at him.

"Have you met Naadia Baji and Humaira Baji before? This is their house. I'm sure they can help you out."

I continue to stare.

"Humaira Baji's sort of scary, don't you think? I mean, not scary scary, but like how I imagine a queen would be scary, you know?"

I'm going to scream, cry, or throw up. Maybe a combination of all three.

"How old are you by the way? I'm eighteen; just graduated high school last week. You look like you're around my age, but you might be secretly thirty with fantastic skin. That'd be pretty funny. Hey, I never caught your name. I'm Raza. I think I said that before . . ."

He. Keeps. Talking.

Finally, his attention is diverted as the back door slides open, Humaira entering.

"Sajal!" she cries, alarmed. "What happened?"

She's already in motion, sticking her head outside to call a cleaning lady to handle the mess.

"Sajal! That's a nice name. Like the actress. You sort of look like her, actually. The big eyes." He turns to Humaira. "This was my fault. Auntie sent me inside to grab this tray to refill outside, but I wasn't paying attention because they were singing 'Bachna Ae Haseeno,' which is one of my favorites, and maybe I shouldn't have tried dancing while holding this tray, and then I crashed into her, and I've been trying to help her clean up. I said she should ask you for a change of clothes or something."

Humaira offers Raza a placating smile. "Oh, don't worry, Raza. I'll take care of Sajal here. Can you do me a massive favor, though? Fawad is being a terrible bore out there and refuses to sing or dance. Can you please rectify the situation, you know, get him in the mood?"

Her voice is sweet and sure, as if she is used to getting everything she asks for.

Raza nods. "Yeah, sure!" He heads to the door, then turns back around. "See you, Sajal!"

I sincerely hope not. His energy levels are at two hundred when I need them to be at zero, like mine.

After he's gone, my entire body deflates, the aggravation leaving me fatigued.

"Let's get you cleaned up," Humaira says, squeezing my shoulder. She leads me to a guest room on the main floor, handing me a towel and showing me where the bathroom is. "Do a quick rinse, being mindful of your face, so as not to mess up your makeup, and I'll be back in two minutes with some clothes."

I do as I'm told. Afterward, when I open the bathroom door, there's a clean pair of clothes laid out on the bed, plus a bag to put my dirty clothes into. I freshen up, feeling a lot calmer than I was.

By the time I'm ready to go outside again, I'm hoping the party will be winding down, but if anything, it's in full swing. The second I step outside, my senses are bombarded: loud music and the warm night and the smell of spicy food.

"Hey, you're back!"

Oh no.

I turn, and there Raza is, with his ridiculous hair and massive glasses and absurd grin.

"Come on, let's go join the singing," he says.

"No, I'm good," I say, trying to be politely dismissive, but this man would not catch a hint if it smacked him in the face.

"You're at a dholki! You have to sing! Come on, the aunties are playing that game—I forget what it's called—the one where they sing a song, then the other team has to sing a song starting from the last letter of the last lyric the other team sang. My bets are on Nabila Auntie winning, but Shahida Auntie has been holding her ground pretty well, too. And don't even get me started on Zeba Auntie, who switches sides like every five seconds."

Where is the mute button? If I wasn't in such a bad mood, I might even be impressed.

"Actually," I say, turning around, reaching for the door, "I'm going to go."

"Oh, where are we going?" he asks, following me. I stare at him.

"I'm going out front for a smoke," I lie. I have never smoked a thing in my life.

"I can go with you."

"I'm going to go smoke . . . weed." Do people say weed or is it pot?

He's startled by this, but still undeterred. "I've never done it before, but I can still keep you company."

I look at him. "Why?"

He shrugs. "Why not?"

I sigh. Then groan. "Let's go sing."

"Great!"

We go join the aunties, sitting cross-legged on the floor among all of them. These aunties are having the time of their lives, singing and laughing and smacking each other. Honestly, an outsider might think they're drunk, but they aren't.

I usually love how rowdy Pakistanis get, especially at weddings, but right this moment, I'm not feeling it. I rub my temples.

"Come on, clap!" Raza says, when he sees I'm not participating. I scowl at him, but he must have no concept of self-preservation because he reaches for my hands, forcing them together into clapping motions.

"I'm going to kill you," I threaten, and he laughs.

"You're so funny," he says.

I clap to keep my hands busy before I actually commit a felony.

But then my gaze strays to Asif and Naadia up on the stage, the way they're talking to each other, heads close, mouths moving quickly as if they haven't seen each other in years and have loads of catching up to do.

Despite all the chaos around them, it looks like they're enclosed in their own private bubble.

I used to feel that way with Haris, sometimes. Like we were the only people on earth.

He'd be close enough for me to see the curve of his dark eyelashes in beautiful detail, and once I remember telling him, "It's so unfair your eyelashes are naturally so long and thick. You're a boy! You don't need long eyelashes!"

He'd laughed, saying, "Sajal, no way you're jealous of my eyes when yours look like that. Every time you look at me, the thoughts flee from my head."

I had smiled, pleased, though I'd continued to tease him, saying, "Come on, as if you have any thoughts in your head, anyway."

"Hmm, that's true. But all the thoughts I have are of you."

How could he have felt that way about me only to break up with me a short month later? Was he lying, then? I don't think he was. His eyes were perfectly clear, his words intensely genuine.

So, what? He just . . . changed his mind? How can someone feel one way about someone and then one day just . . . not anymore? It doesn't make sense to me.

I can't look at Asif and Naadia up on that stage. It hurts to watch.

"Where are you going?" Raza asks when I stand.

"Bathroom," I mumble, then run before he can ask anything further. Inside, I go to the living room, away from the noise. I'm not the only one who needed to reset.

"Need a break?" Fawad asks. He's Asif's older, unmarried brother, even though he's twenty-eight and Asif is only twenty-five. He's sitting on the chair in immaculately pressed white shalwar kameez, a laptop balanced on his knee.

"Fawad Bhai, your brother is grossly in love," I say, collapsing onto the chair next to him. "Like, I love it for him, but still. Major yuck."

"You're telling me?" Fawad replies, taking off his thin-frame glasses to run a hand over his eyes. "He's been like this since they got engaged three months ago." He slides his mug my way. "Here, have a drink." I take a sip of his coffee. It's brutally bitter, but it matches my mood, so I drink half of it. Fawad looks at me. "Jeez, rough night?"

"You don't know the half of it."

He looks at me closely. "Hey, aren't those Humaira's clothes?"

Before I can reply, someone comes bounding in. I groan.

"Hey, where did you go?" Raza asks me. "They're singing 'Ko Ko Korina,' which is the best one! Oh, hey, Fawad Bhai! What are you up to? Work? At your brother's dholki? Shame, shame, shame.

And after Humaira Baji already scolded you twice! Aren't you scared of her?"

"Hey, Raza," Fawad replies, then looks at me, confused by Raza's familiar tone. "I didn't know you two knew each other."

"We don't," I say quickly.

"We just met!" Raza says at the same time. "I spilled a tray of dahi bhalle on her. I thought she was going to kill me. Then I thought she was deaf. Then she said she was going to smoke weed, but we didn't, don't worry! Then we were singing, but then she disappeared—"

Fawad raises a brow, ignoring Raza and turning to me.

"Save me," I mouth. Fawad closes his laptop and stands. He goes over to Raza, drapes an easy arm around his shoulder.

"Hey, Raza, let's go sing 'Ko Ko Korina,'" Fawad says.

"Okay, cool! What about Saj—"

But Fawad steers him away, leaving me in the quiet. Before they can come back for me, I go to the bathroom and run cold water over my wrists, trying to breathe.

In the mirror, I mouth to myself, *Save me, save me.*

Two weeks later and it's time for the big weekend.

There's the haldi ceremony on Thursday, the mehndi on Friday, the baraat on Saturday, then finally the walima on Sunday. Since all the events are on Long Island, we're planning on just staying over Asif's place for the weekend, rather than driving back and forth.

On Thursday, I'm wearing green, and the whole ride over, I'm hoping to God I won't run into Raza there. I'm probably being a little too harsh, since he was just being ridiculously friendly and nice, but I'm not in the market for any new friends or anything else. Once this wedding is over, I'm going to be a brooding recluse all summer.

When we arrive at Asif's, I don't see Raza anywhere, and I breathe a sigh of relief.

We enter the house, which is decorated with yellows and oranges. We head to the living room, saying salaam to everyone. Around us, music plays from speakers, upbeat songs heavy on the drums.

Asif and Naadia are sitting on a bench, and on the table in front of them sit little bowls with the haldi: a paste of turmeric powder mixed with rosewater. There are also little bowls of oil and a platter of mithai, various colorful Pakistani sweets.

"Come, let's go bother Asif Bhai," Mama says, smiling as she takes my hand. I let myself be carried, smiling too.

"Please, Khala, no more oil," Asif says. His black hair glistens, and his kameez sleeves are rolled up to his biceps, his arms covered in the yellow haldi paste.

"Khala, do more, do more," Naadia says, laughing. She's safe from the oil part of the night, since her hair is covered by her hijab. But her arms and face are covered with haldi, too.

"Too bad, so sad," Mama says, rubbing more oil into Asif's hair. She then smears haldi across his already covered cheeks. "And for you, beta," Mama says to Naadia, putting some haldi on her hands.

I follow suit, flicking Asif's face with oil, laughing as he scrunches his face, then I smear haldi gently on Naadia's nose. Mama and I feed both of them little bites of mithai.

So maybe tonight won't be so bad, I console myself, moving away from the couple to give others a chance. We go to take appetizers, and I pile my plate high with chaat before going to sit with everyone. Some of my cousins are here from Pakistan, too, and I talk with them, feeling perfectly fine, laughing as we catch up and fool around.

But then "Sweety Tera Drama" starts playing, and my mouth dries. I remember sitting in the car with Haris, him singing it to me, dancing along while he drove.

"Stop!" I'd shrieked, though I'd been laughing. "We're going to crash! And then my parents are going to kill me!"

"Don't worry, Sajal. I've got you."

The memory causes tears to sting my eyes.

"I'll be back," I tell my cousins, excusing myself. And as I make my way out of the room, the situation only gets worse.

"Yay, you're here!"

It's Raza. He stands in front of me in an outrageously yellow outfit, a green dupatta hanging around his neck. "Good to see you again!" he says, taking a step closer, and before I can even devise a getaway plan, he smears haldi all over my cheeks.

Shock flashes through me. He grins.

My fingers itch to strangle him, but he runs away before I get the chance. I head in the opposite direction, going to the mirror in the foyer.

"For God's sake," I mutter to myself, wiping the paste off my cheeks with a tissue from the front table.

"They got you, too?" Fawad asks, seeing me as he's passing through.

"I'm going to commit murder," I announce to him. "I am actually going to go to jail."

"What's wrong?" he asks, eyebrows furrowed with concern.

"Men are the actual worst."

"You're not wrong." He shrugs, then grows serious, scrutinizing me. "Do I need to handle something?" He switches to Protective Older Brother Mode. I sigh.

"No," I say, waving him off. Raza is annoying, not harmful. Haris, on the other hand . . . "I should have known better, anyway."

He nods. "That's why my rule is to stay away from love. It doesn't exist. And pretending it does never ends well, for anyone."

"That's so cynical," I say, though I pretty much agree with him at this point. "Don't tell Asif Bhai."

He laughs. "Love works for idiots like Asif, don't worry. Like kids believing in Santa Claus. They get their gifts and don't question it."

"*Fawad*, I swear to God," someone snaps. Fawad jolts as if electrocuted.

We both turn to see Humaira entering, looking gorgeous as always, today clad in a bright fuchsia outfit that only she could pull off. The effect is not even a little bit ruined by the scowl she throws Fawad's way.

"Cease spreading your anti-love agenda at my sister's wedding," she says, beautiful eyes flashing. "If Naadia hears a word of this she is going to spiral, and I will make your life a living hell by unstitching all of your outrageously fancy suits."

Fawad's eyes widen. Since I'm his cousin, I can tell he's a bit frightened and amused by her, but he masks it quickly, rolling his eyes.

"Not all of us are children," he says, condescendingly. Humaira does not care at all for his tone. She holds up a hand.

"Just stop." Then she turns to me, face and voice softening. "Boys are dreadful—some more so than others—" At that, she throws a pointed look to Fawad, who smirks. "—but always have hope. Love is very real."

I sigh. "I dunno . . ."

"Statistically speaking—" Fawad starts.

"You are a terrible menace!" Humaira interjects, whipping her head in his direction. The bickering takes off from there, so I leave them be, heading back to the crowd, but before I can join my cousins, Raza finds me.

He looks at me closely.

"What's wrong?" he asks, his voice surprisingly gentle. I wish he was being cheery again so I could be irritated. I can't handle kindness; it makes me feel too soft.

"Leave me alone," I whisper, but my heart's not in it. I don't bother to hide my misery.

He gently takes my hand in his, pulling me along, and I must really be hopeless because I let him. We open the back door on the side of the house and sit by the steps outside, close to Fawad's garden. I take in the sight of ripe red tomatoes, of fresh basil and yellow peppers.

Raza lets go of me, and I sit down, watching as he rummages through the plants until he plucks off a leaf from one and brings it to me. I press it to my nose, inhaling the clean scent of fresh mint.

"Soothed?"

I nod. A moment of silence passes between us.

"You can go now," I say, which I know it is a little mean, since he's just made me feel a little better, but I'm not in the mood for chatting.

He ignores my comment, sitting down next to me. I avoid him, looking the other way, thinking he might leave, not being able to stand the silence, but then he just starts talking to himself.

"When I was a kid, I think I was in preschool, I had to write a letter to my teacher, Miss Lucy, and my mom was trying to get me to address it, but I couldn't understand what she was saying to Miss Lucy. I was like, no there's only one Miss Lucy. Then she was like, okay write for Miss Lucy, and I was like, no, there's only one!"

I turn back to stare at him. He's laughing when I do, but when he sees my unimpressed expression, he winces.

"Tough crowd," he says. He nods. "Okay, my little cousin seriously doesn't know how to talk even though she's four—she's probably running around here somewhere; I'll introduce you—but she calls mozzarella sticks 'ma-cha-cha-cha-cha sticks.'" He cha-cha-cha's as he imitates her version of mozzarella sticks.

He sees my blank stare. "No?" He thinks further.

"Okay, well, not to get philosophical on you, but—" He stops when he sees my reluctant laugh. "What?" He asks, blinking.

"Nothing," I say. He gives me a skeptical glance, dark eyes narrowed behind his glasses.

"As I was saying, not to be philosophical—"

Before I can stop myself, I laugh. I clap a hand over my mouth, trying to mask my smile.

"Seriously!" he cries out, appalled. "I didn't even finish the story. What's funny?"

"You're saying *philosophical* wrong," I point out. "It's not 'philos-phi-cal.' It's 'phi-lo-sa-fi-cal.'"

"Philosophical?" he says, pronouncing it wrong again, and I laugh, really laugh, before I can help myself. His eyes widen with delight. "Philosophical," he says again, and there I go laughing again, covering my mouth with my hand, but he sees.

"Stop," I say, looking away, but I'm still smiling.

"Thank God you smiled," he says. "I thought I would have to do something insane."

"As if you haven't been already?"

But there's no denying the lingering smile on my face. He grins, positively buoyant.

"How are you so cheerful?" I ask, genuinely curious. "It's unnerving. And concerning."

But I really do want to know. Haris dumping me shouldn't have put me in such a bad spot, but it has. We dated for three months, and when school was finishing up, I figured we would have the whole summer ahead of us.

I planned all these cute little dates, imagining picnics in the parks and beach days and all the ice cream we would eat and movies we would watch. I knew he'd be going away for college at the end of the summer, but I thought we would try to make it work.

I liked him enough to want to try.

But apparently he didn't feel the same way; not at all.

"I just don't want to be tied down," he'd said to me, the last time we saw each other, sitting in his car. It used to be one of my favorite things, sitting in the passenger seat while he drove, the car our own little universe with music and light and laughter.

But that day, the car felt too small, and I couldn't breathe.

"What are you saying?" I'd asked.

"I think we should break up." He hadn't met my eyes.

We weren't even done with finals yet. The summer was over before it had even begun.

"But . . . I thought . . . we were going to spend all this time together."

"I'm just not feeling it anymore." He'd shrugged, finally looking at me. And it had been like looking at a stranger. All that love and warmth that used to be in his eyes when he looked at me, that wicked smile always on his mouth, the dimple popping into his cheek—all of it had disappeared.

At that moment, I'd wondered if I'd ever known him at all. Our entire relationship, I'd been sure about two things: how he felt about me and how I felt about him. Turns out I was wrong.

"You're just too much," he'd said. "I think this is best."

I know I'm not too much, but it still hurt to hear, then and now, when I think about it.

It's worse that I'm still so upset about it. He was a jerk. So when I ask Raza how he can be so happy, I do really want to know.

"Life is good," Raza says with a shrug.

"And when it's not?"

"It's still good." I look at him, the easy way he says that, and I can't relate. Maybe I'm being dramatic. Probably I am. "My mom used to do this thing," he continues. "Whenever she saw me, she'd say, tell me something good. Even when I was having a shitty day, and I couldn't find anything to say, she'd press and say, tell me something good." He smiles at the memory, expression soft. "And eventually I'd mumble something dumb like, I'm alive, or I had pizza for lunch, but you know, it sort of always made me feel better. Like, despite the shittiness, there was goodness."

"That's actually pretty sweet," I say, smiling a little.

"Yeah," he agrees. "She passed away a few years back, but it's a nice thing to hold on to. Whenever I'm having a tough time or just missing her, I'll hear her voice saying, *Tell me something good*, and it helps a bit."

Ohmygod. My heart gives out. I had no idea.

"Shit, I'm so sorry," I say, voice shaky. He nods, swallowing. His eyes are misty, but he doesn't look away; he meets my gaze, he lets me see.

"Thank you."

I can't believe he's so ebullient when there's been so much grief in his life, true grief. I'm sulky because of a breakup. Losing one's mother, at any age, is painful, but to lose one's mother so young . . . I can't even imagine.

He must sense how terrible I feel about it because he bumps his shoulder with mine.

"Don't feel bad," he says. "Just come have fun. I want to feed Asif Bhai so much mithai he throws up."

I nod, following him back inside, back to the music and the laughter, and I really try, but it's hard. I sit down on the sidelines after a little while, and he tries to get me to join the dancing, holding his hand out to me, but all I say is, "Please." He must see the tears welling in my eyes because he lets it go.

And then he surprises me by sitting down beside me.

"You don't have to," I say, feeling miserable. "Go have fun."

"I already am." He smiles. He means it, and it's true. Even just watching other people having fun is enjoyable to him. I can see it on his face.

We sit together, and after a little while, when he looks over at me, I offer him a smile.

The next day is the mehndi. My khala's house is a chaos zone with all the family from Pakistan staying there, plus me and my parents, but it keeps me busy. We stayed up late playing cards and ludo, while the adults drank chai and told stories, and while it was great fun at the time, I'm seriously regretting it now, as Mama wakes me up at ten o'clock.

"Chalo," she says. "Have some breakfast, then Asif Bhai is calling everyone to practice your dances for the mehndi tonight."

The dances we were *supposed* to do last night, but we got a little distracted and lazy.

"Mama, ten more minutes," I groan, pulling my blanket over my face.

"Sajal, utho na," Mama says. "Get up!"

She pulls my blanket off and I scowl, but nonetheless I get up. I wash and head downstairs, eating some quick breakfast before joining my cousins in the living room. Asif is leading the cause, breaking down who's dancing with who, and to what song.

"I'm only doing one dance," I say, before he can assign me to more. Asif opens his mouth to object, but I hold up a hand. "Please." He nods, desisting, and I'm glad. I'm not exactly in the mood to make merry, but I can force myself to do one dance for dear Asif.

"You don't like dancing?" someone asks. I turn, and it's Raza. I shrug. Actually, I do like dancing. Haris and I used to dance all the time: in grocery stores, getting snacks; at the mall, shopping; outside his car, at the beach.

My stomach twists. I haven't danced since the breakup.

"I did a dance last year for my cousin's wedding, it was over in Texas, and God it was hot, it was over the summer, too, and anyway, the dance was to 'First Class,' you know, from that movie, *Kalank*, I think it is? My dad is a huge fan of historical movies, so he made me watch it with him, even though it was sort of problematic with its portrayal of Pakistanis, you know, as most Bollywood movies are . . ."

Suddenly, he stops chattering and looks at me. He pauses.

"Hey," he says, eyes warm behind his massive glasses. "Tell me something good."

"Raza . . ."

"Come on," he says.

"I can't think of anything."

"Try. Please."

I sigh. He's not going to leave me alone until I say something, so I might as well.

"I guess . . .well . . ." I look at him. "No one has spilled dahi balle on me today."

My lips twitch. He grins. "Hey, the day is still young, don't jinx yourself."

Despite myself, I smile.

"There's that smile," he says, expression soft. "It seems like you're going through a tough time, and you don't have to talk about it, but I hope it gets better because you really do have a lovely smile."

"It's stupid," I say, cheeks heating. Especially after hearing that his mother passed away, being this upset over my brief relationship and following breakup is dumb.

"I'm sure it isn't," he says. "If you're upset, it must be something."

"No, no it is," I insist.

"Well . . . you're not stupid."

And I don't know why, but that comforts me. Maybe he's right. Maybe it isn't silly to be upset. I did lose the entire summer I had planned, all those imaginings and hopes and memories waiting to be made. That is a loss. And I did lose this wonderful connection and friendship and person that I cared for deeply; that isn't nothing.

And I can accept that it upset me. That doesn't make me stupid, and it isn't embarrassing. I did really like Haris. He did hurt me. There's no shame in that.

I'm allowed to feel all these emotions; I'm *not* too much.

"You know," I say, looking at him, "I actually do sort of feel better."

"Come on." He grins, walking to the rest of my cousins and Asif Bhai's friends. "Let's dance."

The music starts, and we break up into our groups to practice, all of us coordinating and choreographing. Mama and Khala peek their heads in during our practice to giggle and make fun of us, and I'm not even mad because it is funny.

Asif is a good dancer, but Fawad is a hopeless case. He keeps getting frustrated, threatening to quit every other second.

"I have work to do!" he cries, as he messes up another step.

"He's being forced," Raza whispers to me, tone conspiratorial. "I bet Humaira Baji is making him."

"No way," I say, giggling. "I doubt it."

"I'm telling you," Raza replies. "She's scary. Like a queen."

We laugh as Fawad continues to struggle.

But a few hours later, we make some serious headway, and the performances are basically set. And just in time, too. We all have to get ready for the event, which is starting soon. Everyone disperses to get ready.

"I'll see you later," Raza says. I wave goodbye as I head up the stairs, where Mama is already yelling at me to get changed and my cousins are waiting to use the iron and Khala is getting her makeup done.

I get dressed up, and when I glance at myself in the mirror, I smile. I look pretty. I do a little twirl, and Mama looks at me, smiling.

"Meri soni kudi, you look wonderful," she says, beaming. I feel good.

But then we go to the venue, and there's so many people, I feel myself retracting, and my outfit feels too loud, and I want to hide. I want to go home and get into bed.

Just as I'm considering making a break for it, I spot Raza, and for a moment, everything in me calms, which is the craziest paradox because he is the least calm person I know.

He sees me and his entire face lights up. He comes over, and as he does, I take in the sight of him. He looks really good. His hair is doing this lovely thing, falling just so. Even his dorky glasses and his absurd grin look amazing.

"You look great," he says. I'm wearing a hot pink and bright blue outfit, and for a second, I think he's teasing, and I feel insecure.

"It's too much," I say, fidgeting. "My mom made me wear it."

"So what?" he replies, confused. "You look fantastic."

"I don't know . . ."

"People always tell me I'm too much." His face flashes with hurt. "And maybe I am, but it's better to be too much than too little, I think. More fun!"

I look up into his eyes. Even in heels, I'm shorter than he is. Finally, I smile.

"Yeah, I think you're right."

We stay together as the night progresses, and I have loads of fun. We talk and play with the little babies and laugh. After appetizers, all the men leave the hall so that the girls can do their performances, and for a second, I get that feeling, like I don't want him to go.

But he does, giving me a smile that says, *Don't worry, I'll be back*, and I release a long breath. The girls do their dances. Naadia's best friend, Sadaf, does a dance with her sister Haya, and her best friend, Zahra, and it's incredibly well done. Humaira has about a dozen dances, with various friends and cousins, then one with Naadia, herself, before Humaira does a solo dance to "Tere Bin," and everyone's crying.

When the girls are done, the men come back and Asif gets on the dance floor with his boys, pointing and grinning at Naadia, who's laughing and clapping. Asif does his dance, and this is the one with Raza in it. Raza's having the time of his life, singing along and doing the facial expressions and moving so well.

Then the song switches and it's time for me and my girl cousins to jump in, which we do, and I'm focusing on the steps until my eyes meet Raza's and hold, and I just let the music take over.

We're dancing, not together, exactly, not touching, either, but we can't stop looking at each other, sneaking glances between steps. I recall just how much I love dancing and I get carried away, both of us in sync, and when the song ends, my heart is still beating way too fast.

Our eyes meet, and Raza grins.

My heart kicks violently, as if restarting. The realization stops me dead in my tracks.

Oh no.

"I have to go to the bathroom," I blurt, running. As I go, I catch Fawad send a concerned glance my way, while Humaira gives me a pleased, knowing smile.

I ignore both of them, ignore everyone, and rush to the bathroom. My heels click on the floor as I throw the door open and hurry inside, away from the crowds, and thank God the bathroom is empty.

When I arrive in front of the mirror, I see my cheeks are flushed, and there's a ludicrous smile on my face.

I cover my mouth, horrified.

Oh God. I'm starting to like Raza.

Not this shit again.

At the shaadi the next day, I avoid him, like any rational person would do.

I spend most of the night clinging close to my mother—so much so, in fact, that Mama gives me a weird look, wondering what the hell is wrong with me.

I'm attached to her hip while she converses with an auntie whose brown eyes are looking at me a little too closely, like she knows all my secrets. The auntie has dark brown hair in a bob cut, and a mole above the left side of her mouth, but I don't recognize her.

I must be staring because Mama elbows me.

"Sajal, jao na," she says, irritated. "Go hang out with the bacha party. Why are you so attached to me and the aunties? Ajeeb larki."

"Mama, I—" I start, but I don't know what to say. "My stomach hurts."

That's at least sort of true.

"Acha, go have your stomach hurt with your cousins," she says. I try to protest, but she shoos me away. "They've come so far from Pakistan and you're not even paying attention to them. Buri baat. So rude."

Swallowing hard, I go, walking across the beautifully decorated hall toward my cousins. I make it about halfway until Raza falls into step with me, sipping a Shirley Temple.

"Hey, where have you been?" Raza asks, eyes wide and bright. "I've been looking for you."

My stomach twists, and my heart hurts. Oh, I *really* like him. Hence, I can't look at him. It'll just make it worse. I can't let myself fall.

Love is a wonderful illusion, but it isn't real.

"I've just been with my mom," I say. My voice sounds high even to my own ears. I clear my throat. "I think my cousins are calling me, so I'll see you later!"

I try to dash off, but he holds a hand out onto my dupatta, gently stopping me.

"Hey, where are you running off to?" he asks, a little concerned. "Is everything okay?"

"Yeah, yeah! Everything's fine!" But I won't look at him. "I just want to hang out with my cousins before they go back to Pakistan, you know?"

"Right, yeah, of course," he says, still a little confused. "Can

I just say something really quick before you go?"

Panic beats through me.

"Mhm?" is all I can manage.

"Sajal," he says, and I can't bear it, I turn to look at him. He smiles that sweet smile. "I think you're really cool, and I hope after this crazy wedding is over, we can see each other again. I'd love to hang out."

"Like, as friends?" I squeak. He laughs.

"No, not as friends."

I freeze in place, terrified. It's just like how it was with Haris in the beginning, who gave me some of the best joy in my life, only to change his mind and dump me and give me some of the worst grief.

I can't go through that again.

I won't.

"Oh," I say, swallowing the lump in my throat. "Uh . . . no."

He blinks. "What?"

"I don't want to hang out with you," I say. It doesn't sound believable, to either of us. I see the hurt question in his eyes: *Why are you doing this?* But he doesn't ask.

He won't push if I'm being so clear at saying no. Even if he is confused, which he definitely is.

For once he doesn't have anything to say. All he does is nod, and I can't look at him, so I walk away—but not before I see his eyes well with tears.

And I start crying, too.

We're at the venue for the last event and I'm trying to fix my hijab in the hall mirror, but it won't sit right. My eyes are puffy from crying all night; I told everyone I was crying because of the wedding, to which Mama gave me the weirdest look.

"Pagal larki, only people on the girls' side are supposed to cry at shaadis," she said. To which I cried, "Mama, please!" And she said, "Acha, acha, you can cry, ro lo, meri jaan, ro lo."

So I cried all night.

Now I just have to get through the walima, which is the reception from the guy's family, and then I'll go home, and I'll probably never see Raza again. I convince myself that's a good thing, but if it is, why do I feel like it's the actual worst thing?

What if I'm the one who's wrong about everything?

"Are you all right?" a voice asks. I turn to see Humaira, wearing a gorgeous silver and mint outfit, a diamond teeka glittering on her forehead. Her warm eyes are soft with concern.

"Yeah," I say quickly, clearing my throat. "Yes, everything's great!"

Humaira comes to stand with me, a hand resting on my shoulder.

"Are you quite sure?" she asks, voice kind.

My composure melts. "No," I say, about to cry again. "I don't know!" I cover my face with my hands.

"Aw," Humaira says, pulling me into a hug. I don't want to ruin her pretty clothes with my crying, so I try to refrain from full-on sobbing, letting only a few tears slip out. I pull away, sniffling.

"You know how you said love is real, and we have to always have hope?" I say, voice shaking. She nods. "Well, what if love is real, but you're too much of a coward to seize it? And worse, what if you do seize it, but people change and break your heart anyway?"

"Oh, darling," Humaira says. "We're all fools in love. So no, you're not a coward for being scared. Everyone's scared when it comes to love! That's how you know it is real. And yes, people can change, so it is a massive risk, but you cannot let fear of heartbreak stop you from seizing happiness."

"Really?"

"Yes. The trick is not to let fear paralyze you—which is really the trick for anything worth doing in life."

"For once, I have to agree with Humaira," a voice adds. We both turn to see Fawad, handsome in an impeccable suit, join us. Humaira gives him a warning look, and he throws his hands up in peace. "No, truly, I agree. You must never let fear dictate your actions, Sajal. You must always be brave."

Humaira mutters something under her breath, irritated, before turning to him.

"God, go away!" she says to Fawad. His face breaks.

"What?"

"Leave!"

"Why are you being mean to me?" he cries, walking away.

"Go!"

After he's gone, Humaira shakes her head.

"I can't believe he did some akal ki baat . . ." she says. "I might just be impressed."

My lips tug up in surprise. "So why did you yell at him, then?"

"I can't let him know I'm impressed," she replies coolly. "He'll get a massive head about it, and he's insufferable enough."

I laugh, really laugh. I've never seen Fawad put in his place by anyone, but Humaira does it easily; it's funny to see.

"Anyway," Humaira says, squeezing my shoulder, "will you be all right?"

I nod.

"Yeah . . . Yeah, I think so."

We head into the hall, and the walima kicks off, guests arriving and mingling. I spot Raza's father right away, but Raza isn't with him. The evening advances, appetizers open, and still no sign of Raza.

He arrives late, and the sight of him immediately sends my heart into a frenzy. I want to go to him, but on the first try, I lose my nerve. On the second, he's busy, and on the third, he sees me, and I hope.

But then his face shutters and he turns away, avoiding me.

And I know I have to make it up to him. I have to let him see.

I was scared before, still am, but I'm not going to let that stop me. Fawad and Humaira were right; I have to be brave.

And then I get my moment.

"And now a speech from the groom's cousin, Sajal," the MC announces. Swallowing hard, I make my way to the stage, taking the microphone from the MC. Everyone quiets, waiting for me to begin.

"Assalam u alaikum everyone, for those of you who don't know, I'm Asif Bhai's favorite cousin," I say, smiling. My heart is beating a thousand miles an hour, but I can do this. "To Asif Bhai and Naadia Baji, congratulations, I'm so happy for you both." I pause, looking out to the crowd, and my gaze immediately rests on Raza.

He's not looking at me, but I don't move my eyes from him, and then . . . he meets my eyes.

And I immediately cut the speech I had planned and just start talking.

"Love is scary," I say, taking a deep breath. "Opening your heart to someone opens you to the greatest joy, but also to the worst grief if something doesn't work out. And the fear of that grief can stop you from opening your heart, but you can't let fear dictate you. You have to take the risk because it's worth it. Love is always worth it. Choosing to love is the bravest thing we can do."

I stop speaking, taking in a breath as Raza looks at me, only at me. I hope he understands.

Clearing my throat, I look back at the couple. "I'm so happy to see Asif Bhai being brave and choosing to love. May Allah bless you both with infinite happiness and joy, and may He increase you both in love for one another, and may He never let grief touch either of you. Thank you."

I hand the microphone back to the MC, and the crowd claps as I go to hug Asif and Naadia before walking back to my seat. There are more speeches, then finally, dinner, and as everyone eats, I keep my eyes trained on Raza, waiting for him to stand, and then finally he does.

He goes to get a drink from the bar, and I make a beeline for him, heart hammering.

"Raza," I say, voice breaking. He turns and looks at me, and I'm afraid he'll be angry, but his face is blank. "In case it wasn't apparent, that speech was for you," I say, swallowing the massive lump in my throat. "I mean, it was also for Asif Bhai and Naadia Baji, obviously, but like, also for you."

He nods, turning back to the bartender to get his drink, and my heart sinks. This can't be it.

"You aren't going to say anything?" I ask, tears welling in my eyes. He takes a sip of his drink.

"Yesterday you said you didn't want to hang out," he says, adjusting his glasses. "That was hurtful. Because I could tell you were lying, and I didn't understand, and you didn't explain."

"I know, I'm sorry," I say, heart twisting. "I was being a coward, but I won't anymore, I promise. I want to be brave. I want to be cheerful. I love the way you interact with the world." I pause, catching my breath. "And I'd love to see you again."

He thinks about it for a second—then grins.

"Okay," he says. "I accept your apology. And I'd love to see you again, too."

"Really?!" I shriek, grinning.

"Really," he says. I step forward and squeeze his arms, and he runs a gentle hand against my elbow.

"Now let's have some fun," I say, grabbing his hand. He puts his soda down, and we go to the dance floor, where all my cousins and Naadia's friends are beginning to dance. My heart fills and expands with happiness.

The DJ plays "Nach Punjaban" and the crowd goes wild, as it always does when Abrar ul-Haq is played. I cheer with everyone else as Asif and Naadia dance in the middle of the dance floor, their hands linked.

Raza is dancing beside me, and Humaira makes her way over to me, seeing us together. She pokes my side, smiling, and I shrug, putting my hands up in a "What can you do?" gesture. She squeezes my arm, and at the same time, we both grin.

"Oh no," Fawad says, looking at the pair of us. Humaira's eyes meet his.

Seeing the horrified look on his face, she throws her head back and laughs, overjoyed.

I watch the way Fawad looks at her, something glinting in his eyes, and I laugh, too.

When it comes to love, no one is safe. Even the staunchest cynics can be converted, and isn't that such a wonderful thing?

Sehra
SYED MASOOD

"*I*t's going to be an awful wedding."

Inaya Yusuf shrugged as if she were completely unbothered by the fact that my older brother was going to be miserable and alone on the day he was getting married. This indifference of hers was weird for a couple of reasons.

For one, Inaya and I had been friends since forever and our parents had often paid Tariq Bhai to be our babysitter when we were growing up. He hadn't been particularly good at the job, but that's why we'd loved him.

I mean, I'd personally never recovered from being exposed to movies like *The Shining* or *The Exorcist* at around six or seven years of age, but Inaya had. In fact, she had come to adore them. Tariq Bhai's ridiculous passion for horror movies that were cult classics was something she'd inexplicably come to share. It was something, much to my continued and constant terror, they'd bonded over.

In some ways, he was as much family for Inaya as he was for me. She even called him "bhai," just like I did.

So it didn't make much sense that she didn't care he was going to be brokenhearted on one of the biggest days of his life.

Also, I'd always thought it impossible for Inaya not to care about something. There was no good cause, no injustice, no political or environmental wrong that she was unwilling to battle for. She was a fighter. Always had been.

But now, instead of getting riled up that no one from our families or community would attend Tariq Bhai's wedding, she simply reached across our high school cafeteria table and plucked a fry off my plate.

I bit back a scowl. I hated that habit of hers. I'd never told her that, of course. Unlike her, I wasn't about picking fights. I preferred to get along with the world and liked nothing better than when the world got along with me. Maybe this was why horror movies didn't work for me. I didn't like disrupted realities. There was a reason the world was the way it was and it seemed easier to accept it instead of trying to change it.

The only people I ever aspired to stand up to were boss-level villains in video games, and I was just fine with that.

Even if it meant that my fries got stolen on a regular basis.

I shoved my glasses back up my nose in an irritated manner, hoping that this would send a message to Inaya. It was a "get your own fries and stop pretending that you don't eat them" gesture.

It didn't work this time, just like it hadn't worked the hundred million or so times I'd tried it before. She took another fry off my plate.

"I'm serious," I said, deciding to ignore the ongoing theft of my food. "He's going to be all alone."

"Then do something about it, Han," she told me, as if it were the simplest thing in the world.

My name isn't "Han." I actively wish it were, to be honest, because my parents—for reasons they've never bothered to explain—decided to call me Burhan-ud-Deen when I was born.

Burhan-ud-Deen Nishapuri. I'm pretty sure there are bowls of alphabet soup with fewer letters in them.

Thankfully, almost no one called me by my "actual" name because Tariq Bhai, having declared "nobody has time for that," started calling me "Han" when he'd been going through a *Star Wars* phase. It was, in my opinion, the nicest thing anyone had ever done for me.

The fact that the nickname caught on had irritated my parents. They liked having a kid called "Proof of the Religion" and did not much care for space operas. But a lot of things Tariq Bhai did annoyed them. It was his gift.

Needless to say, they still used the name they'd given me, but they were the only ones.

"There's nothing I can do," I said. "You know that."

"You were invited to the wedding," she pointed out. "You could go."

"You know Dad said I can't. He'll kill me."

Inaya pulled my plate toward her and rotated it a bit so she could reach the ketchup. "If you're not willing to die for what you love, what's the point of being alive?"

I rolled my eyes.

That sounded like something out of a movie, something that was easy to say when there was a script out there that would make sure things turned out the way you wanted, that you would be okay in the end. That's not what life is like though.

Inaya doesn't have the same issues with her family that I do, so it's easy for her to be cavalier when handing out advice. Her parents support her all the time. Yes, she's super into activism, but they like that. Everyone does. Heck, even the cynical, jaded Tariq Bhai says she's a "youth community leader" at the mosque, and he says it proudly even though he doesn't care much for the community or the mosque in question.

No one's proud of me like that.

But then I guess I've never given them reason to be.

"You don't get it."

"Yeah, I do," Inaya insisted.

I wanted to explain why that wasn't true, but before I could make myself argue, she was already speaking again.

"You're the one who doesn't get it. You have to take a stand sometimes, Han."

"That's easy to do," I said quietly, "when everything you stand for is stuff people approve of. I know you think you're a rebel, dude, but you're actually . . ."

She raised her eyebrows when I trailed off but didn't say anything. She was going to make me finish that thought. I hated when she did that.

"You're perfect."

Inaya didn't answer, at least not with words, but she did reach over and pinch her earlobes. It was something desi kids were taught to do when they were asking for forgiveness. That wasn't why she was doing it though. This wasn't a gesture of sarcastic contrition. She was doing it to call attention to her giant earrings and her "Mickey Mouse hijab."

Disney isn't in the business of making hijabs. At least not yet, though I guess if you give it enough time, and they can figure out a way to make it profitable, they will be.

No, the "Mickey Mouse hijab" isn't an officially licensed product of a mega-corporation. It isn't a product at all. It's a derogatory term. It's what some people call the alternative style of hijab that Inaya prefers, one that goes behind, not over, her ears. It's because she adores wearing really elaborate, massive earrings, which she thinks look pretty and I think look excruciating and painful.

I don't really know if wearing a hijab this way is okay or not. I've never had to learn the religious doctrine around what is probably one of the most politically charged items of clothing in the history of the world. Inaya would tell me that's my male privilege talking and she'd be right.

But I do know that some of the other girls at the mosque sneer at Inaya's fashion choice. I've heard them make snarky comments about it. They say that the hijab is meant to be a symbol of modesty. It is supposed to repel the attention of men away from you. Wearing flashy earrings does the opposite of that, so in their opinion it isn't in keeping with the spirit of the hijab.

Honestly, I think if anyone else in the community wore it that way, it wouldn't be a thing. But it is Inaya Yusuf's one imperfection, so people pick away at it because there are no other ways to take her apart.

I mean, if social media has taught us anything, it is that human beings cannot resist the opportunity to criticize someone who has accomplished something, attempted something, dreamt of something grand. It is a terrible impulse, but it's part of who we are. When my friend complained about the way her hijab is talked about, I'd shown her a Yeats poem we'd read in class: "Come let us mock at the great."

And you know what? This sounds awful—and I'd never admit this to Inaya or to anyone, really—but I do kind of get it. Having your parents hold up Inaya as a shining beacon of everything you're supposed to be gets old fast. That, I think, is the real reason she gets hate.

"Ignore them," I'd told her, after she'd started to get comments on her Instagram about it.

She'd given me a look that made me think she felt worse for me than she did for herself. "That's your solution for everything, Han."

I wasn't really sure what she meant but it had stung enough that I'd never brought up the topic with her again. Neither had she. Sometimes when your friends hurt you, and if the hurt is small or unintended, it's okay to let it go. It might even be necessary, in fact.

But the truth was that that comment had cut deep. I wasn't sure why. Maybe it had been because of the way Inaya had said it. Like she was saying something ugly about me.

I hadn't made her explain herself. Because if I had, it might've ruined our friendship. She wouldn't have held back. She never does. Inaya would have, as always, told the truth. It's best, therefore, to not ask her questions you don't want to hear the answers to.

Anyway, I didn't think having some people be catty about the fact that you wear your hijab with your ears showing like a mouse was at all the same thing as standing up to your parents and facing the very real possibility that you'd get the silent treatment or slapped or worse. I mean, technically, Inaya was right. She wasn't perfect, exactly, but her issues at the mosque were minor compared to the challenge I was facing.

But I guess we all think we're the ones climbing the steepest hills in life.

I let it go and Inaya, considering her point made, moved on to talk about something else happening in the world, which, in her opinion, needed fixing.

I was feeling pretty low by the time I got home. Inaya hadn't done a good job of cheering me up. Actually, she never did. She wasn't very good at peddling hope. Another imperfection. I'd have to remember it. I considered making a list.

Anyway, that wasn't really the role she played in my life. It was Tariq Bhai who was always there with a quick joke or funny story to lift my spirits when I needed it. But I hadn't seen him for like half a year now and, in his absence, my heart constantly felt like it was sinking.

It didn't help that when I got home, it was quiet. It shouldn't have been. There should have been music and laughter and chatter and guests and streamers and sweets and flowers and people practicing dance routines they'd probably be too embarrassed to actually perform on the day Tariq Bhai was getting married. But all there was was a deep, aching, mournful silence—the heavy sound of love breaking.

In a house that felt like a mausoleum—at least, I imagine that's what it felt like because I've never been in one of those—I found my parents sitting on the opposite ends of a couch in the living room. My father was reading something on his tablet. He'd recently discovered Urdu novels were available for sale online and had pretty much been glued to his iPad since then. My mother was in her usual spot, with her work laptop in front of her, her brow furrowed in concentration.

Between them, carefully folded, sat what looked like a long strip of deep red cloth.

"What's that?"

"No salam?" Dad asked mildly. "No dua?"

I sighed. "Sorry. As-salamu alaykum." After my parents mumbled their responses, I asked again, "What's that?"

My mother glanced at her husband, who answered for them. "It's the turban I wore when we got married. My father put it on for me, along with the sehra. I thought I would carry the tradition on—"

I couldn't keep the excitement out of my voice. "Really? Then you're going to—"

"I was going to throw it away," he snapped. "As I was saying before you interrupted me, I'd kept it thinking one day I'd get to carry on the tradition with Tariq. But what's the point of keeping it around now, now that he's ruined everything?"

"Don't worry," Mama said, "I reminded him that you do exist."

My father sighed, like he wasn't necessarily sure this was a good thing, but said nothing more.

"Thanks," I told Mama, my hopes that they'd changed their minds about not going to Tariq Bhai's wedding dramatically deflating.

She gave me the best smile she could manage. "A woman may someday agree to marry you. Miracles do happen. Maybe Inaya will show poor taste for once."

I made a face. Lovely as Inaya was, we were just friends. For some reason though, the fact that we'd remained close even as we'd grown up made desi uncles and aunties think there was way more to our relationship than just that. Outside of school, we're heavily chaperoned and never alone with each other. Everyone seemed convinced we had latent romantic feelings for each other that would erupt like a volcano someday, and so they were all really vigilant.

It's like all aunties and uncles are obsessed with who wants to have sex with whom. It's a problem.

"Chalo, kis ko bana rahe ho," Mama said. "If only you could be so lucky."

"I'm not interested in talking about Inaya. I want to talk about Tariq Bhai."

That made my mother's knowing smile disappear.

My father, for his part, scowled and turned his attention back to whatever he'd been reading before saying, "We've already had this conversation."

"It wasn't a conversation. I didn't get to speak."

"That's because no one cares about what you have to say, Burhan."

I winced, not because he yelled—he didn't—but because he said it with such an unshakable disregard for my feelings or opinions that it felt cold enough to burn.

Still, uncharacteristically—maybe because I was spurred on by the conversation I'd had with Inaya at school—I went on. "Tariq Bhai isn't dead. Can we stop acting like it? This isn't fair. He just fell in love with someone you don't approve of. Someone you don't even know, by the way, so—"

"He knew the rules," Dad pointed out. "He knew what would happen if he broke them."

"We don't need to arrange your marriages, beta." Mama broke in. "We know the world is changing. But it would have been one thing if he had chosen a Muslim girl from a good family. Have we ever said anything about your relationship with Inaya?"

I resisted, somehow, the urge to throw my hands up in the air.

"It's just that Tariq chose the wrong kind of woman. Of all the people in the world, he picks a godless white one—"

"Her name is Faith."

My father snorted in disdain. He'd never really been a fan of irony.

"You knew how to live your lives," Mama said softly. "Both of you. We didn't ask for much. Just no dating. And no drinking."

"No drugs," Dad added. "No cursing."

"And no gambling."

"And no pork."

"Well, yes," Mama agreed, "obviously, you have to do those basics. Fasting when you have to. Prayers five times a day. Keeping halal. But really that's it. That's not asking too much, is it?"

"There are about a billion Muslim girls in the world," my father said. "He could have picked any of them. But did Tariq do that? No. Because it isn't about love or whatever bullshit he is telling himself. It is about being willful and disobedient, like he always is. He's always wanted to walk his own path. This I will not permit."

"It doesn't seem to matter what you will or won't permit." I grimaced as soon as I said it. I'd meant it to sound reasonable and logical. It had come out sounding like snark. It was the one thing my parents did not tolerate.

Well, that and romantic feelings for non-Muslims, apparently, or violations of any of the laundry list of rules they'd just rattled off.

Neither one of my parents raised their voice. That wasn't really their thing. They never ran hot when they were angry. They just went arctic and stopped speaking to you. It was the only way they knew how to discipline us.

Well, the only way they disciplined me. I'd seen Dad hit Tariq Bhai a couple of times, when he'd done something outrageous like "borrow" the family car or get caught sneaking into a movie with some girl.

My father set aside his tablet and rose to his feet. This used to frighten me when I was younger, not because he'd strike me—like I said, that seemed to be reserved for my brother—but because he could, because of how much more of a physical presence he had than I did.

I was surprised when I wasn't frightened now.

I was surprised at how tall I'd become.

"You have seen babies, haven't you? You've seen how small, how helpless they are. From that, we have raised you up so you can look us in the eye and disrespect us, hmm? You will teach us about the world now? About what is fair and what is not fair?"

I looked down, unable to meet his gaze.

He put a hand on my shoulder. "Be better than Tariq. I thought, always, that he was the strong one, the one on which you would have to rely. But no. You never acted out, never challenged us, and we see now your true value."

I was struggling to study when my phone rang. It was Tariq Bhai. I answered right away, then rushed to close the door to my room. It was good, even if I'd been commanded to cut off all contact with him, to hear his ever-cheerful voice. He sounded, like he always did, like he had just stopped laughing a moment ago when he greeted me.

My parents had named him well, after the morning star. That was awesome. I took a moment to reflect, for the thousandth time, what had possessed them to name me "Proof of the Religion." I was no such thing. I prayed when I had to pray and fasted and everything, but I wasn't proof of anything except that my parents had decided to have sex at least more than once in their lives.

"Ugh. Gross."

My brother seemed confused on the other end of the line. "What?"

"Nothing. I just had . . . an uncomfortable thought."

"And you haven't even heard what I need from you yet."

I raised my eyebrows. "Okay."

"Have they cleaned out my room yet?"

"No."

He let out a sigh of relief. "Good. Listen, I need you to get some stuff out of there before they do. I don't want things to get worse than they already are."

"What could possibly—"

"Just go to the table on the right side of my bed."

"Fine," I muttered. "It's not something weird, is it?"

"Depends on your definition, I guess."

"It isn't going to be like the time you hid a skull in your closet and Mama nearly died when she found it?"

Tariq Bhai chuckled. "No, we're not close to Halloween."

"We're not permitted Halloween," I reminded him. My parents were convinced that due to its pagan roots, it was wrong for Muslims to celebrate the holiday.

"What are we permitted, Han?"

"It's not so bad. Every family has rules. You've just never been good at following them."

He didn't say anything in response. It made me regret my words, made me wonder if they'd been too harsh, especially as I walked into Tariq's room. It was, in its glorious messiness, the complete opposite of my own. I had few things and I kept them organized. My brother was a collector of everything—Funko Pop action figures from a bunch of franchises, parody inspiration posters, and special editions of the many terrible movies he loved—and his room was the definition of clutter.

It made me miss him.

"I've been praying about what to do," I said.

"What do you mean?"

"About your wedding. I'm not allowed to come, but—"

"I don't expect you to be there." His tone was hard but also tired at the same time.

"You don't?"

"I'd love for you to be," he clarified, more gently, "obviously. But even though I need you with me, Burhan-ud-Deen, I know you. I know you like to keep your head down. All you want is to never get in trouble. It's the most important thing in your life."

For some reason that made me want to cry.

Tariq Bhai hadn't used my full name in forever.

"That's not true," I whispered.

"It's okay. Really. Do what you think is right. That's what I'm doing, after all."

I didn't know how to respond to that, so just to have something to say, just to be polite, I asked, "How's Faith?"

My brother actually laughed. "Dealing with family drama, same as me. I don't think they are going to be there, either."

"They don't like Muslims?"

He chuckled. "I think they object to the concept of marriage to brown people in general."

"That's messed up."

"Like you said, every family has rules."

"It's not the same thing," I protested. "Dad and Mama would've been fine with a white girl if she were Muslim. You could have asked Faith to pretend to believe and everything would have been fine."

"How do you ask someone that?"

I exhaled forcefully and took a seat on his bed. "You can't."

"Right. Besides, if you think our parents would have been okay with a white woman or a Black woman or anyone, really, except a good desi girl, you're just wrong. It would've been more uncomfortable for them, because they wouldn't have been able to use religion as a shield, but you know the truth, don't you?"

I didn't answer him. Instead, I opened the drawer to his bedside table. There was a pile of a men's fitness magazine sitting in it. "I'm here."

"Look under the magazines."

I did. "Are these . . . are these condoms?"

"Yeah." After a moment, he rushed to add, "I haven't used them or anything. I just thought I should have them. In case there was an emergency."

I pulled the magazines out and stared at my brother's stash. It wasn't like he had one or two of them. Just like everything else in his life, he'd assembled a collection. There were all kinds of varieties and brands there. There had to be at least a hundred of them.

"Why did you get so many?" I asked.

"Dad always said to be ambitious."

"What if Mama had found these?"

"I was going to tell her I was volunteering at the university health clinic."

I sighed. "You haven't been in university for years now."

"Yeah. I was back when I got them. Anyway, I would've thought of something."

I grinned. "I know you would have."

"Can you throw those away for me before my room gets raided? Don't use them. I'm pretty sure those things expire."

"You know I wouldn't."

"Yes. I know you perfectly, Han."

I'm not stealthy. I trip and fall over things. I make noise as I move around in the world. So I knew that trying to sneak the condoms that Tariq Bhai had amassed out of his room in the cover of darkness, late at night, might not end well. Besides, there was always the risk that my parents would choose today to clean out his room.

I decided, instead, to use my head. Mama was always asking me to get rid of some of my books—she thought I had too many—so I grabbed a cardboard box, lined its base with my brother's expired contraceptives, and covered them with a bunch of older novels that I would've still liked to keep but could live without.

It was the perfect plan.

Mama actually smiled when she saw what I was doing, which had become something of a rare sight lately. "Finally. How long have I been asking you to sort through your novels? I'm glad you've gotten to it."

"You're welcome." I tried to keep the pride out of my voice. Deception completed. I wasn't such a Goody Two-shoes straight shooter, after all.

"Great timing," she went on. "Just yesterday your father and his fellow board members at the mosque were talking about putting together a library. This will be an excellent start."

I frowned. "What?"

"A little library," Mama explained, "at the mosque. To encourage reading. You of all people should think it's a good idea."

"Well—"

She walked over and tried to take the box from me. "I'll give this to the Imam. That way our entire community can enjoy what's in there."

I held on to it, refusing to let go, trying desperately to figure a way out of this situation. My scheme had been perfect. How was it all going so wrong so fast?

"I have it. You can let go, Burhan."

I opened my mouth to protest, but I hadn't managed to think of what to say.

"Burhan?"

"I think maybe I'll keep these books," I said. "I'm having second thoughts."

"Now you're having second thoughts? Right after you heard that they'll be put to use at the mosque? It's definitely the devil that is making you think like that."

"It's not the devil," I reassured her.

She yanked at the box.

I held on to it for dear life.

"Burhan. Ud. Deen. Nishapuri."

I winced at hearing my mother snap my name into tiny little pieces. It meant the fight was lost. I surrendered the condom collection to her care.

"I'll take this over as soon as I can," she said, "but before I do, I thought I heard you talking on the phone. Was . . . was it Tariq?"

"Yeah."

She closed her eyes, then nodded. "How is he?"

"Not so bad for someone who is dead to you."

Mama held up a warning finger in my face. "You don't know what this is like for us. You don't get to judge us."

I bowed my head.

"It's not easy, you know." She took in a deep breath, blinked a few times, then let it out. "Not easy. The most important thing in the world is for parents to control their children, isn't it? We have to guide you, to keep you from making mistakes. This is a big mistake he is making."

"He's twenty-eight years old."

"I know," she said with a smile. "I was there when he was born. Were you?"

I shook my head.

"His Faith will leave him and he'll be miserable. Then he'll come back home, begging for forgiveness."

"You don't know if that is true."

"Okay," she admitted. "Let's say you're right. What happens if they stay together? Let's say they have kids. What will our grand-children be like? Not Muslims, I can tell you that much. Our family tree will be ruined."

The truth was that our family tree had plenty of people—generations in fact—who hadn't been Muslim, who had only converted after the religion was introduced into the Indian sub-continent. It didn't make them less a part of who we had been and who we were.

I wondered if the first person in the family who had become Muslim had faced the kind of condemnation from their parents that Tariq Bhai was facing now.

Maybe the act of becoming what you thought you were meant to be, of doing what you believed you were meant to do, always involved disappointing someone who had dreamt of a different path for you.

"So many hopes we had of him, hmm? We kept your father's turban all these years, thinking that one day you would both wear it. The sehra bandi ceremony becomes less and less important over time. Most boys now, they don't even wear one."

A sehra is basically a veil made up of strings of flowers. I'm not really sure how the mechanics of it work, but it's made to hang in front of the groom's face. They probably pin it to his turban or something. Anyway, it's meant to signify modesty and it is super old-school.

I hadn't actually seen a real sehra in my life. Most grooms now just go with a turban if anything. I'd only seen it in pictures of my parents' wedding, when my dad had worn one. My grandfather had put it on him. I guess Dad hoped to perform at least a portion of what was a fading tradition.

There was a Yeats poem for this, too. Something about the ceremonies of innocence being drowned.

"We should go to the wedding," I said. "Dad should wrap his turban for Tariq, like he always thought he would."

"We can't. We have to—"

"There's nothing left to do, Mama. You've tried. But he's going to do what he's going to do. Not going to the wedding doesn't help him. It doesn't guide him. It just hurts him. And it hurts you. And that hurts me. So please. Let us go."

"A little pain is good sometimes," she said. "It can send a message. There's still time. He'll change his mind. You'll see."

On the day of Tariq Bhai's wedding, I put on my very best shalwar kameez. The kurta was a deep green raw silk with silver buttons and it was matched with a simple white pajama. I planned to wear black dress shoes with it.

I even used some of my brother's hair products and some of his cologne for once. Vanity wasn't typically one of my flaws, but I had to admit that I liked how I looked.

Then I went downstairs to tell my parents I was leaving.

I'm not sure why I did it.

At least, I'm not sure if there was one reason. There were many.

It was because Inaya, dramatic as her advice was, had been right. You have to stand for something.

And because my mother had been right, too. A little pain can send a message.

And because my father, quite by accident, had made me realize how tall I had become, and it seemed like that should mean something.

Or perhaps it was just because Tariq Bhai had called me Burhan-ud-Deen and I didn't think I could bear it if he ever did that again.

"I told you that you cannot go," my father reminded me, once again rising to his feet, once again smaller than he had been before. "I forbade it."

"I heard you."

"Then you know I will not allow this."

"What I don't know," I told him, "is how you will stop me."

Dad stared at me like he didn't know me at all.

"You are wrong." I glanced at Mama. "Both of you. I've been thinking a lot about this, about what I should do. About what's important to me. You know that I always listen. I always do what you ask. Everyone thinks it's because I don't like to argue or fight and, sure, that's true. But also, I love you, so I obey you. That doesn't mean you control me. It just means that I trust you to be right. But you aren't this time. You aren't today. And I love Tariq Bhai, too, and just now he needs me more than you do."

"Burhan. Ud. Deen. Nisha—"

"You know what, Mama?" I said. "Call me Han."

"Why would you do this?" Dad sounded confused.

"I . . . just told you."

"No. Why open defiance? You could have snuck out, tried to hide what you were doing. It would have at least shown some respect to our authority."

"I'm not sneaking around because I'm not good at it. Because I'm not doing anything wrong. Because I want you to come with me. But if you can't—if you won't—there is something I need from you."

The first person I saw when I got to the courthouse was Inaya Yusuf, dressed in an elaborate purple short kameez and gharara, embellished with gold sequins. She was, of course, wearing a matching hijab—in the disdained Mickey Mouse style—and large golden hoops for earrings.

I couldn't help but grin when I saw her. "What are you doing here?"

"Waiting for you," she said simply.

"How'd you know I'd come? I didn't."

Inaya smiled, shrugged, and gathered her dupatta around her. "You look nice."

"Thanks. So do you. Very . . . plum."

"Thank you? Your scarf is a nice touch. Red is a good color on you."

"It's not a scarf. Come on. Let's go."

We drew a few curious looks and more than a few smiles as we made our way through the courthouse. When we found Tariq and Faith, we realized we had guessed completely wrong as far as the dress code was concerned. He was wearing a black suit, with no tie, and she was wearing a simple white dress with red diagonal stripes.

"We're overdressed," I noted.

"Just a little," Inaya agreed. "You go first."

I took a deep breath and walked toward my brother and the

woman who would soon be my sister-in-law. They were sitting together on a bench. His head was bowed as he leaned forward, elbows on his thighs. She had her arm wrapped around his and was whispering something. They looked good. But they looked alone.

I cleared my throat as I got closer. Tariq Bhai looked up, jumped to his feet, rushed over, wrapping his arms around me in a bear hug. I laughed because he hadn't done that in . . . well, ever, actually, now that I thought about it.

"I can't believe you're here, Han."

"I guess you don't know me as well as you thought."

He chuckled as he pulled back, but his eyes were full of tears. He turned to Faith, who was introducing herself to Inaya. "Babe, it's Han, he's my . . . he's our brother. And that's Inaya. His . . . girlfriend?"

"What? No. Dude," I told him. "Not the time for jokes."

"Definitely not," Inaya said at the same time. "I have standards, you know."

"It's nice to meet you both," Faith said quietly. "Thank you for being here. It means everything to us."

"You cut it close, though. It's almost our turn."

"Sorry," I said, unwrapping the long, deep red strip of cloth that I had wrapped around my neck in what Inaya had called a scarf. "It took a while to get through to Mama and Dad."

"You told them you were coming here?"

I nodded.

"Why?"

"I wanted to get you this. It's dad's turban. From his wedding. He was going to do a—" I made a spinning motion with a finger at Tariq's head. "I thought I'd . . . I mean, if you want, I could try to put it on."

"Dad sent this?"

I nodded. That wasn't exactly true. I'd asked for it, but my parents had allowed me to take it, so for the moment, it was true enough.

"Okay." Tariq wiped at his eyes. "Yeah. Sure. I'll sit and you can do your thing."

"Do you even know what you're doing?" Inaya asked.

I shrugged. "How hard can it be?"

It turned out that wrapping a piece of cloth around someone's head and shaping it into a turban—or even something that would pass for one—was a lot more difficult than I'd thought it'd be. After I'd tried three or four times, and Tariq Bhai's hair was a mess, Inaya started to help, which made things worse somehow. Faith, for her part, just looked on, with equal parts amusement and horror.

I was getting pretty desperate when I spotted a desi auntie with a bob cut standing nearby, waiting to be let in just like us, apparently, though she was alone.

"I'm sorry," I said. "We're having some trouble here." I held up an end of the hard-won cloth I'd brought with me. "Can you help?"

She smiled. "There are probably videos on YouTube that will show you how to do that."

"I can't believe," Inaya said, "that you didn't think of that."

As Faith started looking up tutorials on her phone, Tariq asked, "Did you also write a poem?"

"What?"

"A poem in praise of the groom," my brother explained. "In some parts of the world, that's also called a sehra."

I shook my head. "That's not going to happen. Be grateful for what you have."

"I am," he said.

Ten minutes later, I was done with the turban.

As Faith took one of his hands to lead him inside, Tariq Bhai reached over with the other to mess up my hair in what was, I suspect, both a gesture of affection and payback for what he had just suffered through. I grumbled under my breath and tried to fix the damage but had to admire his efficiency.

The auntie who'd helped out with the YouTube suggestion went past—maybe she felt invested now and wanted to see the ceremony—and I started to follow when I felt Inaya bump her shoulder into my arm. I turned back to look at her.

"There's something I want to say," she told me, which was odd because Inaya usually spoke without preambles.

"Now?"

"Yes. It's probably a temporary thing and I'll forget later. Also, I'm not sure if I'm going to be sentimental enough again anytime soon to say it, so there's no time like the present."

I waited for her to go on.

Inaya smiled up at me. "It's just . . . I'm so proud of you, Burhan."

Unexpectedly and without warning, I felt myself choking up.

It was, of course, because of what she'd said. But also because I was so glad I had decided to be here, and it was so terrible that my parents weren't. And it was because I agreed with Inaya—I was really proud of myself, too—and I didn't know what to do with that feeling. It was kind of new.

The door that everyone had walked through earlier opened, and Tariq Bhai poked his head out. "If you guys don't mind, I'd really like to get married now."

"Han's being all emotional," Inaya said. "It's weird."

My brother looked at me more closely. "You okay?"

His turban looked crooked and clumsy and like it was moments away from unraveling. Would my father have done a better job with it? Absolutely. But I'd done the sehra bandi ceremony, and that was something.

Because maybe the real tradition was not about having a family member perfectly place a piece of cloth on your head. Maybe the real tradition was just having someone there to do it in the first place.

I smiled. "Yeah. I'm good."

Fate's Favorites

JASHIE BHUIYAN

Stranger.

The word has been wrapped around Nivali's ankle in loopy black writing for the longest time. She doesn't remember a time when it wasn't.

It doesn't bother her much—all it means is that she hasn't met her soulmate yet. From time to time, Nivali wonders what's written on the other person's skin. Whether it also says **Stranger** or something else entirely.

She's sixteen, carrying four different bouquets, trying to make sure that this godforsaken wedding doesn't implode because of her older sister's excitable mood swings, when she notices black ink swirling around her skin.

Beautiful.

She stares at her wrist incredulously for a second before reaching out for her sister, Tiana, fingers tangling in her shirt. She doesn't know where Ma and Baba went—probably organizing something else for Tiana's wedding—or more likely, *yelling* at someone they hired for the wedding—but it doesn't matter. "*Tiana.* Tiana."

"What is it?" Tiana says distractedly, not even looking over as she inspects the rest of the bouquets. When Nivali tugs on her shirt again, Tiana finally turns around with an exasperated expression on her face, but she freezes when she catches sight of Nivali's wrist. "Is that—?"

Nivali nods, brushing her fingers over the word to make sure it's really there. The realization sinks in when the ink doesn't smudge and her head snaps up, scanning the crowd around them. They're at a mela in preparation for Tiana's upcoming wedding, just a few weeks out. There are hundreds of people around her, all of them squeezing together to get the best deals, haggle for the best prices, and there's absolutely no way for her to figure out which one of them is fated for her. It could be the girl standing by with red highlights in her hair, eyes focused on her phone, or the boy riding his bike through the marketplace, carrying at least six different plastic bags on his handlebars.

"I don't—what am I supposed to do?" Nivali asks Tiana, feeling short of breath. Tiana offers her a comforting smile that does little to console her.

"You wait and hope for the best," she says, squeezing Nivali's wrist gently.

Later, when Nivali is walking toward her Baba's Honda Civic, carrying a garment bag with her lehenga for the wedding, she's too distracted by the dress to notice a pair of eyes following her curiously.

"I'm so glad I don't have to match with you for once," Nivali says to Tiana, who snorts, shaking her head. They've spent their entire lives wearing matching outfits for functions, and both of them are beyond tired of it.

"I'd honestly kill Ma if she even *tried* to make us wear matching outfits on my wedding day." Tiana flips her dark hair over her shoulder. "Enough is enough."

Nivali's grin threatens to break her face in half. She's barely aware of her feet as she approaches the car, slipping inside and making sure not to accidentally wrinkle her lehenga in the process. All she can think about is how excited she is for her sister to finally get married, and to her soulmate, nonetheless.

Nivali misses the word ***Heartbreaking*** across the back of her own neck.

Two weeks before the wedding, Nivali's sitting in her bedroom, practicing swirls of mehndi on her legs, when she notices a new word on her thigh. ***Unforgettable***. It makes her smile for three days straight. To know that her soulmate—the one person in the world that completes her—is thinking these thoughts about her, even if they're subconscious to some degree, makes her feel warmer than the sun. She studies the word for longer than she needs to, mesmerized by her soulmate's handwriting before she gets pulled into shaadi planning once again.

It's the day of the mehndi party and Nivali is in the bathroom, wet hands gripping the sink, knuckles straining as she tries to breathe through the panic in her chest.

She glances up at the mirror for only a second, but it's enough to see ***Talented*** scrawled across her collarbone, and she manages to finally suck in a huge breath.

As she's doing that, the door to the bathroom opens—it's a

gender-neutral bathroom at Tiana's request, and Nivali was happy to insist on it when their parents pushed back—and someone steps inside. Nivali's body turns without permission, hoping and praying it's not her sister. How could Nivali have messed up Tiana's mehndi just *days* before her sister's wedding? When Tiana trusted her over more experienced henna artists? Over actual professionals trained for this? There's still bile rising in the back of Nivali's throat, humiliation making her face burn bright red.

It only worsens when she bumps into the intruder, water splashing from her hands onto the boy's shirt.

"This is my last straw," Nivali says almost to herself, only slightly on the side of hysterical. "Oh my God. Oh my God. I'm so sorry, I'm so—"

Instead of meeting an angry expression, she looks up to warm brown eyes and the brightest smile she's ever seen in her life. "You're fine, I promise," says the boy, and something inside of Nivali twists and turns, coming alive. "Are you alright?"

"I—I'm fine," Nivali says, taking a step back in shock, but somehow the stranger is unbothered, still grinning. His smile is beautiful. So is everything about him.

"Nivali Khan, right?" asks the boy, tilting his head. "The bride's younger sister?"

Nivali can do nothing but nod, pressing her lips together to keep from saying something ridiculous like *The crinkles by your eyes make my heart flutter and I don't know why.*

"I'm Aman Chowdhury," the boy says, holding his hand out. Glancing down at it, Nivali startles at the word ***Beautiful*** written there, just along his pointer finger. It seems someone else knows exactly how stunning Aman is. But maybe it's not Nivali's place to complain, since someone once wrote ***Beautiful*** across her skin, too.

Willing herself not to act like a complete and utter idiot, Nivali takes Aman's hand in her own and quietly says, "It's nice to meet you."

"Likewise," Aman says, still grinning before he falters slightly after giving Nivali another once-over. "Are you sure you're alright, though? You look a bit pale."

Nivali wants to melt into the ground. Her skin is a medium brown, so for her to look pale is an absolutely atrocious thought. The idea of her anxiety being visible, something people can see, makes her want to shrivel up and hide for the rest of her life.

"I . . . I messed up my sister's mehndi," Nivali admits, shocking even herself. Something about Aman feels trustworthy. For the first time in a while, it seems like her instincts are right because Aman's face softens at her words.

"You've been doing mehndi all night, haven't you?" he asks quietly, squeezing her hand once before dropping it. "I saw your designs on some of the other aunties. They look really good. One mistake doesn't mean anything, you know that, right?"

Nivali can't help the nervous laugh that escapes her. "I don't know about that."

Aman seems personally affronted by her response. "I'm serious, Nivali. They're not tattoos, it's not the end of the world. I bet your sister has already forgiven you if there's even anything to forgive."

Nivali blinks, astonished that this practical stranger has that much faith in her. It almost makes her want to believe it, too. She doesn't feel quite as anxious anymore. "You really think so?"

"I know it," Aman says, before reaching in one of the pockets of his kurta, pulling out his phone. "Do you have an art Instagram or something? I'd love to follow it. That way when you're famous one day, I can say I knew you from the start." A smile tugs at the edge of his mouth. "Maybe a selfie, too?"

"Are you pulling my leg?" Nivali asks incredulously, but she's biting down on her bottom lip to keep from smiling as she stares at Aman's earnest expression.

He simply laughs, moving closer to Nivali, warm cheek brushing against hers for half a second as he says, "Cheese!"

Nivali finally lets her grin break loose as the camera on Aman's phone snaps a picture. Before Nivali can ask to see the photo, Aman suddenly holds out his finger, gesturing for her to hold on. "One moment, I swear."

Then she watches as he dashes out of the bathroom, leaving only silence in his wake. She blinks a few times, perplexed, but her heart rate has calmed down significantly, so she can't even really be upset.

She forces herself to take a deep breath, focusing on counting to ten before she exhales. Aman is probably right. Tiana knew Nivali wasn't a professional when she asked her to do her wedding henna—she asked because Nivali is her sister, because she wanted Nivali's art on her body regardless of how good it is. Nivali is so used to worrying about what other people will say, what other people will think, especially in crowds like these, where there are judgmental aunties and uncles alike looking for an excuse to tear into her.

But maybe it really is okay. Maybe Tiana really isn't mad.

The bathroom door swings open again and Aman comes through the door, holding a tube of mehndi in his hand. "Can I have your autograph?"

Nivali's mouth falls open in surprise. "Oh my God, you're insane."

Aman shrugs, handing her the tube anyway. "Is that something you should say to your biggest fan? Who's going to run the Nivali Khan fan club if I leave?"

Nivali bursts into quiet giggles. "My sister, probably."

"So how could she ever be mad at you?" Aman asks, his eyes bright, and something in Nivali's chest finally settles.

"You're right," she says, and now her face is red for an entirely different reason. "Should I make out the autograph to my second-biggest fan then?"

Aman sighs dramatically. "If you must."

Nivali doesn't do that, but she does draw a flower in the center of his palm, taking gentle care not to mess up any of the petals. When she's done, he admires her handiwork with a faint smile.

"Well?" she asks.

"Perfect," he says, but then his expression flickers slightly, focusing on something over Nivali's shoulder. "Uh, I'm really sorry to bring an end to our lovely conversation, but I really do have to pee."

The bathroom stalls. Of course. Jesus Christ, her mental breakdown kept the poor boy from actually using the bathroom. "I'm—I'm so sorry," she says, flustered beyond belief. "Please, by all means. I'm sorry for holding you up."

"It's okay," Aman says, lips pulling up again. "It was worth it."

And then before Nivali can register what's happening, Aman leans in, whispering, "You've got this," in her ear before he dashes off into one of the stalls.

Nivali stands there for only a second, dazed, before she realizes she should probably exit the bathroom.

It's an hour later that the blouse of her saree rides up and she notices the word *Artistic* scrawled across her hip.

A few hours later, Nivali is lying in Tiana's bed, scrolling through her phone as quietly as possible. She came into Tiana's bedroom earlier, intending to ask for forgiveness, only for her sister to pull her into a hug and then refuse to let her go for the rest of the night. Normally Nivali would have left, since the two of them have incredibly opposite sleeping schedules during the summer—Tiana has a 9-to-5 job, and Nivali has recurring insomnia that keeps her up until late morning.

But this may be one of the last nights Nivali can spend the night cuddling with her sister. In less than a week, her sister will be marrying Mohammed, and as nice as he is, she doesn't think he'll want Tiana's younger sister coming over and climbing into their bed at random hours of the night.

So for now, Nivali will make do with what she has.

As she's scrolling through Instagram, a notification appears that makes her stop in her tracks.

aman_chowdhury started following you.

So he really did look up her art Instagram after the mehndi party. Nivali smiles to herself, following him back without thinking much of it. A moment later, an influx of notifications come in as he goes through her different art pieces and likes all of them. Her smile only widens.

A voice whispers *fate* in the back of her mind but she barely hears it, losing consciousness to sleep. She also doesn't notice the word **Enthralling** on the inside of her arm, but it's there all the same.

On the night of the gaye holud, Nivali is tracking the guests a little too closely. There's the pot-bellied uncle who always burps a little too loudly; there's the auntie with a bob cut and a small mole above the left side of her lip that Nivali always finds herself looking at without meaning to; there's the cousin who always sneakily (or not-so-sneakily) pulls out his vape at every possible opportunity; there's Mohammed's sister who's a little too nosy and keeps asking Nivali if she's gotten her first soulmark yet—even if the answer is yes, it's none of her business because Nivali refuses to become the talk of the party. Brown functions are like shark tanks. One drop of blood and they come swarming, demanding an arm or a leg, wanting to chomp into you until there's nothing left.

Thankfully, Nivali has managed to mostly sneak under the radar by wearing full sleeves and carefully wrapping her orna around any remaining skin that shows. Since marks fade with time and Nivali only has two right now, she should be fine, given nothing shows up on her forehead like a flashing neon sign. At any rate, everyone's eyes are on Tiana in her stunning yellow salwar kameez as people come up and smear turmeric across her beautiful brown skin.

Nivali decided before the event even started that she would wait until the end to apply anything on her sister. It feels more special if she's one of the last to do it. She asked Tiana to reserve a spot on her cheek just for Nivali.

Ma and Baba are busy fussing over Tiana anyway, and Nivali definitely wants to avoid that. There have already been one too many instances of people telling Nivali she's next, as if she isn't seven years younger than Tiana and still in high school. The fact that Tiana's getting married at twenty-three already feels far too young to Nivali, but Tiana also met her soulmate when she was ten, so it evens out a little bit.

Nivali scratches at her rib cage, where no one else can see but she knows the word *Lovely* is written, having seen it while she was changing earlier.

Either way. Nivali doesn't really care much for her soulmate right now, anyway. She's too busy looking for a familiar face in the crowd.

It's hours before she finds him. Or rather, he finds her. She's sitting at one of the tables, idly pushing around a piece of rasgulla in a small dessert bowl. Her orna is covering her head to keep people from paying attention to her. Usually, she'd spend the night with her family friend, but Zareen is being held hostage by the aunties because they caught sight of her soulmark. She only got it a few months ago, but she's managed to keep it mostly under wraps. Zareen told Nivali to save herself, and Nivali absolutely listened, saluting her once in solidarity before tucking her tail and making a break for it.

"You know, they just replaced the gulab jamun if you wanted that instead," Aman says as he slides into the seat beside her, and Nivali's head snaps up in surprise.

"Aman," she says, a touch too breathless.

"Nivali," he says, leaning his elbow against the table and smiling up at her. "I've been looking for you."

"Oh?" she says, before she remembers to reel herself in. "Well, I've been around. What did you need?"

"You've been hiding," he says instead of answering her question, poking her arm. His skin is warm to the touch and Nivali tries not to shiver in response. She always runs cold.

"Can you blame me?" she asks, tilting her head to gesture at a cluster of aunties gossiping about a recent engagement of a couple who—if Nivali is hearing correctly—are not soulmates. It's actually not that uncommon for people to be in relationships with people who aren't their soulmates, especially among the younger generation, but every desi elder Nivali has come across seems aghast at the idea of fraternizing with anyone *other* than your soulmate.

Nivali can't say she cares much. It'd be nice to meet her soulmate, sure, but she knows that not everyone does. And just because they're her soulmate doesn't mean they'll definitely end up together. She likes the idea of someone fated for her, but she also wants some choice in who she's with. It's a complicated thing to think about. Right now, she just considers them a comfort, someone who is always with her and seems to think the best of her until proven otherwise.

"They're pretty bad this week," Aman acknowledges, rolling his eyes and bringing her back to the conversation. "It's always soulmate this, soulmate that."

"Right?" Nivali says, shaking her head. "I wish they'd find something else to talk about. Thank God Tiana and Mohammed are soulmates, or I imagine this wedding would be a lot more insufferable."

Aman nods, reaching for a fork to stab the rasgulla Nivali has been playing with. She's about to playfully argue against it when she falters at the words written on the back of her hand. *A dream come true.*

At the aborted movement, Aman looks at her curiously, but then he notices what has Nivali's attention and stops short. Quietly, he asks, "Do you know who it is?"

Nivali glances up from the words, her mind still reeling. Someone out there thinks that she's *"a dream come true"*? Not for the first time, Nivali burns with wonder as to who could be thinking these things about her and *why*. "No," she says, equally quiet. "Do you know who yours is?"

In reply, Aman rolls up the sleeve of his sherwani to show the word **Whimsical** on the inside of his elbow. "Can't say I do. Who would call me whimsical, though?"

Nivali ignores the irrational pit in her stomach screaming of jealousy and shrugs instead. "You're pretty whimsical," she murmurs, looking away.

Aman hums in reply but doesn't say anything else.

Three days before the wedding, Aman posts a picture of him and his friends on Instagram. Nivali likes it immediately and only later notices the words **Twin Flame** on his forearm. She seethes for half an hour at the stranger who would dare to say something like that about Aman before Tiana comes in, freaking out over which earrings she should wear for the wedding, distracting Nivali completely.

At least for a few hours, until she's lying in bed upset about it all over again. She doesn't know why she likes Aman as much as she does already, but the idea of him having someone out there fated for him makes her want to burn down buildings. Sometimes soulmates can be so *annoying*.

Across the dip of Nivali's collarbones are the words **Charming** and **Sweetheart**. When she posts a picture on her Instagram story where the marks are visible, she notices Aman views it. After that, he stops replying to the nonsensical conversation they were having in their messages right beforehand. The next day, when he does reply, his response is dry and bare. He seems more distant than he's ever been, and Nivali decides right then not to post her soulmarks again unless she has to.

Surprising no one and everyone simultaneously, Zareen's family decides to host a small party in celebration of the wedding. At first Nivali thinks it'll be only the bride's side, but then Zareen's older brother, Naveed, comes rushing in saying that the groom's side will *also* be attending and everyone needs to go to the kitchen immediately to help make more appetizers.

Nivali locks gazes with Zareen across the room and both of them roll their eyes before following Naveed into the kitchen. A handful of their family friends follow in suit, all groaning. The parents are too busy decorating or running errands outside, buying sweets and actual meals from the nearby restaurants.

"Pass me the potatoes," Naveed says a few minutes later, and Nivali dutifully obliges as Zareen goes to set the stove. Elsewhere, some of the other boys are being put to work, Tahsin, Sheehan, and Nabil mixing together a large bowl of jhalmuri. "Also, is it true you got your soulmark?"

Nivali nearly spits out her Tang-infused sharbat. "Excuse me?"

Naveed's eyes widen and he looks at Zareen with a guilty look on his face. "Sorry. Was I not supposed to know?"

"I'm gonna kill you," Nivali says to Zareen in a deadpan voice.

Zareen smiles sheepishly. "What's a secret between siblings, Vali?"

Nivali continues to glare at her, but Zareen comes over to hug Nivali until she gives in with a sigh, returning the embrace. "You are so annoying."

"Yeah, yeah," Zareen says, tweaking Nivali's nose before returning to the stove.

"So," Naveed says, calling her attention back to him. "Do you know if your soulmate is that guy you like? Zareen, what did you say his name was . . . Aman?"

"Zareen Mahmud, I swear to God."

"Sorry! Sorry!"

Naveed catches Nivali around the waist, holding her back from strangling his sister in an untimely death. "Oh, calm down, Vali, I'm not going to tell anyone."

Nivali turns to narrow her eyes at him. She doesn't have a brother, so he's the closest she has, and she knows enough to know that's a bald-faced lie. "You are literally the worst at keeping secrets."

He goes to refuse but stops short. "Well. Yeah. But I'll do better this time!"

"Let's all take a breather," Zareen suggests kindly, and then immediately tucks her tail and disappears into the distance, shouting for their other family friend, Raisa, to save her.

Nivali stares after her in exasperation. To be honest, she hadn't even considered that Aman might be her soulmate. It feels too impossible to even hope for. No, she's certain that there must be someone else out there who looks at Aman and thinks **_Beautiful_** and **_Whimsical_**.

But she wishes there wasn't.

For a while, Nivali manages to forget all about it, too distracted by the sudden flurry to make appetizers when the first guest shows up far earlier than expected. Naveed rushes out to call his parents and beg them to come home at the same time that Raisa hands Nivali a huge platter of food to fry.

That's why, when Nivali is turning over a piyaju and sees Aman in the corner of her eye, she accidentally flips it onto the counter by mistake.

"Shit," Nivali mutters, and she hears more than sees Aman laugh brightly somewhere behind her.

"You alright?" Aman asks, coming over with a paper towel to clean up the mess she made, but not before poking her playfully in the stomach.

She releases a nervous giggle that dies in her throat the second she actually sees him. He's as gorgeous as ever and it feels so unfair that Nivali almost stops breathing entirely.

That's when Naveed chooses to enter the kitchen, holding a box of sweets. He doesn't look up as he walks in, simply saying, "Vali, I think these are expired. I tried one and it tasted like shit," while inspecting the back of the box. "Do you want to give them a try before I toss them?"

Aman's entire expression changes, eyebrows raising and his hand falling from Nivali's waist. His eyes are on Naveed, watching him almost coldly.

Nivali can see the assumption Aman is making even before Naveed says anything, and she mentally cusses Naveed out seventeen times in her head for causing issues and problems for her. It probably doesn't help that Naveed is wearing Nivali's orna around his neck, since he noticed it kept slipping off her shoulders and into the food earlier, and took it as a precaution.

"Just throw them out," Nivali says, and hopes she doesn't sound as miserable as she feels. Naveed's soulmark is across his collarbone, the word *Silly* that Nivali absolutely did not put there, stark against his dark skin.

Except the word *Silly* is suddenly wrapping around Nivali's forearm, too. Aman's eyes dart to the word immediately before flashing back to Naveed. This cannot be happening. This cannot be happening.

She already knows who Naveed's soulmate is—and so does he, given it's his girlfriend of two years. So why are the planets colluding against her right now?

Naveed shrugs, walking over to the trash can and throwing out the box of sweets. He still hasn't looked up. Nivali is going to kill him.

When Naveed does look up, his eyes widen and he sizes Aman up with appraising eyes before smirking at Nivali. She hopes Zareen is ready to plan her brother's funeral, because it's inevitable at this rate.

"You must be Aman," Naveed says, holding out a hand for Aman to shake, which he takes almost gingerly.

Maybe Nivali will just throw herself out the window. That seems like a decent plan.

"And you are?" Aman asks, voice sharp.

Nivali is two seconds from legitimately kicking Naveed out before he can do any more damage, but Naveed *laughs*, letting go of Aman's hand to throw an arm around Nivali's shoulders that she doesn't really appreciate. "Well, that doesn't really matter. What I would like to know is, what are your intentions with Vali over here?"

Naveed then proceeds to poke her cheek like they're five and nine years old all over again. Nivali scowls at him, but he just laughs, ruffling her hair.

"Zareen, come get your stupid-ass brother!" Nivali finally shouts, unable to take it any longer. "When is Lily getting here?"

"She's already here!" Zareen calls back from the other room.

A moment later, Nivali's savior, Lily, appears in the kitchen doorway. "Is my boyfriend bothering you again?"

"Always," Nivali says and shoves Naveed away from her, in the direction of his soulmate. "Please get rid of him."

Lily snorts but obliges, grabbing Naveed by the arm and pulling him away from the kitchen. "Come on, silly. I told you not to try those expired sweets."

Naveed pouts. "But, babe, I—"

He disappears from view as they turn around the corner, leaving only Nivali and Aman in the silence of the kitchen. Finally, Aman turns back to her. "Family friend?"

"Family friend," Nivali agrees, trying not to let her relief show too visibly. "For now."

Aman smiles, though it's fainter than usual. "I have my fair share of annoying ones, too. For what it's worth, he seems nice. How long has he been with his girlfriend?"

"Two years," Nivali says, and resists the urge to scratch at her soulmark. She wonders what it must be like to know the person you're dating is the person meant for you. It's so obvious in the way Naveed and Lily are together, in the way she always grounds him, in the way he always knows how to make her laugh.

Will it be like that for her, too?

Will it be like that for Aman?

"Are they soulmates?" Aman asks, even quieter.

"Yes." Nivali breathes. The word **Darling** shows up below Aman's ear, and something dark and red burns in Nivali's chest.

Aman nods, his smile flickering. "Must be nice." He looks away from her, his head hanging low. "I'll see you outside, yeah?"

"Of course," Nivali says and misses the word **Bittersweet** on her ankle bone. "I'll be there."

Aman falters for a few seconds before he offers her one last smile. "Sounds good. You should check on the piyaju before you come out, though."

"Oh fuck," Nivali says before turning her attention back to the stove. "Oh fuck!"

The sound of Aman's laughter carries from the living room. It's a comfort if nothing else.

The day before the wedding, there's another party, hosted in Nivali's own house. The entire first floor is covered in red and orange decorations, and the smell of samosas and shingaras wafts through the living room from the kitchen. The upstairs is mostly off-limits, but Nivali and Zareen sneak up there anyway, joined by Raisa. After a while, some of the other teenagers follow suit. She's not surprised when she sees Aman, but she is surprised when he comes into her room with two of his family friends trailing after him.

"Nivali!" he says in greeting. There's something different in the air between them, an unspoken tension that carries in each of their movements, even if they try to ignore it. "Fancy seeing you here."

Raisa nudges her painfully in the ribs, all too aware of Nivali's blooming crush. At this point, the better question is, who isn't? Nivali didn't even know Aman until last month, since he's from Mohammed's side of the wedding, but now she's hyperaware of his presence.

"Hi, Aman," she says, offering him a wave. "What's up?"

But he's not looking at her. He's looking at the various paintings hung across her walls, all signed off with her signature.

"These are sick!" one of his family friends says, taking a closer look. "Where'd you buy them?"

"She painted them," Aman says before she can clarify, and his voice warms her to the bone. "Didn't you, Nivali?"

Nivali nods, trying to ignore the flush climbing up the back of her neck. "Yeah. I'm really into art."

"You're a prodigy," he says, and it's almost reverent. Zareen lets out a high-pitched giggle at Nivali's side and Nivali has to resist the urge to smack her.

"It's nothing," Nivali says, waving him off. But for the rest of the night, Nivali can't help how much she smiles, much less acknowledge how impossible it is to look away from the stars in Aman's eyes. Something in her gut is tightening to a point where it's almost painful.

Only later, when Nivali's showering off her makeup and sweat, does she notice the word **Prodigy** across her navel and narrow her eyes in wonder.

Nivali has a theory, but it's a dangerous one. One she's not willing to voice aloud, but she finds herself paying closer attention to Aman's soulmarks than anyone else's. The day of the wedding, he's around, helping to prepare for the ceremony, patting Mohammed on the back, carrying boxes into the venue, adjusting flower pieces and setting down chairs, and Nivali can't stop staring.

The word **Confident** wraps around Aman's wrist, the word **Brilliant** on the back of his neck, the word **Handsome** across his cheekbone, the word **Loud** on his jawline, the word **Patient** between his fingers.

On Nivali's own body the word **Wonderful** is written down the length of her arm only to be replaced with **Friendly** on her shoulder and then the word **Cheeky** on one of her cheeks (which Zareen naturally finds hilarious).

After the wedding comes the reception, and there's loads of music and laughter and food and just bright, burning happiness, and still, Nivali has eyes only for Aman.

She watches him from her seat, watches as he dances in the middle of the crowd to "Deewangi Deewangi," and wants him to look at her so badly she doesn't know how to put it into words. Aman finally glances her way, and when their eyes meet, Nivali swears there's a spark, and she wonders if Aman feels it, too. She can't ask, but when Aman winks playfully at her, Nivali finds herself standing up without her own volition.

She makes her way through the crowd until she's coming to a stop in front of Aman and her eyes drop to where **Dearest** is written down the side of his neck.

"Care to dance, Nivali?" Aman asks, and when she nods, he grins a dazzling smile, and covertly pulls her through the crowd until they end up in a mostly uncrowded hall outside the main hall. God knows what the aunties would say otherwise. They pass one of them on their way, the one with the small mole on the left side of her lip, but she only smiles at them like she knows what Nivali's thinking.

Aman wraps an arm around Nivali's waist as "Main Agar Kahoon" starts to play, another classic from *Om Shanti Om* (2007), and she wraps her hand around the back of Aman's neck, thumb brushing along the soulmark.

Aman leans in close and when he speaks into Nivali's ear, she can't help but shiver. "Who do you think caused the word **Enticing** to be here?" As Aman says it, he presses his thumb into the side of Nivali's arm.

Nivali exhales deeply before muttering, "Doesn't matter."

At that, Aman pulls back and raises his eyebrows. There's more there that he isn't saying, all of it covered up by a facade of mischief, but she can see it all the same. "Is that so?"

Nivali merely shrugs, and then because she's slightly stupid and slightly reckless, she pulls Aman in by the neck and kisses him. To her immense relief, Aman kisses her back, fingers tightening where they're digging into Nivali's skin.

When they pull away, the word **Dearest** has disappeared from beneath her thumb and instead **Great Kisser** appears beneath Aman's eye, and Nivali feels delirious from how happy she is.

"Hey," she says, nudging her nose into his. "Can I ask you something?"

He hums, carding his fingers gently through her dark hair. He looks exasperated and fond at the same time. It sends something fluttering in her stomach. "Of course."

She smiles softly. "What do you think of me? Like, if you had to describe me in one word, how would you?"

Aman's brow furrows like Nivali has thrown him for a loop. His fingers pause, resting against the curve of her shoulder as he thinks. His brown eyes are intense when he looks at her, scanning her features like it'll give him the answer he needs.

"I can't," he finally says, looking down. "You're lovely, you're charming, you're funny, you're talented, you're sweet, you're caring—you're everything."

Neither of them breathe for a second, and then, as Nivali predicted—hoped—the word **Everything** shows up neatly on her wrist. Without saying a word, she holds her arm out toward Aman, who glances up and inhales sharply.

"Nivali." Aman breathes, eyes locked on the soulmark. "This— this says **Everything**."

"It does," Nivali says, and swears her heart stops when Aman lightly brushes his fingers along her soulmark, as if unsure it's really there.

"Does this mean you're my . . . you're my soulmate?" Aman asks, and his bright, beautiful brown eyes meet hers.

Instead of answering, Nivali grins and pulls him into a kiss. Aman's laughter spills into her lips and rings loudly in the hallway, even with the music from the wedding booming on not far away.

The Wedding Biryani

NOREEN MUGHEES

The hushed whispers lull as I take the stage. My heart slams in my chest as I get ready to speak. Zayn locks his gaze on me for a second. His eyes, the color of sun-drenched honey, are distracting, but I am resistant to his wicked charms.

I think.

Zayn Malik has tripped me up twice already; I'm not going to lose to him again. He doesn't play fair; he cheats, and he steals my favorite Rumi quotes. And if it weren't enough, uff Allah have mercy! He's hella distracting.

Like right now, he runs a hand through his luscious locks and they fall mesmerizingly slowly, with a curly lock hanging right above his left brow. Like a peacock dancing in full glory circling the poor female.

The first time we met, he carried me across the stadium because I twisted my ankle. I was so taken by his gesture, and he seemed nice, like knight-in-shining-armor nice. The very next day, he completely ignored me in front of his friends.

Eyes on the prize, Zayna, block these tantalizing images of his perfect hair and that square jaw.

Once I take the podium, he leans on the desk and presses on the buzzer. His lips curve upward as if issuing me a challenge with a glance, before saying, "Your time starts now." I clear my throat and speak effusively about environmental justice and how the poor communities in places like Camden are always left out because marginalized communities often live in cramped urban areas with not enough open, green spaces, which makes cleaner air a challenge. On how developers target pristine areas and destroy natural habitats because rich people want privacy and large lots away from poor and often colored communities.

"And time." Zayn presses the buzzer, making me stop right before I speak out the kicker. The line I had been practicing for days.

"Can I get a minute to finish?" I lock eyes with him, daring him.

"Sorry, then I would have to do that for the other team as well," he says without any hesitation.

I am angry but count to ten in my head to calm my rapid exhales. "And that's exactly what you did for them, you gave them longer."

"Because they had a rebuttal."

The teacher who's moderating nods her head in approval.

I huff internally, controlling the rising anger because I have seen Zayn give other teams a few seconds to finish and sometimes even when they didn't have a rebuttal. He knows I can beat him and all the others if he'd let me finish.

He doesn't.

"Rules are rules," I retort.

"And I didn't break any," he claps back.

"This is where I say that Zayn is correct." Mr. Sherman, our English teacher, who's afraid we're gonna break into a fistfight, intervenes.

When I huff off the stage, there's pin-drop silence, as if I have done something wrong.

When he's onstage he gets a round of applause. From all. I hate that he gets to be Mr. Popular here, too. I hate that ever since he joined, our little club has grown, most of them his fangirls.

Afterward, I take out my frustration on my Fitbit, which I had set to beep ten seconds before my time was up as a warning. Of course, I had forgotten to take my device off Mute, so it was partially my fault.

"I want to smack his smug face," I seethe as I talk to my best friend.

Deepika, my sister from another ammi, sighs and puts a hand on my shoulder and squeezes it like she always does to calm me down. Deepi and I have been friends since she was the only other brown girl in my kindergarten who brought Indian food in her lunchbox.

"Zayna, c'mon. You've gotta admit, he is kinda cute, in a very Zayn Malik way." She puts air quotes around Zayn Malik, referring to his actual name.

I have this urge to roll my eyes, but instead of saying something, I slam the door to my locker a little too loud. Loud enough for Maddy and her friends to look our way.

Deepi darts her gaze in their direction, then in mine. "Uh-oh." Deepi waves in their direction and smiles. Lately, she's been doing this a lot. Wanting to hang out with the popular ones rather than silly old me. Maybe it's also because she has a crush on Maddy's cousin, who's half desi. Danny is cute in a very sweet way. I just wish Deepi didn't have to suck up to Maddy to get to Danny. Girls and their crushes, the ruin of so many friendships.

Maddy saunters in our direction and then addresses Deepi, completely ignoring me. "Hey, D. P., we're heading to the mall.

Danny wanted me to ask if you wanted to come with?"

Why can't she just say "with me"? And why does Deepi not mind Maddy calling her "D. P."? Deepi on the other hand smiles with a fervor I personally reserve for pistachio kulfi.

"Sure. I'd love to," Deepika replies with a smile wider than the moon.

"Okay, I'll pick you up. I hope your parents will approve." Maddy side-eyes me and flicks her hair.

Ya Allah! I want to say something so badly, but I let it go; this is exactly what Maddy wants. To get to me.

I didn't recommend Maddy for the debate team. What she doesn't know is that it wasn't personal. I just wanted more people of color to be in the group, so I recommended another desi girl for the team. And it wasn't like Maddy had any real interest in the team, she just wanted to get face time with Zayn.

I have no idea why Zayn is so popular with girls. I mean yeah, he's the soccer wizard and my opponent on the debate team, so a nerd and a jock. He's half Indian and half Moroccan and has the best features of both descents. Head full of long curly hair and eyes that have bewitched half the girls in our high school. Not me. I know the type and steer clear. Being that my father was such a lothario.

My dad's relationship with us is complicated. You would think any father would be eager to participate in their daughter's major life events. Not him; he had to be shamed by his own daily to participate.

"Mom's working an overnight shift and Dad won't be home until eight. So they won't even notice I'm gone," Deepi says with a wry smile. And it makes my heart twist a little. I know her parents are both doctors, but I wish they would spend some time away from their patients and with their own flesh and blood. Her older brother went off to college, so I know she's seeking attention outside now, in Danny and Maddy.

I swing away from them to prevent my tongue from uttering fifteen lashes at Maddy.

I mutter under my breath, "When did you start to care about how others truly feel, Maddy?"

Maddy points her index finger and talks with gritted teeth. "What, are you cursing in another language at me? Or are you chanting some black magic spell? It won't work, my mom sages our house every week."

"And yet she keeps missing." I say it loud enough for her to hear it this time.

Maddy narrows her gaze at me, her skinny finger quivering. "Did you just call me a witch?"

"I don't have time for this, truly. Because unlike you, I have to work to help my mother keep a roof over our heads. See ya later, Barbie." I sling my backpack on my shoulder and stride toward the front of the building, where I'm sure Ammi is about to pull up any minute.

Deepi follows me after telling Maddy how I'm having a bad day and other excuses I never need for her to make for me. Honestly, I couldn't care less.

"Where was this speed in gym? Slow down a tad, please!" Deepi catches up to me and then leans forward with hands on her knees to pant.

I run my hands up and down my frame and retort, "I hate gym, 'coz I'm not exactly skinny, ya know?"

"Stahpp with this, you're not fat! Don't listen to the desi aunties fat-shaming you at the masjid." Deepi shakes her head in disgust. Then she does the arm cradle thing again.

"Well, my mother is one of them, nowadays, always hiding the sweets from me, and pointing salads in my direction," I say, as I push open the main door leading outside.

The line of cars in the pickup area forms within minutes, and I spot Ammi's old black Honda in the front. My mother is never late. She is a picture of punctuality, unlike so many other Indian parents I know.

"Go hang out with your loser friends, then come home. Ammi's making vegetable biryani for a large party." I nudge her ribs and smile.

"I can't promise. It might be late and I wanna be home before Appa gets home." Deepi scans the parking lot for her ride. A neighborhood auntie picks her up and is never on time.

"Come home with us, if your ride isn't here." I look in the distance and follow her gaze as she scans the line of cars.

"I can't. Maddy is picking me up, remember?" She waves in the direction of a maroon SUV in the distance.

"I hope you won't turn into them. You know how much I hate skinny Barbies. Not too long ago we'd make fun of them for their entitlement and being so superficial." I pat her shoulder and give her a side hug.

Deepi lets my hand fall but straightens her back. "They're not all like that, you know. Give people credit."

"Are you defending Maddy? She treats people with even an inch of body fat like they're gluttons. You should not hang out with these witches, because they're changing you as well."

"You know what? Maybe I should hang out with someone who's not ready to push everyone away. It's not our fault your father left your mother, you know? It's like constantly walking on eggshells with you, not knowing what pisses you off. World's shit right now, for literally everyone." Deepi's voice breaks at the last part.

I shake my head and take deep breaths. The ones closest can hurt you the most. They know your scars and can twist that knife where it hurts most.

Imagine you're in a peaceful meadow, and ignore the jabs from the best friend turned flamethrower. *It's up to you how you react to people. Remember, you're in control.* I repeat the mantra my shrink has taught me and shake my head and mutter, "There's no boy in the world worth your best friend. But if you don't care, I don't either. Have fun with your plastic friends."

I don't stay back to hear Deepi's retorts. Here, surrounded by my peers and school staff, I want to have the last word and not let her push me to the brink. Before I lose it like before. I don't want to be the fire-breathing brownie again.

The summer breeze smells of rain. The charcoal-colored skies are making it darker than usual, matching my current mood.

Ammi slithers the car to the curb next to the stairs leading to the school. She brakes and snakes the car up a few times. She's probably on her phone and not using hands-free. I have told her numerous times. And usually, she's safe, but when she's in a parking lot, somehow all bets are off.

I open the back door and see trays of food occupying most of the back seat. The smell of chickpea curry, fried bhaturas, and sweet semolina halwa fills the car. No place for me to sit, so I swing to the front.

"Ammi, please buy a minivan, the food's taking up the entire back seat. And the front seat has your purse." I pick up her purse and move it.

She glares at me but tells whomever she's on the phone with: "Yes, I will be there in five minutes, inshAllah."

After she hangs up, I push my palms in a namaste pose to plead, "Five minutes? Ammi, I'm hungry. Can we go home, please?

I don't want to be delivering the trays and get stuck in the auntie brigade's cross-examination about my college plans and how I need to find a good Muslim boy."

Ammi shakes her head as if her chai has turned dark and bland. "Not true. Soofiya Baji is so kind. She's given me a list of all her former clients and even recommended me to them. These orders are keeping a roof over our head. Be grateful."

"Uff, Ammi. Soofiya Auntie's daughters are married to wonderful men and she has a comfortable pension. Thanks to Daniel, her house is paid up. All she has to worry about is throwing baby showers for Sana. What's the big deal if she sends a little business your way?" I ignore the pangs of hunger worsened by the fact that the chola bhatura smells perfect. Spicy and lots of coriander with caramelized onions on top.

Ammi drives at the speed limit on the highway in the left lane. People give her dirty looks and take over. One even honks and mutters a curse.

She honks back and yells, "Tere baap ki aankh."

I chuckle. "Did you just say 'your father's eye'? What kinda curse is that?"

"You think I will stoop to his level. But he should know just because I wear a scarf over my head doesn't make me an easy target." She adjusts her hijab and continues at 55 miles per hour on the highway.

"Ammi, can you move to the middle lane, maybe? You're obstructing traffic." I wave at the cars cutting in front.

"Chup karo badtameez. My car, my rules. Don't be a passenger seat driver," Ammi rebukes me.

A torturous five minutes later, we pull over next to Sana and Daniel's beautiful house and I help Ammi bring all the trays inside. Once I slide the trays on the kitchen counter, I skedaddle. Ammi sticks behind to chat with Sana's mom, Soofiya.

My Instagram pings with updates from Deepi and her mall pics. I turn my phone on silent to avoid the updates. While she enjoys boba and Danny, I'm stuck here listening to my stomach gurgle, triggered by the smell of food still lingering in the car. My mother is still gossiping with Soofiya about the masjid aunties while I wait in the car.

Ammi finally heads back, and once she sits, she rubs her hand excitedly and says, "I have a big order and this one is for the wedding."

"It's the desi and Yemeni wedding that the masjid is sponsoring." Ammi's eyes light up. "It will be so good to have a food tasting, and it's for a good cause."

She means the wedding that Yasin Malik and Zayn are helping out with as well. My stomach bottoms out when I ask, "You mean the masjid-sponsored shaadi that Uncle Malik is helping with?"

"Uffo. Which else? Why so many questions? We'll help out. Everyone else is. The bride and the groom are both recent immigrants and no family is around to help." Ammi is clearly irritated. She has no idea how much I hate Zayn's guts.

I try to think of other things to say to her to get out of this job. It's probably not even a job she'll charge for either. Knowing her, she will do it as a duty toward helping the fresh-off-the-plane couple.

Ammi looks both ways and inches out of the driveway. "The one where Mr. Malik is cooking Middle Eastern food?"

"Yes, how many more desi-Yemeni weddings are happening soon? Concentrate, beti. We have so much work to do. Yasin

Malik's son, Zayn, is helping him. You should be more like Zayn."
Ammi shifts the gear while simultaneously giving me the "was-in-labor-for-twenty-six-hours-with-you-and-look-how-you-turned-out" look the one that makes me want to hide.

"Zayn and I are nothing alike. Thank Allah!" I mutter under my breath.

Ammi curses another driver's beard. He made the mistake of honking at her when she pulled out of Soofiya Auntie's driveway. Then, when she's finally on the road merging on the highway, she remembers. "What were you mumbling earlier?"

"Ammi, do you really need me there?"

She stays quiet but grips the wheel tighter. After several long seconds, she replies, "Who do I ask for help? Your pregnant sister who's due any moment? Or the middle daughter who's constantly working long shifts at the hospital and goes to medical school full time? Or my deadbeat husband who left us and never gave me any support after? Haan, bolo? Who do I ask for help, when my almost eighteen-year-old daughter is too busy to help?"

Ammi lays on the guilt thicker than ghee on roti. I want to retort, "Why haven't you divorced him? And why do I still have to take his name, even though he has refused to pay child support for the last six years?" but I don't, because that'll just fan those licks of anger rolling through her. Plus, I know she's hurting, and I don't want to say things in anger that'll just push her past her breaking point.

I clench my teeth and retort. "I'll help, but Ammi can you make sure we set up early and leave? I don't wanna stay for the whole thing."

Ammi pulls in our driveway and parks. She turns to me and her eyes soften. "Beti, all the girls your age love going to weddings. Why do you hate them so much? It'll be fun, we get to see everyone in the community after such a long time."

Marriages have forever been ruined by my parents. I also don't like the big to-do with week-long celebrations and parties. It's a waste of food and resources. If I ever get that far, mine would be a simple nikah with just family. "If" being the biggest question. Or, I might be happy just surrounded by books, cats, and chai.

Not just that, every time I think of any big social events, my mind is filled with memories of loud screaming and arguing from every time we'd go out as a family when my parents were together and me and my older sister in our rooms, scared. For a cheating asshole, my father was a jealous man, pointing to Ammi, accusing her of trying to entice other men.

Ammi would try to defend herself by saying how she caught him talking to women on his phone, and it would escalate.

My mother couldn't give my father a son, and that was per-haps her biggest shortcoming. So when he had a chance, he found another woman who gave him that and dropped us like hot daal.

I cross my arms. "Yeah, I have no interest in being the target of aunties who will pinch my cheeks and comment on my weight judgingly."

Ammi's lips thin in a straight line. "This world is full of all types of people. If they annoy you, you smile and file them away. The more you harp on how they treat you, the more miserable you will be."

"Yeah, it may have worked for you, but doesn't work for me. The smiling thing." I don't mean to be curt, but this whole exchange, especially the idea of me working with Zayn, is making me edgy.

"Bas! Enough of this bakwaas." She smacks my shoulder to accentuate the "you're talking nonsense" comment. "Help me unload the groceries and prepare for the next catering order."

As the skies open up, Ammi grabs the umbrellas and shoves another one in my direction. "Make sure to bring all the bags inside."

As I pull my hood over and jog to the trunk, I wonder if I can both completely avoid Zayn and help my mother out.

Avoiding Zayn Malik was never going to be easy, but I never thought it'd be impossible. The second I step inside the community center's kitchen, he is there. The huge kitchen suddenly feels small. The quartz counters gleam in the overhead white lights.

He is dressed in a slate gray shalwar kameez and his hair is tied in a ponytail. An errant curl lingers on his forehead and so does my gaze.

"Like what you see?" He waves his right hand and smiles.

"Please don't kid yourself. I'm not one of your fangirls who melt at a wave." I shake my head and pivot around him to start settling up.

"Someone skipped their chai today. Don't worry, I'm an excellent tea maker. How do you like your tea?" He pulls out a ceramic white cup from the overhead cabinet, fills it up with water, pushes the cup inside, and presses a button on the microwave.

"You're not making chai in the microwave, are you? And who exactly said you were a good tea maker? One of your gori fangirls?" I scoff as I open multiple drawers to look for a cutting board.

"How else am I gonna boil water?"

I check the cabinets above and say, "In a pot? Do you know where they keep the cutting boards?"

"What are you cutting to shreds besides my ego, soniyo?"

He can flirt in all the languages I know, I'll give him that. *Soniyo* is the equivalent of "a pretty girl" in Punjabi, and the way it rolls off his tongue is sort of melodic.

"Your ego is no match for my cutting skills," I jab and duck underneath to suppress a grin. I move the pots around but still no sign of the cutting board. I wish Ammi had given me a cutting board.

His voice comes from the other side of the counter. "I think I found the area that is used to cut things, complete with a set of knives. Although, telling you where the knives are might not be in my best interest."

I stand up too quickly. "Ouch." My yelp reverberates as I see stars after bumping my head against the quartz kitchen counter.

He rushes next to me and helps me lean back against the counter. He moves in closer to check on the gash. His breath smells of lemon-flavored gum, as he blows on the cut on my forehead. "Lemme see if there's a Band-Aid somewhere. Please don't pass out."

He rushes back with a first aid box. I hear the tear of a package and then the squeak of an antiseptic ointment. He cleans the cut.

My eyes tear up from the burn, and he covers the cut with the Band-Aid. When I open my eyes, I gaze into his. I look for signs of treachery and lies but instead I find them comforting. Like a warm haleem on a cool winter night. The ice around my heart for him thaws a little.

I look away because it's hard not to get swept up in how he looks at me, his eyes focused on me like I am the center of his universe. Throwing all I've held dear off-balance. And this isn't the first time. When we're in the debate club together, sometimes our eyes meet and I feel like I'm glancing inside his soul. When his eyes shine in a color similar to the filter coffee Ammi makes in the winter evenings, it tells me he's had a good day. Sometimes they're darker, like the Nestlé milk chocolates Ammi used to buy at the Indian grocery store. That tells me he's upset.

As I get up slowly and move to where he's cleaning out the cutting space, I tell myself what I always tell myself before I am in the same room as him: Zayn Malik is a player and just because we have similar names doesn't make me anything like him. He is to be avoided at all costs.

He pulls out onions from the grocery bags on the counter. "I can chop onions if you'd like. I promise not to mess up."

I open my mouth to retort but then glance at the big clock and change my mind. I'm behind schedule if I want to sneak out of here before the crowd gathers. I should take all the help I can get. Ammi has totally forgotten about me.

"Okay. Just because I'm in a rush. And if you mess up, you have to leave me alone." I cross my arms and give him my sternest glare.

"Aye-aye, soniyo. Now can we put our knives away? Let's pretend we like each other, even if you don't," he says as he peels the red onions, getting ready to chop them.

"Don't you mean 'we'? And you say this as you're reaching for a formidable-looking knife."

"I like you plenty. And I meant the figurative one."

I let his comment sink in. Did he just blurt out he likes me? Maybe this is what he tells all the girls. I concentrate on measuring the cups of rice to put in the big pot to wash.

He puts his AirPods in, and for a bit, the only sounds are of him chopping onions, that thwack-thwack of the blade hitting the counter. The quiet is nice, as it lets me keep my walls up. Those icicles harden around my heart again.

I wash the rice and soak it in a pot. Then I take out from the fridge the huge containers with marinated meat that Ammi had left last night. The recipe Ammi had written in Urdu and English now calls for frying onions.

Onions. Ugh! I have to break this peace and approach him. I step up behind him and say, "Hey are the onions all done? I need them for the baghar. Did your ammi teach you how to chop, because my aunts and my sister never let any male family members near a chopping board. My brother-in-law had to get stitches the last time he tried to chop onions."

I stand there for a beat before tapping him lightly; maybe he didn't hear me?

Zayn's hands quickly halt and he drops the knife.

He grazes my hand, and I feel his touch in my nerve endings. I jerk my hand back.

Zayn swings around and searches my face.

Talk about being hypersensitive to his touch, even if it's a simple brush of fingers. This isn't something I've experienced before. No other boy sets these fireworks. Worst of all, he's so unlike any of my previous crushes.

I feel this connection in our mutual loss of a parent. For him it's literal, and for me, it's metaphorical. Another similarity is that our mothers are strong women with deep cultural ties, and finally, he's a debate nerd like me.

He moves to the side to let me scoop up the onions in the container. His voice is deep and a little troubled when he speaks. "Can I ask you something?"

My hand holding the container of evenly sliced onions shakes; his closeness and his impenetrable gaze unnerve me. I reply without looking directly at him, "I guess so? As long as it's cooking related."

He crosses his arms, the corded forearm muscles flexing, temptingly. "Do you really hate me so much that being in the same space makes you skittish? And can we please not talk about my mom?"

I'm a little taken aback by his question because of how on point he is, except he truly doesn't know why he makes me skittish.

I don't know why he does. And I'm not sure I'm willing to risk my sanity to find out. This is why I look him straight in the eye and get into my bitch mode. "I don't spare enough thoughts on you to hate. But from what I can see you have a long line of admirers already."

He gives me a wry smile. "Maybe the one person I want to really hang out with doesn't give a shit about me. And maybe all the things those people say about you are true, too."

"And here I thought only desi aunties fat-shamed." I let out an exaggerated sigh, almost feeling guilty of turning this argument in a direction I'm sure he didn't intend.

He swallows hard, making his Adam's apple bob. "That you're quick to judge and push people away when they want to get close. That even your closest friend hangs out with others now."

He means Deepi. Even though he doesn't say it. That comment is like a match to the anger already roiling through my veins.

I jab my finger at him. "You know nothing about me. So stop. Thanks for cutting the onions but that doesn't give you a right to comment about my personal life. And I thought you said you liked me? You got some messed-up way of showing it for sure."

"Look, all I'm saying is that maybe if you let people get close—"

I cut him off before he goes any further. "And end up like my mother? No thanks."

I swing away from him and step outside after grabbing my phone. I need a break from him and everything before I lose it.

The back of the community center where the kitchen sits is still relatively quiet. Most of the noise from the people setting up lights and other decorations is up front, where the main entrance is.

I text Deepi as I wipe the tears. **What have you told Danny about us?**

She calls me instead of texting back.

I clear my throat to clear the remnants of the tears.

Deepi says in a sleepy voice, "Wassup?"

I suck in a breath and say, "Zayn said that we're growing apart. What did you say to Danny about us?"

The rustle of sheets on her end tells me she's still in bed. When I hear her voice again a few seconds later, she sounds stressed. "Zayna, I would never. Trust me, please. They must've seen us argue, and you know people talk."

"No, but Zayn said it with such confidence."

"When did you and Zayn become best friends?"

"Zayn and I—we're not friends. Maybe he's just talking shit. I don't know, Deepi, you've been so busy with your other life lately that it's been tough, you know?"

"All we do is fight, so I need a break from that sometimes. Besides, you did not tell me you and Zayn are hanging out. Wait until Maddy finds out."

My voice is shaky because I feel so spent. "Not a word about this to Maddy, please. And it's this catering gig my mother has to do where we have to share a kitchen. Can you believe he had the nerve to say I pushed you away, and this is why you're with Danny."

Deepi's voice is pensive, as if she's looking for the right words before shelling a life truth at me. "Well, he's right about only one thing. That you tend to push people away. From the first time you meet someone, you're betting on them to betray you. And that, meri jaan, is so not normal."

I like that she's calling me by sweet nicknames again, but I don't love that she's dishing cold, hard truths.

"According to you I should just swoon and plan my wedding with him? Come on, Deepi—"

The back door swings open. Zayn pokes his head out. "Planning your wedding, nice! Anyway, I came out here because I'm wondering if I can slip the baklawa in the oven? My father bought dessert for tonight's event. I stuck it in the fridge, for now."

Deepi's excited voice comes back on the phone. "Is that Zayn? My, my! Even his voice is swoony. How are you not melting? My nani jee used to say, 'Give people a chance. You may learn something.'"

I wipe the sweat on my forehead with the back of my sleeve. "I am melting, just not the way you'd think. I'll talk to you later."

Deepi cannot help but impart one last bit of advice before hanging up. "Hey, please be nice to the sweet boy; he's still recovering from his mom's passing."

The kitchen now smells of nuts, honey, and buttery dough. An older man with his back toward me is arranging trays on the counter.

"Assalamualaikum." I greet the older man who is busy fiddling with the knobs on the wall oven.

"Waleikum Assalam," he replies in a deep voice. Zayn introduces this man as his father. When he finally turns around, a surprise runs through me as I recognize him. But only now do I notice the striking resemblance. The same hazel eyes and that dimpled smile. He has kind, gentle eyes and a patience about him that Zayn clearly lacks.

"Zayn's mother made perfect baklawa. She tried to teach me. It'll never be as good as hers, but we try. You want to help?" Mr. Malik asks as he pours a dark honey-colored syrup over the tray.

"Sure. I love baklawa. I want the recipe so I can try it out, too."
I sidle next to him and watch as he carefully pours. The sizzle of
the hot syrup over cool pastry sheets fills the air along with the
smell of sweet honey.

Mr. Malik, Zayn, and I prepare the baklawa trays, then cover
them with plastic wrap and set them aside.

The timer on the oven beeps as he sets it for four hours. "I'll set
the timer on the oven so that you both don't forget about it."

"Oh, I haven't even started with my biryani, so I'll keep an eye
on it if Zayn wants to leave. I think I've got this." I hold the oven
door open as Zayn slides in the last of the trays.

"Do you want to come to the Qabrastan with me, son?" Mr.
Malik looks at Zayn.

He flits his gaze in my direction and his jaw hardens. "Can we
do this another time, Baba?"

I take the rice and disappear to another part of the kitchen. The
kitchen is part of an open floor plan in the community center's basement, so even though it's not tiny by any standards, voices carry.

Mr. Malik's soft but irritated voice reaches my ears. "You're our
only child. She would've wanted you to visit her grave, son. Maybe
it'll help give you some closure? Remember the grief counselor
brought that up? Maybe you can write to her and bring a letter to
read to her, if it helps?"

Zayn's reply is in an even more irritated tone. "You wanted
me to be here, so I'm here. Today is tough, Baba. I want to be in
a happier place, this is why I'm here to help with the wedding. I
can't, I'm not ready—"

"Are you ready to pray? Because that's the least you can do. The
masjid is so close, at least attend the dhur prayer and pray for her
soul? I have to go, but it would make your mother happy. That's all
we can do for her now."

A shuffle of feet and the door opening and closing lets me know someone has left. I stay put and resist the urge to check up on Zayn.

Losing his mother cannot have been easy. My stomach twists into a knot, and I wonder how he is feeling. They mentioned today's date; is it some type of anniversary today? I feel his loss in my bones, although mine is alive; it stings, this abandonment. This loss that's a big black hole in my heart. It's worse for him, because his mother was a loving, caring one who was always there for him. Our whole community lost a wonderful member when she passed.

I busy myself in cleaning the rice I had soaked earlier and start to cook it. Ammi's recipe calls for it to be cooked only partially.

I search my pocket for my phone. Then, the counter. It's not there.

"Looking for this?" His voice startles me.

Zayn waves my phone and smiles. His smile isn't like anyone else's I know. It's open, hearty, and inviting. Gosh, when he smiles like this, it just makes the sun brighter, the air fresher.

"Yes. Thanks." I hold out my hand to get my phone back.

He shakes his head, then asks, "How much of my family drama did you hear?"

"If I lie and say nothing, will it make you feel any better?" I gaze into his eyes. Threads of red run through, telling me he is holding back tears.

He puts a hand to his heart and says, "Uff, so you're telling me you actually have started to care about me?"

Part of me wants to tell him to back off, because he's starting to affect me in a tiny way. Especially because today, if it is an anniversary of some sort, must be hard for him. I move in closer, hoping to comfort him; maybe just for today, I can put my boxing gloves away.

"I am but human. And I am so sorry about your mom. I only met her a few times, but she was a genuinely wonderful person." Zayn's mother, Layla, was a beautiful woman. Tall and slim, she had a strength to her. Her serene face fills my thoughts, and I feel his loss, so much.

"I will give you your phone back, but you have to trade something about you that no one knows. Only fair because you heard a lot of my shit." His face is more relaxed now, unlike moments ago.

It's comforting to know that I can soothe some of his sadness, or anger, whatever made him sad earlier, away. This happy-go-lucky classmate of mine has so many layers to him.

Ammi always said to be patient with people, and understand that sometimes we're all made of stone, like Rumi said. *Like a sculptor, if necessary, carve a friend out of stone. Realize that your inner sight is blind and try to see a treasure in everyone, their pain, their love.*

I scan my memories for an embarrassing one and wonder which one I should share with him—something that won't backfire if he ever uses it against me. Maybe the one about dancing?

"Why are we sharing secrets? Are we that level of intimate friends? I don't think so," I say over the sounds of sizzling onions in the big sauté pan. I go over to add star anise, mace, zeera seeds, and cardamom to the mix.

The ground powdered masalas Ammi keeps in a round box with small circular containers, so many memories of Ammi cooking fill my brain, triggered by the smell of the baghaar, this particular one had all the members of my household asking Ammi if she was cooking biryani. I take a pinch of garam masala from the box and mix it in with the onions and the spices; next I scoop freshly minced garlic and ginger paste and then paste from the Jersey tomatoes from our summer garden.

Zayn pops a cardamom pod in his mouth and says, "Well, even if we are none of that, it's only fair. Come on, it could be a harmless one. Something like I hate pickles on my sandwich, but still eat it because I don't want to disappoint my father."

A smile escapes my lips and I quirk up an eyebrow. "Well, that's specific enough to be true. Okay, I'll give you one. I love dancing but have never danced in any weddings, ever. Too scared."

I drop the pieces of marinated chicken one by one in the now-browned onions as he stirs the baghaar around. "Never danced? Like not even in girls-only henna parties?"

My face heats. Maybe it's the heat from the flame, or his cardamom-scented breath, or the fact that he's folded his sleeves up and now his biceps flex as he stirs the chicken around. I move away from him to avoid his closeness affecting me.

Thankfully the call for prayer from the masjid reverberates on the speakers inside the community center, which is a few buildings over.

"I'm going to head over to pray, are you coming as well?" I ask, rolling up my sleeves and shutting off the flame.

"It's complicated, my relationship with Him." He points to the roof.

"You mean the coordinator of events, whose office is upstairs?" I tease him, knowing well he means his relationship with Allah.

"You know what I mean . . ." His voice changes a bit; I know he's still hurting.

A dead parent is unlike anything I've ever experienced. Just the thought of losing my mother lances my heart in infinitesimal places; I can't even imagine what saying a forever goodbye to a loving parent feels like. My father is an asshole of the highest order, but when he was around and did pay attention, he could be somewhat kind. But it's different when a mother, whose entire life revolved around their only child, goes.

"I'm so sorry. One for overhearing the conversation between you and your father earlier. I'm not asking you to have faith; all I ask is be patient with yourself. When my nani passed away last year, going to her grave helped. Because I felt like I was talking to her. Not saying that's what it'll do for you, but maybe it'll help?" I squeeze his shoulder and lock gazes with him. I want to hug him, and tell him it gets easier.

He leans into my touch. Then says, "You know how I hurt because you do, too."

Hurt I do, but I push it down, and it comes out as anger. Oh how it hurt, when my father abandoned me, and while we live in cramped quarters in a small townhome, I heard news of him buying a big house across town for his new family. Or when I still hear rumors of him going on Disney vacations with his new family. When the community looks at my mother and me with pity. It sucks, but it gets better.

He extends his hand. "I'll make a deal with you. I'll go to Ammi's grave if you come and dance with me after the wedding dinner tonight. I'll save you a spot by the gazebo in the back."

"Let me get this straight, you will go visit your mom's grave, the one you've been avoiding going to for months, for a measly dance?"

He raises his hand and nods. "Do we have a deal?"

Ammi says to always look in someone's eyes to gauge if they're telling the truth. I look into his. His pupils are wide and his gaze steady. He is not lying, I know that.

"Deal." I shake his hand and he covers his other hand over mine and lingers.

"Zayna." Ammi's voice booms, and we both move away.

As Ammi goes on about how I didn't soak the rice for enough time and that I didn't fry the onions to the perfect crispy texture, I wonder about the lines from Maulana Rumi's book. Maybe the way to live is to really live a better life, one where we help each other heal.

Was I helping him heal, or did he actually help me?

Ammi waves a spatula in front of my face. "Zayna? I have everything under control here. Your sister will be here to pick you up soon. Go home and get ready for tonight. I took out a nice shalwar kameez and left it on your bed. Also those jhumkas that you love, I'll let you borrow them, but please, those earrings belonged to your nani, so if you lose them . . ."

Ammi is letting me borrow Nani's jhumkas. Today is a hell of a day! I don't even let her finish before I prattle, "I won't, I promise!"

When I check my phone, there's multiple notifications waiting. First, I check Deepi's message.

Did you see, you're tagged on Zayn's picture! It's now viral.

I reply, **Wut r u talkin abt?**

She texts me, **Check your Insta.**

I had put my Insta on mute for notifications because Ammi gets curious if my phone pings too much. But my Instagram followers have doubled.

The post has a picture of a grave and a hand on the name. It's his mother's grave.

The text underneath the picture breaks my heart as I read it.

One year to this day, I lost my Mama. She was my pillar of strength, my best friend, and the best confidant you could ever ask for. I never wanted to visit her grave because part of me kept thinking if I don't see her disappear in the ground, she will come back. She will walk through that front door and put on her house slippers and ask me to bring in the groceries from the car. I refused to give her slippers away.

Grief is irrational and annihilates all hope. But today, I found a little pocket of joy again, in form of a friend. Friendship from someone I had always hoped for, but never actually thought would happen. So thank you to a fellow lover of Rumi. Because of you, I had the courage to do this. And yes you were right, talking to her here at her grave helped.

I know Amma listened to everything I said, because after I confided in her, I felt lighter again.

Freer again, joyful, and above all hopeful!

PS: I hope you have the dancing shoes ready.

XO

I look at the tags and he hasn't just tagged me, he's tagged the entire debate team. I exhale and sprint outside to get ready for the dance tonight.

I will, in fact, meet Zayn for a dance at the wedding tonight.

The wedding was a beautiful affair. The nikah took place in the backyard of the community center. The stage was partitioned off for the nikah, the bride and groom sat separated by strings of flowers, and the bride, Bushra, sat opposite her groom, Salman, separated by the flowery curtain.

The qabool hais were said in a shy voice by Bushra, and in an enthusiastic one from Salman. The Qazis declared them married.

Salman peered through the flowery curtain, and this is when I see Zayn. He was right behind Salman as he crossed over to get a first look at his now wife.

Salman lifts Bushra's bridal veil and gives her a chaste hand squeeze. As he gazes into her eyes, he says, "I love you."

I look up to see Zayn locking eyes with me. He smiles and mouths, "Wow."

I smile and lift an eyebrow, as if to say, "Who? Me?"

He nods affirmative then tips his head in the direction of the gazebo as if to say, "Don't forget about your promise."

Ammi breaks our wordless conversation and pulls me in the direction of aunties. "Come, they all want to praise you, Zayna."

An auntie approaches me, still holding a plateful of biryani. She smiles and says, "This biryani is exquisite. Can you share the secret ingredient with me?"

This auntie is older and has a mole underneath her lower lip, so I know for sure this is a face I'd remember. I wonder if she's new to this community.

She waves a hand across my face. "Still with me?"

"Sorry. I don't know of any secret ingredients. It's the biryani spices, rice, and chicken." I parrot the list from memory.

"Oh, but there is. I think he knows." She tips her head in the direction of Zayn, who's busy mingling.

"Huh?" I stare blankly at her.

She pats my shoulder then swings away; before she leaves, she smiles over her shoulder and winks. "The secret ingredient is love, beti."

After Ammi racks up catering orders and biryani praises, I help to distribute the wedding favors that I and other girls from the community helped make.

Before dessert, everyone mingles, and I venture out to the gazebo.

The sun is about to set and the sky has an orange hue that bathes everything in that golden light at this hour.

The song "Kesariya" plays, and Zayn waits for me right underneath the gazebo, with two dessert plates filled with baklawa.

"Are we dancing or eating?"

"Both." He smiles as he extends a plate of baklawa in my direction.

A Confluence of Fates
PAYAL DOSHI

The Ballroom at the Taj Mahal Palace Hotel in Colaba glittered with an air of Victorian elegance. Crystal chandeliers spilled bejeweled hues over the vaulted ceiling and the sprawling turquoise carpet adorned with yellow motifs.

The hotel, a historical jewel of Mumbai, always left Alia in awe. Either that or it was the butterflies that had set up camp in her stomach at the thought of meeting Jehangir. Alia tried to keep a poker face, upset her own body was betraying her. She hadn't seen Jeh since they graduated high school five years ago. Until this wedding, she thought she'd never lay eyes on him again.

Sana grabbed Alia's arm. "I did a quick scan. He isn't here yet."

"I don't care if he's there," Alia said, a little too quickly.

"Really?" Sana and Pooja cocked their perfectly threaded brows.

Alia knew fully well she couldn't fool her best friends. "Forget Jeh. Where's Kavya? I'm dying to see her outfit."

It was day four of Kavya's sister Naina's extravagant five-day wedding festivities. After a decade-long relationship, Naina and her fiancé, Cyrus, were tying the knot by having two weddings: a

Zoroastrian ceremony to honor his Parsi and Iranian heritage and a Hindu ceremony to honor Naina's Gujarati heritage.

"Wait a second." Pooja narrowed her eyes, her rani-pink eyeliner giving her white and gold Anarkali kurta a bold pop. "You're telling me you're not the least bit nervous to see him?"

"If anyone should be nervous, it should be him." Alia faked bravado.

The memory of the last time she'd spoken to Jeh was scalded into her mind like a hot, sizzling burn. In retrospect, it was silly, but it was the first time she'd been betrayed and humiliated by a boy. And infuriatingly, she remembered every detail like it was yesterday.

"After all, isn't *he* the one who lied to me?"

"She's got a point," Sana said, gesturing toward the waiter carrying a tray of mutton kebabs. She popped one into her mouth. "Oh, these are delicious."

"There she is." Alia waved, relieved to have spotted Kavya, the fourth of their quartet.

Kavya shimmied over, dancing and sashaying past the gold Corinthian columns wrapped in strings of white roses and jasmine. She struck a pose, showing off her mango orange ghaghara choli embroidered with gota-patti flowers. The flare of her skirt could easily put Marilyn Monroe to shame.

"You look absolutely gorgeous!" gushed Pooja.

"Beware, all the aunties' eyes are going to be on you for their darling, suitable sons!" Sana winked. The bells on her crop top and dhoti pants jingled, adding a playfulness to the cool, artsy vibe she exuded.

Kavya guffawed in her signature belly laugh. "A hard pass, thank you!"

A procession of well-dressed and well-jeweled guests began streaming in. They hugged and chatted, quickly filling the tables bedecked with gilded Chiavari chairs, stiff white tablecloths, and lavish peach and cream-colored floral centerpieces. Waiters dressed in black meandered around them, balancing trays of cold drinks and appetizers.

"By the way, I bear important news." Kavya rubbed her henna-colored palms in glee. "I heard Cyrus's mom telling him that his cousins will be here any minute. You know what that means!"

Alia took a breath to stop herself from turning into a glop of anxiousness. Jehangir was Cyrus's younger cousin.

Pull yourself together!

"At the cocktail party last night, I heard Jeh's single with a capital S!" Pooja practically sang. She'd been in a relationship for years, the longest amongst them, and got way too excited at the possibility of making new couple friends.

"Did you plan this? Because the *three* of you seem more excited about seeing Jeh." Alia placed her hands on her hip. Her bangles matching her chiffon blue saree tinkled like bells on a ghungroo.

The girls smirked when a guest tapped Kavya's shoulder.

"Your mom's looking for you."

Kavya's mother was waving furiously at Kavya to join her. She looked elegant in her sea-green silk banarsi saree, which she had draped in the Gujarati style with the pallu over her front instead of dangling at the back. A gold necklace with emeralds gleamed on her neck.

"Shit, I gotta go; the ceremony's starting. Find a table. It's going to be fun!"

Thup, thup, thup!

Farzana, Cyrus's younger sister, tapped the microphone. She

looked all grown up at fifteen in a traditional Parsi gara saree bordered with an exquisite spread of birds and leaf vines embroidered in white silk. She stood on stage beside a bronze lamp lit with a diya along with two lagan ni khursis, regal armchairs fashioned from teakwood and chosen by the bride's and groom's families, on which the wedding ceremony was to take place. Later the chairs would become a part of the couple's new home.

"Hello, everyone!" Farzana said as the guests quieted. Kavya hurriedly stood beside her. The light of the crystal chandeliers sparkled off her diamond earrings. "As many of you know, centuries ago, Zoroastrians migrated from Persia to India and in more recent times from Iran. Since most of our family descends from Iran, we're going to be celebrating a wonderfully entertaining Iranian Zoroastrian custom called 'Baleh!'"

"In this ceremony," Kavya continued, "the groom-to-be's father, uncles, and brothers must convince the bride-to-be and her father—my sister, Naina, and my dad—that she's making the right decision in choosing Cyrus as her partner. After the groomsmen plead Cyrus's case, Naina must be convinced to say 'Baleh!,' meaning 'Yes, I agree!' Naina might have been dating Cyrus for ten years but today is the final verdict! Will Cyrus make a worthy husband? Take a seat and watch the drama unfold!"

The guests descended into a game of musical chairs as everyone rushed to find a seat. A comical debate ensued between Cyrus's cousins and uncles trying to decide who got to go on stage while Alia, Sana, and Pooja ran toward the first trio of empty chairs they could find closest to the stage. Soon, the cherry-picked groomsmen gathered in a line.

And there was Jeh, standing before Cyrus, last in line.

They were both dressed in a dugli, the traditional Parsi ensemble of a white shirt with bows along the front and white trousers.

The only difference in their outfits was the fetah, a flat-topped ceremonial hat that Cyrus wore on his head. Jeh whispered into his ear, and a boisterous laugh erupted from both cousins. A lock of wavy hair fell over Jeh's forehead, and Alia took a long, desirous breath. He flashed someone his signature side smile. She noticed his slightly crooked incisor in a row of otherwise immaculate teeth just as she had the first time she'd spoken to him.

It was a Thursday in the middle of ninth grade. She was in the school canteen. The memory was so vivid, Alia could see herself walking to a table precariously balancing a plate of samosas and three packets of chips while lost in conversation with Pooja, Sana, and Kavya. Just as she was about to sit down, someone swiped the chair from under her. Alia squealed, nearly falling on her bottom when a boy grabbed her.

"I'm so sorry!" he said.

Apparently, he'd been in the middle of a conversation, too, and absentmindedly pulled a chair for himself to sit on. After several profuse apologies, Alia assured him it was okay, then returned to her friends with one sentence: "Shit, he's cute."

"Are you going to take a bite or simply ogle at Jeh with a kebab on a toothpick stuck in your mouth?" Sana asked, a grin spreading over her face.

Alia quickly unskewered the kebab with her teeth and willed the rising heat on her cheeks to keep from spreading. Why was she this bothered by him?

Sana slipped her arm into the crook of Alia's elbow. "Be honest. Do you still have feelings for him?"

"He was my high school crush, Sana! We're nineteen and in college now, remember?"

"It was unrequited though." Pooja heaved a dramatic breath, laying her hand on her chest.

"If only it was as romantic as it is in books and movies," Alia said through cheeks tucked with kebab.

Had she attended the cocktail party last night, she would've seen Jehangir, and their awkward meeting would've been over and done with, allowing her to enjoy the wedding without her stomach flip-flopping as it was right now. But she had to miss the party. Her dad's blood pressure had shot up and he'd been hospitalized. No matter how many times he made her promise that she wouldn't let his sickness define her every waking moment, she wasn't going to leave his side. *As if, Dad.* He was her whole, entire world.

"If I was still into boys and if you weren't ever into him, I'd definitely make a move," Sana said. "Jeh's got that cool and broody vibe."

"Cute or not, just once I'd like him to apologize for what he did. Though I doubt he even remembers."

"You two were close to being something," said Pooja.

"Well, it was for the best," Alia said, growing annoyed. "Anyway, after the Sahil debacle, you know I'm done with relationships."

Her friends grimaced at his name and Alia sucked in her breath.

"You're right," Pooja said. "I'm all about your seven-year plan to achieve girlboss dreams."

"Don't mock my plan!" Alia almost tossed a spring roll at her.

"I'm not! If anything, I'm jealous you know what you want to do with your life, unlike me who has no clue whatsoever."

"It's high time something works out for me, and if it's going to be my education and job goals, then so be it," said Alia. Between her dad's illness and her breakup, the last year had well and truly been the crappiest year of her life.

"Hey, I'm counting on you to become the next Indra Nooyi or Mindy Kaling." Pooja looked at her in all seriousness and then grinned slyly. "So I can benefit from your fortune as your best friend."

"One of her best friends," Sana corrected. "I'll gladly partake in some of that dough. My artist's salary is going to be pretty bleak."

"Don't we make a cheery triad?" Pooja laughed as a round of cheers went around the Ballroom.

Naina walked in, arm in arm with her father, making her grand entrance. She looked ethereal in her white lace bridal saree embroidered in gold silk. Dark kohl accentuated her bright brown eyes, and she wore a messy bun off to the side. A loose curl dangled beside her ear. Cyrus basked in her beauty as though she was a vision he couldn't tear himself from. She chuckled, lighting up the room, and sat on one of the lagan ni khursis. Her father, dressed in a pale lilac sherwani, took his place behind her.

One by one Cyrus's father, his four uncles, and three cousins stepped onstage, fanning out on either side of Naina and her dad. Cyrus sat offstage with his mother, Parveen Auntie, sending warnings to his cousins to not embarrass him. Jeh cocked him a look and everyone laughed.

"May the ceremony begin!" Kavya mimicked a drumroll and handed the microphone to Cyrus's uncle, the first groomsman in line.

The room turned silent.

"Dearest Naina," Cyrus's uncle began as the guests doubled over in chuckles anticipating an amusing reason as to why Naina should accept Cyrus's hand in marriage. "Ever since we learned about your upcoming nuptials, we ingrained into Cyrus three very simple words that we promise Cyrus will always say to you. They are, 'Yes, my dear!'"

Alia and her friends snorted at the dad joke while Naina, playing her part seriously, conferred with her father.

"I'm afraid that isn't a good reason for us," he declared. "We will need a lot more convincing."

"We're not giving up our Naina that easily!" Naina's best

friend, Swati, shouted and all of Naina's twenty-person friend group hooted.

Cyrus's oldest cousin stepped forward to make his case.

"Make it a good reason, Ardeshir!" heckled Farzana.

"Oh, be certain that I will. You see, Cyrus and I are only one year apart and in the years that we've grown up together, Cyrus has always had a soft spot for the . . . ahem . . . fairer sex. I know this because he first fell in love when he was five and—"

Jehangir discreetly motioned to a waiter carrying a tray of appetizers and sneakily popped two Russian pattices into his mouth. Alia's eyes widened, amazed at his audacity and sheer lack of self-control when it came to food. Some things never change, she thought, unaware of the smile peeking from her lips. She savored her own fried chili and chicken cheese pattice while watching the show of Jehangir Khambata as if snuggled in the darkness of a movie theater.

Since their "meet-cute" in school, they had spent nearly a year playing the eye-contact game. She searched for him in between classes, in the school corridors, during recess, or on the basketball court, where she found him shooting hoops and looking drool-worthy in shorts. She had no idea how he felt about her, though she'd seen him glancing at her on more than one occasion. But it was only when Virag, one of Jeh's friends, asked out Muskaan, one of Alia's friends, that Alia and Jeh began talking. They texted far into the night. They wished each other luck on their respective tests. They knew each other's weekend plans. It was mostly platonic, and for a while she knew more about what was going on in his life than her best friends' lives. And then came the flirtations, the one-on-one hangouts, and the inside jokes, like when he confessed his favorite ice cream was banana and strawberry and she looked at him like he had said mud-slush.

"What? It's the best!"

Alia faked a gag. "Fruit flavors should be banned as ice cream flavors. Give me dark chocolate, coffee, or salted caramel any day."

After school that day, they rode together in a rickshaw, arms touching. His mission was to get her to taste the banana strawberry ice cream at the nearest Baskin-Robbins. In return, he promised to taste the coffee flavor. They both hated each other's ice cream but spent the better part of an hour chatting until Alia's phone rang, with her distraught mother on the line worried about where she'd been. Jeh immediately flagged down a rickshaw and dropped Alia off at home. As she got off outside her apartment building, he promised to take her to the best wada-pav in the city. Alia couldn't wait.

In the years that followed, Alia rarely had a bite of street food without thinking of Jeh and their countless food escapades. He always had a dozen food places he wanted to try out. They weren't fancy; they were street stalls and hole-in-the-wall restaurants, but to this day it was some of the best food Alia had ever eaten. They had toured the city tasting delicacies from the famous dosawalla in Ghatkopar's Khau Galli that served twenty-five types of dosas (she had had the Manchurian dosa, and he the Maggi cheese dosa) to Bademiya in Colaba for its paneer and chicken kathi rolls that melted in your mouth. For her part, she introduced him to the places her dad used to take her family to—the stall selling crispy, golden medu wadas after they'd collected shells on Juhu Beach, the restaurant opposite CST train station selling pav bhaji drowning in oodles of butter, and the tastiest pani puris in the world (she was prepared to wager on that claim) at Elco Market in Bandra after a day of shopping on Linking Road.

"Hurry, get up!" Kavya whispered, and Alia's plate nearly fell from her hands. As they ushered out of their seats, Kavya's eyes skittered in panic.

"What happened?" asked Alia. She'd clearly missed all the juicy details about Cyrus's first tryst with love since another uncle was now speaking.

"Cyrus excused himself before Ardeshir came on and now Zubin Kaka is nearly done with his turn, and Cyrus isn't back yet!"

They swiveled to look and rightly so, he wasn't there! Parveen Auntie was holding a forced expression as her eyes skimmed the ballroom. She called on Jehangir who was standing closest to her. Quick words were spoken, and Jeh disappeared into the crowd. A younger cousin took his place.

"Naina is freaking out. No one knows where Cyrus has gone."

"You think he got cold feet?" asked Sana.

"He's been madly in love with Naina all through college. There's no way!" said Pooja.

"Chill! He probably had to go to the loo because he needed to go . . ." Alia clamped her lips shut, unable to help herself.

"Poo!" Sana and Pooja answered, bursting into giggles.

Kavya's mother rushed toward them, and they piped down their laughter. Alia's heart dropped to her toes. Jeh was walking beside her.

"Girls, can you please help Jeh look for Cyrus immediately? Kavya, get back to the ceremony right away. The guests can't know anything is amiss."

"Of course, Auntie," Pooja said as Kavya dashed off toward the stage.

"Let's pair up; it will be faster and more efficient." Sana winked and Alia gaped at her. She opened her mouth to refute the suggestion, but Sana and Pooja had already taken off in the opposite direction.

Unbelievable, thought Alia. Even in a time of crisis.

"Hi," Alia said, reaching to tuck an invisible strand of hair behind her ears. Finding no loose strand, she dropped her hand to her side.

"Hey . . ." replied Jehangir. A sheen of sweat glistened on his forehead, and he smiled nervously. "This is crazy, isn't it?"

"Yeah, really crazy . . ." A whiff of his cologne, a cedar-woody-musky scent, wafted over Alia, and her nerves raced at the speed of light. "Erm—"

"Any ideas about where we should look for him?"

The ceremony was nearly halfway through the line of groomsmen. Time was ticking.

"Right, er—maybe we can ask if someone has seen him?"

"Great idea."

Alia politely squeezed past uncles in suits, sherwanis, and duglis, keeping an eye out for Cyrus lest some of them had cornered him into a chat or worse, bad puns about married life. But she didn't spot Cyrus's mop of curly hair anywhere. With barely a foot between them, Alia and Jeh made their way through chatting aunties, running children, and nervous waiters who hoped no excited guest bumped into them and spilled the food onto the Taj's expensive carpets.

Alia tapped one of the waiters. "Excuse me, have you seen the groom? He was sitting right beside the stage."

"Yes, ma'am." The waiter turned toward the wood-paneled arches. "I saw him rush toward the restroom about ten minutes ago."

"Thank you!"

Alia and Jeh ran into the vestibule outside the ballroom toward where the waiter had pointed. A crowd of guests swarmed the food counters.

"Wait here," Jeh said, and dashed off into the lavatory. Alia scanned the area for Cyrus.

As the seconds passed, she found herself back in tenth grade, on that ill-fated day five years ago. They were six months from giving their board exams and graduating from school. Mrs. Bose, their physics teacher, was absent that morning. Rain fell in sheets, slamming against the classroom windows. The benches lining the windows were soaked and her classmates squeezed, three on a bench, into the middle rows. Needing to pass thirty minutes, the class broke into groups.

Alia blinked, watching the memory unfold as if she were a fly on the wall. She, Kavya, Sana, Pooja, and three other girls were sitting on top of their desks, coming up with the silliest ideas for a group project they had to submit in two weeks. Jeh was deep in conversation with the boys, making predictions about the T-20 cricket matches that were going on. Every now and again, he glanced at her. One time, she caught him staring unabashedly. At some point, the two groups merged, talking about movies, school assignments, and Farewell Day—the day they got to dress up, the girls in sarees and the boys in suits, to bid adieu to their schooling years—an Indian version of prom.

Someone asked, "Are we bringing dates or going solo?" Jeh's eyes fell on Alia. A flush rippled through her body and she pretended she was cool either way.

"Want a chip?" she asked, eating from a packet of Magic Masala potato chips she'd bought from the canteen. Jehangir was sitting diagonally opposite her, their knees grazing. Her other knee grazed against Veer but that didn't send any pangs of desire cascading through her whatsoever.

Jeh nodded, taking a handful in one helping.

"Hey, I said 'a' chip! These packets are seventy-five percent air, twenty-five percent chips!" Alia waved the packet away from his prying hands.

"What do I do with one chip?"

"Don't you know no human can come between Alia and her Magic Masala chips? The girl can get ferocious," Kavya warned with a knowing expression.

"True," admitted Alia. "They're the guiltiest of my pleasures and you should be so lucky I offered to share one with you."

Jeh joined his hands. "Pray allow me one more chip, thou, I pleadest. I promise to buy you ten more packets, but don't deprive me of my deepest yearning for potato chips. My stomach growls in abject hunger."

"Wow. That was the worst mishmash of the poorest Shakespearean and God knows what else!" She laughed, tilting the packet toward him.

"And yet somehow I convinced you to share." He cocked his eyebrow, and Alia's heart exploded into tiny little heart bubbles.

"He isn't there," Jeh said, walking back. "I even checked the two banquet halls adjacent to the ballroom."

Alia broke out of her reverie and cleared her throat.

"Where should we go next?"

Jeh looked around. "Let's try the Taj lawns. Maybe Cyrus needed some air and sauntered there for a bit?"

Alia nodded and they cut through the throng of guests milling around the chaat counter. As they passed the pani puri station, Jeh held Alia's arm. His eyes lingered over the fried, golf ball–sized puris filled to the brim with spiced potatoes, drizzled with sweet tamarind and spicy green chutney, and then dunked into a tub of icy mint water.

"Jeh, we don't have time!"

"Please, just one! We need the sustenance to keep our minds alert to locate this fool called my cousin."

The pani puris looked mouthwateringly delicious, and if there was one type of food Alia couldn't resist, it was any form of Mumbai chaat. She let out an exaggerated breath, and then grinned, turning to the young man making the puris.

"Two, please?"

Like a magician, the man's hands moved with skilled precision, fashioning a plate of pani puri in seconds. Alia placed an entire puri into her mouth and Jeh did the same. Their eyes met the moment the puri cracked and the sweet, spicy, and tangy flavors frolicked with their tastebuds. Jeh stepped closer. With a delicate touch, he wiped away a drop of mint water trickling down the corner of Alia's lips.

She froze.

"Didn't want it to ruin your saree."

Before she remembered her manners, he handed her a paper napkin.

"These aren't as good as the Elco Market pani puris," he said.

The napkin remained in Jeh's hand as Alia stood shocked he had referenced their past. Her breath deepened, trying to keep a straight face.

Respond!

"A-agreed. They're still pretty good though," she said, relieving him of the napkin.

A silence fell between them after Jeh asked for directions to the gardens. Alia hitched up her saree to go down a flight of stairs and her heels echoed in the absence of conversation. She thought of a dozen banal things to ask like, 'How have you been?' or 'Isn't it way too hot for February?' But as the spotless marble corridor stretched ahead, their past trailed them like a dark, skulking cloud. Jeh got off the last step and stopped before her.

"I'm sorry for the way things went down between us."

Alia stared. He'd come right out and addressed it. She thought about pretending to ask what he was talking about, but his directness left her reeling.

"It's not a big deal. We were kids," she said, continuing on her way. She didn't want him to know she was still affected by something that happened years ago.

He stopped her again. His eyes traveled over her face, and she felt them land on every part of her skin. Hot pinpricks bloomed over her.

"That doesn't excuse how I acted. I should have explained myself." He paused, his eyes searching hers for forgiveness. Alia took a breath, reminding herself not to buckle over her stilettos. "I should have told you about her. It was complicated, and you know how everyone in school got when they found out someone had a girlfriend or boyfriend. I was ridden with guilt and confused . . . and . . . I want to apologize. I've thought about reaching out and clearing the air so many times."

Alia was back in that classroom again.

The rain poured. They were being silly and flirtatious over a packet of chips. Little did she know, in a matter of minutes, the dreams she had built around him would shatter to pieces.

This time he only took one chip. He dipped his head in thanks and they looked at each other long enough for Alia to zone out about what was being discussed around them.

A boy spun a pencil box on the desk. It stopped at Jeh and a girl named Diya.

"Truth or dare?" she asked.

"Truth," he replied, nonchalantly.

"Is it true you have a girlfriend?" Diya's eyes pranced with mischief as the color dropped from Jeh's face. Everyone oohed and ahed and those closer to him bombarded him with *'what?!'* For a split second, Alia wondered if they were talking about her. Had people noticed all the time they were spending together?

"Come on, spill the beans!" said Diya. "We've heard rumblings from the Parsi colony!"

And just like that, Alia's heart crash-landed. She didn't need to hear him utter the words to know, yes, he had a girlfriend.

"Tanaz, right?!"

Jeh looked at Diya like she had outed him.

"Ooh, is she the one from the convent school, St. Anthony's?" another girl asked.

As the voices of his friends besieged him, his cheekiness, flirtation, and silliness vanished and not once did he meet Alia's eyes. She wanted to get up and run home. They'd spent so much time together, had countless conversations, ate so much food, even shared the same spoon numerous times, and *not once* had he alluded to having a girlfriend.

Alia shot him a disgusted look. She held back her rage and the tears threatening to fill her eyes. He had lied by hiding the truth, to both her and his girlfriend. She felt worse for poor Tanaz, who had no idea what he was doing behind her back. Alia flung him another look. This time he glanced up, shriveling under her simmering, humiliated, and hurt-filled stare.

After that day, Jeh avoided Alia. He was never around when the group hung out. If he was, he'd leave early without conversation or eye contact. Their phone conversations ended. Their texts stopped. Alia had no intention of talking to him either. By the time Farewell Day came around, the two groups had disbanded. Muskaan and Virag had broken up and Alia had no reason to seek Jeh out. The last time she'd seen him was when everybody was taking pictures on Farewell Day. Their eyes locked briefly, but because of her ego and the fact that he hadn't once apologized, Alia had turned away.

Now, five years later, Alia looked into Jeh's eyes again. This time, her heart wouldn't stop fluttering, and it made no sense. Was it the apology she had been waiting for or did she actually have feelings for him? Time might have healed her wounds, but it had left an ugly scab, one that burned whenever someone lied to her.

"But you didn't clear the air," she said, realizing she wasn't ready to accept his apology yet.

His dark eyes grew somber. "You have every right to be mad at me."

Be cool, Alia. Be cool. She heard Kavya's voice and then Sana and Pooja's inside her head.

"That's true, I do." She angled her chin at him and tucked a wave of hair that had slipped over her cheek. "But for now, we have a groom to find. Once we do, you can resume apologizing. Sound good?"

Jeh broke into a sideways smile and arrows of heat went shooting through Alia's body.

Finally, they made it to the hotel's sprawling gardens. Wafts of sea breeze plump with heat and humidity blew over them as the waters of the Arabian Sea shimmered in the distance. Bouquets of marigolds were being brought out by the hotel staff along with stacks of burnished gold Chiavari chairs. Alia wasn't surprised the hotel was prepping for another wedding later in the day. Weddings in India were a perennial business, and in the cooler months from November to February, everybody wanted a breezy, outdoor venue. Alia and Jeh circled the lawns, hardly noticing the majestic arches of the Gateway of India and the rustle of pigeons flocking to the skies.

Jeh tried Cyrus's cell phone again. There was no answer. They went back inside and inspected the lobby filled with guests. They peeked in the hotel's coffee shop and hurried through the corridors lined with ornate mirrors, portraits of Indian maharajahs, and a photo wall of famous guests from Amitabh Bachchan to Barack Obama. They fast-walked through the leafy portico with rattan chairs, past the grand staircases, and the swimming pool with sun-bathing guests sipping chilled beverages.

Cyrus wasn't anywhere. For the first time, panic seeped into Alia, but she was determined not to give up hope. There had to be a logical explanation.

"How stupid we've been!" Jeh slapped his forehead. "He must be in his room."

Of course! The families of the bride and groom had booked rooms so they could freshen up and have a place to rest between the ceremonies.

"Where are you going?" Alia asked as Jeh sprinted past the elevators.

"We've booked two rooms. I have the keycard to my room and Parveen Fui has the key to their room. Keep a look out—I'll be back in five!"

By the time Alia nodded, he had loped out of sight. Tall as he was, she could see the top of his head bobbing through a sea of people.

"Aliaaaa!" Sana and Pooja ran toward her.

"Did you find Cyrus?" Alia asked eagerly.

"Nope," said Pooja. "We're on our way to the parking lot to see if any of the drivers have seen him."

"Naina is going to kill him if we ever find him," Sana said, and then held Alia's hand. "Tell us, how's it going?" A smirk filled her face as an identical one appeared on Pooja.

Alia bit down her smile and glanced to make sure Jeh wasn't close. "Can you believe he actually apologized?"

"He did?!" Pooja looked positively ecstatic.

"Oh god, I feel so ridiculous."

"Alia, you're as pink as a pomegranate!"

"Ugh, I know! What's wrong with me?"

"He's coming!" Sana grabbed Pooja to duck out of sight.

"Make us proud!" she yelled.

"And don't go all serious on him. Be naughty, not nice!" Pooja winked before disappearing into the crowd.

"Sweet Caroline," Alia's dad's favorite song, began playing as Jeh approached, flashing Cyrus's room keycard.

"Oh my, who do we have here?" the meddling Auntie said, squeezing between Jeh and Alia. "Is she the girlfriend you're not telling us about, Jehangir?"

Jeh grew mortified. "No, she's a friend, Auntie." He tried to skedaddle away, but she jiggled closer, scrutinizing them with a wine-flushed look.

"We went to school together," Alia explained.

"That's how it begins!" She chortled, spilling wine from her glass. "He's our *mitho dikro*, our sweet boy, Jeh!" She pulled his cheeks, making him bend down to meet her face. A tomato would've paled at Jeh's reddening cheeks. "Now, hurry you two—the ceremony is about to end. Only two more left! I had a bathroom emergency, but I'm rushing back inside to hear Naina's decision!" As if there was any chance Naina was going to say no. Although after Cyrus's current antics, Alia wasn't as sure.

They nodded to say they were coming and raced toward the

elevators. Jeh pressed the up arrow. He thrummed his feet, impatient for the doors to open.

"How's Parveen Auntie doing?" Alia asked, sneaking a furtive glance at him. How did he look so hot in an outfit that had two big bows in the front?

"She's very worried. Naina is really trying to hold it together, too," he said, pushing the elevator button several times.

Ding! The doors opened.

Jeh pressed the sixth-floor button, and a Tchaikovsky symphony played. The elevator swam with the scent of his cologne.

First floor.

It started to get hot. Alia moved her hair to the side, giving her neck and chest room to breathe. Sparks of heat exploded under her skin as the kaleidoscope of butterflies in her stomach took flight. Maybe it was the "Waltz of the Flowers," or that she was a hopeless fool, but she felt she was in a period film about forbidden lovers doomed for love. Or maybe it was because they were standing an inch apart.

Second floor.

Alia could practically taste the heat emanating from his body.

Third floor.

She squeezed her eyes shut.

Fourth floor.

"Was I imagining it all or was there something between us?" Alia asked, louder than she intended.

She didn't meet his eyes, staring instead at the shiny elevator doors mirroring their hazy reflections. When he didn't respond, she turned to him.

"You weren't imagining it . . ."

His eyelashes were long, much longer than hers, and he held on to her gaze while her body melted under her.

"I've thought about it several times," he said, glancing at his shoes.

Fifth floor.

"Thought about what?" She wanted him to say the words.

He took a breath. Maybe he was nervous, too.

"Us," he said. "You and me and what we could have been."

Alia held her breath, hardly realizing it. How many times had she imagined those words in her head? His hand in hers. His fingers lost in her hair. Her laughs buried in the bend of his neck.

Ding!

The sixth-floor doors opened and a boy scampered in. His mother glared at him and apologized, but Alia was grateful for the intrusion. She waved the kid goodbye and stepped out. Jeh followed her with a look that asked if she was going to respond, but with a blink, he let it go.

No boys, Alia. And definitely no childhood crushes to derail your life plans. You got him to admit he felt those feelings, too. Isn't that enough?

Jeh was halfway down the cream and gold carpeted corridor.

"607 and 608," he said, arriving at the rooms.

Jeh unlocked Cyrus's door and they barged in. The clothes Cyrus had worn in the morning lay folded on the study desk and on the floor were open suitcases with a bridal trousseau for Naina. An extra keycard and half-empty bottles of mineral water crowded the TV console. Wedding gifts piled high on the sofa-chair and two sarees wrapped in tissue paper rested on the bed. A freshly steamed sherwani for Cyrus to wear for the Gujarati wedding ceremony hung on a wardrobe knob along with a larger-sized sherwani and blue suit, presumably his father's. Jeh threw open the bathroom door—save for perfume bottles, Parveen Auntie's makeup paraphernalia, and toiletries, there was no one there. They left the room and Jeh opened the door to his cousins' room. The mess assaulted Alia's senses. There was no denying they had partied last night—but more important, there was no sign of Cyrus.

"Fuck!" Jeh yelled, slamming the wall with his hand. "Where is he?!"

Alia looked back at Cyrus's room. She'd seen his parents' clothes for the Gujarati wedding and the reception after. She'd also seen Cyrus's sherwani for the Gujarati wedding, but she hadn't noticed his clothes for the reception.

"There has to be another room," she said, darting out of Jeh's room.

"What do you mean?"

"I didn't see Cyrus's suit for the reception, which means he and Naina must have their own wedding suite for once they're officially married. His reception clothes have got to be there and so might he!"

Jeh ran forward to hug her. Realizing what he was about to do, he swiftly dropped his arms and rushed into Cyrus's room. In seconds, he was out with the keycard Alia had seen on the TV console—this one had a different room number than the other two rooms.

"You're incredible," he beamed. "There's only one keycard to this other room when there should be two. Cyrus *has* to be there."

The elevator dinged and they flew out, racing toward the room. Alia could hardly breathe as Jeh slid the keycard into the key slot of the Lotus Suite. Inside, the balcony doors were open, and the muslin-white curtains flapped violently, almost reaching the wood-engraved four poster bed. A cell phone peeked from within the folds of the disheveled bedsheet. Alia stuck her arm out to stop Jeh from taking another step. Curled into a ball on the hand-knotted rug, between the bed and the suite's charming colonial furniture was Cyrus—swollen and puffy faced. Jagged wheezes left his mouth as his arm shook trying to reach his leg; his fingers curled around a massive . . . glue stick?

Jeh sprang into action. "Quick, turn him over! He's had an allergic reaction."

Alia helped Jeh roll Cyrus onto his back. Thankfully, he was conscious, although his face and neck were covered in hives. Jeh uncapped the "glue stick," which Alia realized was Cyrus's anti-allergy injection, and jabbed it into Cyrus's thigh through the trousers of his dugli.

"One . . . two . . . three . . ." Jeh counted, and he jabbed him again. After a few minutes, Cyrus's wheezing subsided. Alia rushed to get him water while Jeh helped him sit up.

"We found him!" Alia said to Kavya, who answered on the first ring. "He's had an allergic reaction. We're in his and Naina's wedding suite."

Within minutes, Cyrus's parents, Naina, and Naina's parents were in the room profusely thanking Alia and Jeh.

"It was the peanuts in the green chutney, I think," Cyrus said hoarsely, as Naina hugged and kissed his swollen face. "I had a pattice and some of it must have touched the chutney beside it. I should have been more careful."

He turned shamefaced toward Naina. "I'm sorry, baby . . ."

"I'm just glad they found you," she said through tears slipping down her cheeks. "Next time, you're not putting a morsel of food in your mouth before checking with me, understood?" She kissed him again, cradling his head in the curve of her neck. "That is the condition of my saying 'Baleh!' without the groom being present!"

Everyone chuckled and relief washed over the room.

"I should win 'Best Wife Award' for that alone." She shook her head, teary-eyed.

"You are the best of everything in my life," he said, stroking her loose curl. "Let's hurry so I can bind you forever to this unfortunate mess you've agreed to call your husband before you change your mind!"

"First I need to know if you're completely fine." Naina stepped aside to make space for Cyrus's father, who was opening up the doctor's bag he always carried with him.

As they waited for Cyrus to be examined, Alia nodded at Jeh, suggesting that she was heading back downstairs. It filled her heart to see love like Naina and Cyrus's—strong, honest, and pure. She pressed the elevator button to go down.

Ding!

Alia stepped inside as a rush of air skimmed past her neck.

"Care to join me for a ride?" Jeh asked, his hand stopping the doors from closing.

Alia arched an eyebrow. "Care to explain?"

"Parveen Auntie wants me to pick up some antihistamines for Cyrus. Although Naina's weaving some pretty spectacular makeup magic on him as we speak."

It was always the smallest things. A rickshaw ride together. A shared meal on the street. Discussing their favorite TV shows. Chatting until 3:00 a.m. This wasn't a big moment either, but here he was asking her to go along with him again.

Alia knew she was sliding down a slippery slope, clearly having underestimated her feelings for Jeh. But she threw caution to the wind. After everything she had been through last year, wasn't she entitled to ride out her emotions for at least one day? Besides, what was the worst that could happen? An hour alone with Jeh couldn't possibly derail her life plans.

"Uber or taxi?" she asked.

Minutes later, they were riding down the narrow lanes of

Colaba Causeway in a blue Tata Indica "cool cab" in search of a pharmacy. The afternoon sun streamed through the windows, warming Alia's arms in spite of the full blast of the AC. They drove past century-old buildings, from the British Raj to fancy pubs and the iconic Leopold Café. Alia glimpsed the bullet holes on the café's exterior walls, and her chest tightened. The café had left the bullet holes there in defiance of the Mumbai terror attacks in November 2008. She was only five on that horrific night when terrorists roamed the streets of Colaba spraying the café with gunfire and grenades.

"It's hard to believe we're celebrating in a place that was ravaged by bombs, blood, and death," Jeh said, reading her thoughts.

Alia untethered her gaze from the café and turned to him. Jarringly, she remembered the Taj Mahal hotel was the worst hit that night. Guests and staff had been held hostage for days as bombs exploded, sending blazing flames through the open windows.

Everyone had said the city survived because of its resilience. But Alia knew it was the people who were resilient. No matter a tragedy personal or collective, time left them one option alone: to keep moving forward. It's what her dad said to her every day.

"We're going to miss the wedding ceremony," Alia said, frowning at the bumper-to-bumper traffic. Horns honked and exhaust fumes mingled with the perfume of tuberose blossoms.

"We'll probably only miss the Achu Michu," Jeh said as the traffic light turned green. By the time their cab moved a foot, it turned back to red.

"What's the Achu Michu?"

"It's when the groom's mother welcomes the bride into the family. She places a red tikka on her forehead, makes her wear a garland of red and white flowers, and gives her a . . . what was it . . . oh yeah, a coconut wrapped in string along with a bouquet of flowers. The bride's mother does the same to the groom. Before you say anything, I only know this because my sister got married last year and my mother went over it a thousand times." He shook his head.

"Hey, there's nothing embarrassing about knowing your traditions. Besides, it sounds lovely. Now I wish we wouldn't miss it. Seriously, will the city ever be rid of traffic jams?" Alia leaned forward, hoping to find an open road, but a river of cars met her eyes.

"I'm not complaining," Jeh said, getting comfortable in his seat. "The more traffic, the better." That side smile again.

"Well, aren't you turning on the charm today?" Alia laughed at his directness.

Jeh shrugged. "Just stating facts."

Alia didn't know if most girls were like her or not, but when it came to boys, she analyzed her every word, intention, and thought. Then there was Jeh. When he needed to run away from a situation, he did so without a second's hesitation. He didn't care about what the repercussions would be or what she would think of him. Now that he seemed interested again, he was openly flirting with her, not worrying about how direct he was being, in fact, wanting to be direct as if their past had been wiped like a clean slate.

"So, what's your game plan, Jehangir?" She faced him, not meaning to seem accusatory or threatening, just matter of fact.

"Jehangir?" he repeated, wide-eyed. "Shit, you're serious."

She toyed with her bangles, looking at him.

"I don't have a game plan," he replied, as if the words held an unsavory connotation. "I've always enjoyed spending time with you, and I'm glad I got the chance again after all this time."

It was a satisfactory answer. In fact, it was a good answer. But it still bothered her. Boys acted on whatever they felt like in the moment, and it could change one moment to the next. Maybe Jeh saw her today, and it rekindled some feelings. So he was making the most of their time together. What about when the wedding was over, and they went back to their separate lives? It wasn't as if she wanted him to profess his love for her and make a commitment—gosh, no—but what was the point of being charming and flirtatious if there was no end goal? Didn't he realize that his behavior could allude to a possibility of something more, especially because of their past, when in reality he probably wasn't sure if that's what he wanted in the first place?

"Well, I'm glad you're getting that chance," she said, rather curtly, and his face deflated like a balloon she'd pricked out of spite.

Wasn't that just her luck with men? She either attracted those who were overly possessive or those who didn't feel compelled to take the next step. It was for the best, she realized, reminding herself that she was categorically done with relationships after she'd broken up with Sahil, her boyfriend of two years.

Jeh glanced out the window. A hawker selling toy planes peeked in. Seeing no kids, he walked to the car in front. She bet he was wishing there was no traffic now. Just as Pooja had predicted, her self-righteousness had turned a perfectly lovely conversation sour. Alia tried to come up with something to lighten the mood when he turned to her.

"I heard you're majoring in finance."

The question threw Alia off. How did he know? All she knew was that he'd picked the field of science after they graduated from school while she had chosen commerce. If she had to guess, he was studying engineering?

"Yup. I plan to get an MBA in International Finance after we graduate."

"Here or abroad?"

A rock dropped in Alia's stomach. When she disclosed her plans of studying abroad, her and Sahil's relationship had quickly tumbled downhill.

"Why do you want to risk our future—long distance is not easy—for a few years of freedom and fun?" Sahil had lashed out. "You know as well as I do it's only about the flashiness of having a degree from the U.S. than the actual studying that everyone goes there for."

"Are you serious right now?" Alia retorted. "I want to learn to live by myself, experience a new country, and prove myself in a global setting. And I'm coming back! Don't you want to see what life is like outside India? Live a real-life adventure?" The anticipation of her future felt like fairy dust on her feet, itching to make her fly and explore what lay beyond the safety of the only life she knew. It was her dad's dream for her. Perhaps the only one he'd be alive to see come true.

"Oh please." Sahil's nostrils flared. "Everyone who leaves gets too tempted with the lure of the West to come back. Prey stuck in a spiderweb, I say. And you want to be just like them. If you want to get ahead in the corporate world, you'd be wise to start working as soon as we graduate. My dad even got you a job in our company! Think about how amazing it would be to work together. It's baffling that you just don't see that!"

"I want to earn my own place, Sahil. I don't need your, your dad's, or my own father's help."

The same argument had gone on for months until Alia had called it quits. When Sahil realized there was no chance of a reconciliation, he turned belligerent, calling her selfish and coldhearted, among other choice words she preferred not to remember. Since then, Alia had sworn off boys. She wanted none of the drama until she had reached a point in her career when she could focus on finding love without compromising on her dreams.

"Abroad," Alia said defiantly, even though it might've been an inconsequential detail to Jeh. "Either the States or Australia."

"I'm not surprised you've got it all figured out."

"I like having a plan," she said. "Well, actually a seven-year plan."

"Do you now?"

She laughed, slightly embarrassed.

"Can I ask what it is?"

He was serious.

"You'll think I'm crazy. Most people do when I tell them what it is. I mean, it's not an out-there, unconventional, crazy plan or anything. It's pretty standard, potentially boring to most. It's just thought through, I guess."

"So, you care about what people will think?" He leaned forward.

"I mean, I-I don't," she stuttered with an awkward laugh. "I didn't have a great experience with my ex when the topic came up, and I've stopped caring about defending it to others who don't understand it." She sunk deeper into the corner of her seat, folding her hands against her chest.

"You shouldn't have to. Most people seem more interested in hearing their own opinions instead of listening to what others have to say." He paused. "But I would love to know more if you're comfortable talking about it."

It had been a long time since someone asked Alia what she really wanted. And here she was dumping her emotional baggage on him.

"Okay, here it goes," she said. "Finish my bachelor's of business management degree with a specialization in finance, hopefully with top scores; get an MBA in international finance on scholarship either in the U.S. or Australia, since those are the only two countries where we have family; and gain work experience for three years before moving back to work for a top consulting firm."

He pressed against his seat, watching her. Alia raised an eyebrow.

"It's a fantastic plan. I'd kill to know exactly what I want to do. What's surprising to me is that you want to come back."

"Is it that shocking?"

"Yeah. Most of us who plan on studying abroad rarely have plans of coming back, especially before we've left."

"That's true," she said. "I don't want to be too far from my family in case . . ." Alia stopped herself, not wanting to talk about her dad's health. "Besides, India is so different from when the last generation left to go abroad to study or work. If you ask me, there's been a bit of a brain-drain since, and frankly, I don't want to add to it."

Jeh laughed. "Can't argue with that. Yours is a brain we certainly don't want to drain away to the West."

"Ha ha, very funny," she said, thwacking his arm. He held her hand, his fingers intertwining in hers. Blood coursed through Alia like waves in high tide.

"I don't have set goals like you," he said. "I'm afraid if I don't meet them, I'll disappoint everyone and become a disappointment myself. I haven't figured out who I want to be and where I want to be quite as much as you have. I wish I had," he scoffed at himself. "I meander. I feel my way through things to gather more clarity. After we graduated, I took up science. I thought I wanted to be an engineer. I hated it. I changed to arts, taking up economics. I was good at it, but it didn't motivate me enough. I'm studying law now. I think I like it. I'm enjoying the challenge and the creative aspects of a case. But my grades aren't very good yet." He paused a beat. "I like you, Alia. I have since school. I've been a coward, there's no doubt, but hunting down a missing groom and picking your brain stuck here in traffic has been the most exhilarating thing I've done in a long time."

Alia had to do everything in her power to stop herself from sliding over to taste his lips in a kiss she'd dreamed of a million times. But she stayed rooted.

"Am I something you need to feel your way through, meander by, and explore before getting clarity on knowing whether it's what you want?" Her mouth miraculously formed coherent words when all she could feel was a sweaty mix of red-hot, heart-pounding sensations in places she dared not admit.

He let go of her hand. "The opposite, in fact. There's something between us. Something chemical, something electric, something elusive that I've never felt with anyone else before. I'm scared to bungle it up like I'm so great at doing."

Alia's breath stopped on its way to her lungs.

"Seeing you again feels like . . . a confluence of fates."

A horn honked and the brakes slammed. Alia nearly rammed into the seat ahead.

"Forty-seven rupees," the driver said without turning around.

Alia broke out of her trance and glanced at the large green lettering of "Noble Chemists" over a busy shop. It peeked out from underneath one of the columns of an old historic building, a type of colonnade architecture designed to protect people from the rains during the city's torrential monsoons.

"Let me help?" Jeh offered as Alia stepped out of the cab and tried to maneuver her saree and high heels over the potholed road. He helped her up the crowded footpath and she slid her necklace under the folds of her saree.

"I should have thought about where I was bringing you . . ."

"Don't worry, I've learned the art of handling snatchers and boob-friskers in my time." She mimicked fiercely elbowing a person. "Plus, today, I've lucked out with a big, strong man to protect me, haven't I?" she said with a grin.

"Dhyan se chalo!" she reprimanded a man who walked straight into her shoulder without a care in the world. He looked chastened, and Jeh pulled Alia close. There was an intimacy, a familiarity, one brewing for five years. Her body pressed against his as it pushed past other unwanted ones. Their palms glued to each other. Their fingers interlocked. When they reached the front of the pharmacy counter, he drew her in front of him, towering behind her to make sure no one intruded her space.

Alia was as grateful for the crowd as he'd been for the traffic. The cacophony of loud voices, prescription requests, hustling bodies, sweaty arms, and cawing crows blended into a symphony of sounds of her beloved and chaotic city. They drowned her anxiousness, her confusion, and she let herself rest on him. Her stringy backless blouse pressed against the bows of his dugli. The skin on her back caressed the sturdiness of his chest. As they waited for the pharmacist to bring out the medicine, his hand found its way to her waist, and he let it linger.

Alia exhaled slowly. Why did his touch feel so natural, like coming home? She could have turned, and her lips would have found his.

Jeh paid, and they left the shop hand in hand. As soon as they found a spot free of people, Alia slipped her hand out of his. If he was taken aback, he didn't show it. They stood close, looking for a free cab.

"The only option is Uber Pool," he said, checking his phone. "Otherwise, the wait is fourteen minutes."

"Let's pool it," she said.

Standing on the street, the bustle of the city pulsed in her veins. Tapering fronds of skinny coconut trees fluttered in the wind like fingers playing a piano. Alia faced Jeh.

"So, you want to go abroad and not come back?"

"I haven't decided either way . . . For now, I'm deliberating between an MBA or an economics degree to go with corporate law. Although the best-laid plans of mice and men often go awry, don't they?"

Alia's desire surged. Did he have to go quoting literature?

"Frost?" she ventured, not wanting to sound dumb.

"Robert Burns."

Alia felt the twinge of defeat, though Jeh didn't seem affected by her poet mix-up. A crimson bloom twirled loose from a gulmohar tree and fell beside her. The Uber arrived. Jeh shuffled into the front seat while Alia squeezed into the back with two other passengers. He turned, asking with his eyes if she was comfortable, and she nodded, trying not to further crease her saree.

They made it just in time as the priest dressed in white robes and a white paghari was making Cyrus and Naina sit facing each other. Naina's pallu was draped around her head and she looked the picture of a demure Indian bride. Four married women walked up onstage and held a sheet of cloth hiding Cyrus from Naina's view. Thankfully, his face looked much less swollen.

Kavya waved Alia and Jeh over. Jeh joined them after handing Parveen Auntie the bag of medicine and pulled a chair beside Alia. Her friends couldn't contain their grins and Alia silenced them with a sharp look.

"Everyone's eating already?" Jeh eyed the tables with several guests halfway through their meal, including all of them at Kavya's table.

"It's nearly two o'clock now, and I'm starving," Kavya said, taking a bite of chapati with sali murghi, a gravied chicken topped with deep-fried potato straws. "Indian weddings are so long; you have to eat to get through them."

Sana nodded, diving into her dal rice and fish patio. "The main reason we attend them is to feast!"

"Well, I can't bear to look at all this food and not partake." Jeh pushed his chair aside. He turned to Alia. "Coming?"

The priest's voice boomed. "In this ritual called the Ara Antar, the white cloth symbolizes the separation that has existed between the couple. I shall now——"

"Let's be quick," Alia said. Her knotted nerves had begun to loosen at the sight of the scrumptious food, but she didn't want to miss any more of the ceremonies.

Who're you kidding? You obviously can't seem to resist spending more time with him.

Alia hushed her conscience and hurried behind Jeh, who was already in line at the lunch counters. Her eyes travelled over the endless array of food.

"Don't worry, there's a method to the madness," he said with a devious glint. "Personally, I like to begin on a sweet note."

"Oh, a switcheroo?" She raised her brows.

He grinned and served Alia a substantial dollop of sweetened yogurt, adding a portion of Parsi sev, which he described as vermicelli cooked in sugar with cardamom, nutmeg, and a garnish of silvered almonds. "On to the savory portion—first up is lagan nu achar, a Persian dry fruit pickle of carrots, raisins, and dates. Next, we have kid gosht, a lamb stew in a cashew gravy—utterly delicious—followed by patra in macchi, a quintessential Parsi delicacy of steamed fish wrapped in banana leaf and dressed in green chutney." Alia smiled. He sounded like a contestant on *MasterChef.*

"Lastly, we cannot forget the lagan nu custard, a Parsi version of crème brûlée, which believe it or not, must be had in between bites of the other food to heighten the sweet and savory flavors of the meal."

Alia readied her stomach for what was to come as Jeh's gaze hesitated over the saffron-pistachio ice cream and malai kulfi.

"Can we at least come back for dessert?!" Her stomach was about to burst even before taking one bite.

"You're right," he replied, and Alia remembered his undying love for buffets, with their all-you-can eat allure. With their plates towering with food, they made it back to the table. Alia sat down and turned her attention to the ceremony.

With the sheet of cloth still separating them, the priest placed grains of rice in Naina and Cyrus's left hands. He then placed Cyrus's right hand within Naina's, and they broke into surprised grins. Even after ten years together, it was plain to see that the touch of their hands sent a rush of giddy happiness through them.

"Why is it important for you to have a plan?" Jeh asked as if he was suddenly mystified by the notion.

Alia slipped a spoonful of lagan nu custard into her mouth. Was this his way of asking where he might fit into her plans? Had he read into her non-reply (and intimate body pressing and hand holding) as her agreeing that their meeting was "a confluence of fates"? Alia started heating up again. Now who was guilty of sending signals they shouldn't be sending?

The truth was it wasn't about what Jeh was thinking. If Alia truly had to answer his question, she had to talk about her dad, the one subject she spoke to no one about except her inner circle. It hurt her to talk about it. To accept that this was her reality. What a terrible luck of the draw she had. Most people her age had healthy parents. They didn't grapple with grief or hospital bills or the idea of death on a daily basis.

Alia put down her spoon and looked Jeh straight in the eyes. She had to be honest. Didn't she hate it when people hid the truth?

"When Dad got sick, everything in my world fell apart. Nothing made sense. Nothing we did helped. We were spectators watching the most terrifying show of our lives. All we could do was manage what Dad was going through while trying to make it slightly easier for us and him. So, I started making lists—medicine lists, doctor visit lists, grocery lists, to-do lists. Those grew longer into plans. Now, I need them. They give me a sense of control even though I know we don't truly have any. But it stops my mind from wandering down 'what-if' scenarios, which after what happened to Dad, only end in horrible imaginings. With a plan, I don't stray. I stick to the line and walk on it. It keeps me efficient because I'm reminded every day that time isn't a luxury for everyone."

Jeh's lips wavered, wanting to say something, but he seemed unable to find the words. Alia turned to look away.

"It's never fair when something so cruel happens to someone, especially to your own family." His voice was tender. "But the way you're handling it and looking to the future is really impressive. Your dad . . . he must be so proud. He's raised a strong woman."

She was used to leaving people speechless, uncomfortable, or overly sympathetic when they learned about her dad. But Jeh hadn't patronized her. He'd met her where she was, in a complicated tryst with reality.

"I shall wrap the string around Cyrus and Naina's hands and join it with a final knot to symbolize the bride and groom's desire to unite as a lifelong couple," the priest expounded, interrupting their moment.

Jeh drew Alia's attention back toward him.

"I'd come back for you."

A breath escaped Alia's lips.

She remembered for a second how she had felt leaning against his chest. How her burdens had momentarily floated away. Her dad had been that person once. The one she could count on. The one she turned to when the challenges came. "Forge ahead, Alia, and make your mark. I'm always here," he used to say. She was afraid of nothing knowing he was there. He was her support, her rock, her pillar of strength. And then that pillar cracked. It splintered to pieces. Now she had to be her own pillar. Her family's pillar. At least she was trying to be, building it brick by brick. How tempting it was to give into that illusion again. . . .

Alia smiled. "Don't tell me girls fall for that line?"

"I sure hope they do." He grinned.

"You should want to come back for you, Jeh. You shouldn't have to give up on your dreams and plans for someone else—surely that's not romantic . . ."

"Some might find the proclamation flattering."

"Ah, big, strong words," she teased, fully aware of being guilty of entertaining the possibility of allowing the distraction of a boy into her seven-year plan. "Some might say flattery is hypocrisy dressed in the sweetest of lies."

Jeh laughed, a big belly laugh. "Rolling with the punches, Sharma!"

Alia chuckled, glad for the burst of levity. She noticed he was sitting closer to her, his plate of food neglected for the moment.

"In all seriousness, I don't want to be responsible for anyone's major life decisions. Being responsible for mine alone is hard enough."

"Maybe you are a major life decision."

Words—they were so powerful and yet so easily dispensed. Half of Alia wanted to shout, "Yes, make me your life decision!" The other wondered about the meandering he usually needed to do before being certain of himself. Was it the heat of the moment or was he truly aware of what he was saying? Alia wished she could be fooled easily.

"That's a big life decision to be sure of when you aren't so sure about yourself."

"Ouch!" His hand flung to his heart.

"Oh no, I didn't mean it that way." She grazed his hand. If her relationship with Sahil had taught her anything, it was that she wanted—needed—to put herself first. For all the fireworks, shooting arrows, and butterflies she felt, who was she if she left one boy's arms only to run into another's chasing the illusion of safety? She wanted Jeh. Every pore of hers yearned for him. But she also yearned for the dreams she'd hoped for in her life.

How could she possibly let herself down?

"We're still versions of what we are to become," she said, spinning the bangles on her wrist. "Works-in-progress, if you will. Wouldn't you say we have some living, discovering, and maturing to do before settling into our final selves?"

"Is there such a finality? Isn't life a perennial work-in-progress?"

If Alia didn't blink, her eyes would've watered, but Jeh didn't break his gaze. Her palms, the nape of her neck, and the skin under her clothes turned sweaty.

"There is added symbolism in the ritual," the priest said, tunneling through the tension between Jeh and Alia. "While the thread that binds them is weak and can be broken easily, it gains strength when wrapped seven times, symbolizing the time they will put in, the trust they will build, the respect they will gain, and the love they will foster. The bond then becomes strong, enough so that it cannot be easily broken, if at all."

Alia tried to maintain her outward cool.

Breathe, Alia. Small, easy breaths.

"What are you trying to say, Jehangir Khambata?"

His eyes fixed on her, and his lips parted. She ached to hear the words and yet she was terrified of them.

"Cyrus, stop daydreaming about the honeymoon and make sure you go first!" an uncle yelled.

"Naina!" shouted one of her cousins. "Do it as soon as the sheet drops!"

Alia's friends looked at Jeh, confused about what was going on. Alia glared at the stage. Did everyone have to interrupt them at the most inopportune of times?

"Watch what happens when the sheet drops," Jeh said, flatly, their moment lost.

As the priest finished the seventh encirclement and invocation, the aunties let the sheet fall. Promptly, Naina lifted her hand and threw the grains of rice on Cyrus's head.

"She did it!" the guests chanted, and Naina was officially declared to be the one fated to wear the "pants in the relationship."

Cyrus winked at her. "Was there ever a doubt?"

The thread ceremony ended, and the priest commenced the final wedding rituals. Cyrus and Naina faced the guests as the priest sprinkled them with rice from a silver thali containing rose petals and a silver goblet filled with coal, sandalwood, ghee, and incense.

Alia turned to Jeh. He had bent forward, elbows resting on his knees, and his eyes focused on her.

"You should know I've sworn off boys until I've met my goals," she said, before he asked her a question she couldn't refuse.

"Why?" He grew serious.

"Relationships require work. Chemistry and inexplicable feelings are good places to start, but they aren't enough." Also trust takes more than a day to earn, she wanted to add, but she kept silent.

"I completely agree."

Alia wondered if he realized they had only one shot to get it right this time. If they went too fast, they could self-combust. They'd be done. Finished. They'd get no do-overs. He might be okay, but she couldn't bear the thought of losing someone else who held a piece of her heart for so long.

She looked at him, wanting him to understand her. "Maybe we become the people we are meant to be first?"

His lips pinched in a frown, and Alia's heart pounded like a yo-yo against her chest. He was not getting it. She straightened a fold in her saree and angled a glance at him.

"You don't get a second shot at second chances. You get just one shot."

There, she said it. Her truth. Out loud. She wasn't going to let him hurt her like he did again.

Jeh leaned back. It might have been an inch, but it may as well have been the seven seas. Alia's heart crash-landed for the second time.

Now, he's got it.

Her self-righteousness and emotional baggage had pushed him away. Though in the end he hadn't fought for her or for that "something elusive that he had never felt with anyone else before." In spite of standing her ground, Alia didn't feel victorious.

"The thing is though . . ." He bit his inner cheek. "There is one thing I do know about myself."

His eyes seared into her.

"I want to see the person you are meant to become, Alia. Entirely on your terms, either as a friend, or if I should be so lucky, more than one. But this time, I'm not letting you go."

Alia caught her breath. The seconds stretched into eons.

He had fought for her, after all. On her terms.

"I'd like that very much," she said, finding her voice through a smile she couldn't contain.

Jeh broke into his big, gorgeous grin. From the corner, his eye twitched and something struck Alia. Rice and rose petals rained in their direction and the spell between them broke. Cyrus had swung Naina into his arms.

"I now pronounce you husband and wife!" the priest said, his cheeks blushing with excitement. "May your union founded on love and understanding begin."

Cyrus leaned in to kiss his bride.

The guests cheered as Jeh held Alia's gaze. A torrent of dazzling pink petals showered over them.

A Wedding Recipe
for Disaster
SARAH MUGHAL RANA

There were many unwritten do-nots on one's wedding day, but pickling vegetables in mustard oil would top the list.

But it wasn't my fault.

I had always pictured my wedding day as a romantic affair—where I'd be perfumed in gulab and my hands would be swirled in maroon mehndi dye, and I'd cherish the processions. But that was a long time ago, when I assumed weddings were nothing more than an excuse to dress up in lush red and gold fabric, and the heavy baggage of family drama threatening to suffocate the celebration didn't exist. I knew better now.

Last night—after toiling for hours reviewing my ammi's notes on which aunties to avoid and which to converse with on my wedding day, what topics were banned in discussions with all my relatives, and which jealous families to watch out for—my nerves were a boiling pot of Kashmiri chai threatening to bubble over, a mix of sweet and bitter.

So yes, today in a fit of nerves—and perhaps cold feet—I'd

ventured down to the kitchen after the dawn prayer of Fajr. And for the past hour, I'd been pickling vegetables, because what else could I do at five o'clock in the morning?

With a sigh, my eyes flitted down at my hands. Haldi stained my fingers. The kitchen counter was powdered too in the bright yellow spice. My gaze caught on the stack of unopened mail on the marble top, a familiar flyer featuring pickles and curry decorated in bold fonts making my stomach turn.

KHAN FOODS—GRAND OPENING MONTH INCLUDES SPECIAL DEALS AND COMBOS FOR THE BEST AFGHAN-PAKISTANI FOOD IN TOWN!

I resisted the urge to crumple it. I hadn't spoken to Osama Khan in over a year, not since that day.

No Salama, don't think about him. It's your wedding day.

Technically, it wasn't my wedding day—it was the first of a week-long celebration that my Ammi had always dreamt for me. Weddings didn't last a day in Pakistani culture. We squeezed in the engagement, the nikah, pre-wedding rituals, the wedding celebration, and then post-wedding reception called a walima. Today was my nikah—a *modest* party for me to sign the wedding contract and begin a new chapter of my life. By modest, I meant the party would still boast a healthy hundred-something crowd in a pretty garden before a feast of mouth-watering food, with aunties and uncles decked out in their finery.

"Salama!"

Oh no.

"Salama!" my Ammi whisper-yelled again from behind me, and slowly, guiltily, I turned around.

Ammi's eyes dropped to my hands and, fingers clutching her

dupatta to her mouth, she gasped so loudly, I flinched. "Tobah, tobah!" she screeched before pulling at my arms. "You idiot daughter, what have you done!"

"Ammi, I can explain—"

"Your hands, oh your hands!" She wailed like it was Judgment Day. "Look at the turmeric; what will the mehndi artist do in her touch-ups! The flowers look yellow!"

"It's only five a.m. I can wash the spices out before the girl arrives!"

"You idiot daughter," she repeated before thwacking my head. "Such a grown girl and still you do idiot mistakes. The spices will stain your skin!" She sniffed around my shoulders and hair before wrinkling her nose, unimpressed. "You will also take three showers. I worry that no matter how much attar we spray on you, only Allah can take away the mustard oil smell. We don't want Ismail to run away, horrified."

Ismail Abdullah Chaudhry was my fiancé. "I think he's used to this smell by now," I muttered. "He's Punjabi. What Punjabi household doesn't smell like delicious curry and achaar?"

Ammi pinched my cheek too hard. "He's a good son, a Punjabi boy, unlike others. Now he will have to put up with his mustard-smelling bride." She reached up and smoothed my still-damp hair—I washed it the previous night.

There was a lump in my throat, but I couldn't swallow it down. "Unlike others," I repeated. I didn't question who the *unlike others* was meant for.

Ammi drifted to the kitchen counter, wiping it down with a damp tablecloth to clear away the sprinkling of spilled haldi and black cumin seeds. Her hand paused, brows crinkling at the stack of mail envelopes.

"Why is this nonsense here?" Ammi snapped, and if there

was a way to violently lift a Khan Foods flyer, Ammi had accomplished it.

"It came with the mail," I said quickly.

She crumpled it in her little fist. "I just know Baji Ruqayyaah intentionally had her employees mail the flyers to our house."

"Ammi come on, that's ridiculous,"

She held up a hand. "Enough beta. I know you've always had a soft spot for this ridiculous family."

"Ammi, of course not—" I tried to play it off.

"But I am done giving them the benefit of the doubt." Ammi turned up her nose. "The Khans think they're better than our Sheikh Pickles." Ammi began ripping the flyer and I withheld a sound that was a cross between a snort and gasp.

The rivalry between our family businesses was borderline comical. Afghan-Pakistani pickles versus our Punjabi-Pakistani pickles—the perfect recipe for ethnic fights, quite literally, through food.

The Khans were Pashtun who moved from Mardan to Lahore two decades ago, becoming my parents' neighbors. They emigrated to America at the same time as my parents, opening up an Afghan-Pakistani pickle small business at the same time as my parents. Each accused the other of copying them. And well, the rest was history: Our families competed for the best farmers markets, the best product managers, distribution networks in the biggest Arab and Indo-Pak grocery stores, co-packagers, factories, and now major retailers.

In all that time of cursed food business politics, we were neighbors until the Khan family grew their enterprise and abruptly moved to a different city, to the relief of Ammi.

I hadn't seen them since.

Last I'd heard, their son, Osama, had entered a commerce

program in some top university to continue to expand the family business into restaurants all over the state.

"Salama?"

No, you're doing it again. Do not think about him. I swatted memories of Osama away.

"Salama!" Ammi repeated, shattering my reverie. "What is wrong with you? You look so sullen!"

"I'm not!"

"Ah." Ammi shook her head. "You miss Ismail."

I resisted the urge to scowl. Wasn't this why the marriage was happening in the first place? My parents adored my fiancé. Ismail was a good Punjabi boy, well educated and a family friend. The perfect match in my parents' eyes. Family caste was at the heart of politics around marriage.

I couldn't ignore the resentment weighing heavy on my chest.

Maybe Ammi caught the trembles in my hands or maybe she figured—since I hadn't gone to sleep after dawn prayer—that I had cold feet. Ammi was always good at knowing the little things that were unspoken.

Tutting her tongue, she said, "Since you've spiced the vegetables, let's finish preserving it, and *then* you can go take three showers."

She rolled up her sleeves and began quartering the lemons, carrots, chillies, and green mangos. I blinked and watched her rhythmic movements, the ritual of tradition possessing her, something I was still trying to mimic.

After grinding the mustard, nigella seeds, and the rest of the salt and spices in our clay pots, we sprinkled it onto the quartered vegetables. This recipe was passed from my great-nano to my nano to my ammi and now to me.

Afterward, we laid the mango and carrot to dry outside as the sun rose, and it was as if we'd both been snapped out of the peace of ancestral ritual.

Ammi pinched my cheeks again, but more gently. "Today is a big day, jaanu. During Fajr prayer, I asked Allah to bless you with so much. For a happy, prosperous wedding and marriage. I know your brother isn't here, but if he was, he'd be shocked to see his sister all grown at nineteen years."

"I know," I said softly. The mention of my brother, Abbas, who died years ago in a car accident, always felt like a raw wound. My throat pinched together, eyes stinging (and not from the waft of spices). It's why my parents fawned over me—I was all they had left.

Ammi sniffled.

"Oh Ammi, please don't cry. You don't want swollen eyes on the day of my nikah," I pointed out.

She sniffed harder. "We will smell like haldi and onions because of your idiot mistakes. Now go upstairs and wash those stains. Use Dettol if you must." She pecked my forehead. "And even if you smell like haldi, Ismail would be the bigger idiot for running away," she whispered into my hair.

My lips cracked into a smile but on the inside, I couldn't help but think, *How horrible am I that a part of me hoped the groom would run away?*

12 MONTHS EARLIER

"Salama ma'am, the son is here at the reception asking for you."

I paused looking over the inventory ingredients, directing my glance at our (now) best sales representative for in-store demos,

Kassim, my baba's brother's sister-in-law's son. As a new Punjabi immigrant, he was living in our basement. He had an adorably annoying habit of always calling me ma'am at work, like I was incredibly important, even though I was his older cousin and I'd told him to stop on many occasions.

"Who is it?" I asked.

Kassim stared down nervously into his hands and half whispered, "Him. The enemy's son."

"Why are we whispering, and who is 'him'?" I half whispered back.

"He is right here," a familiar voice cut in from behind us.

Kassim straightened sheepishly while I froze on the spot.

On seeing him, my pulse stuttered, just like it did every time we interacted. And like all those times, I ignored it.

Like the professional I am, I elbowed Kassim hard before nodding my head in greeting to Osama, the infamous son of Khan Foods. Osama was nineteen, a full year older than me, with light brown eyes that caught the light in a nice way that I didn't like thinking about, and unruly short curls framing his handsome brown face.

Osama took two steps toward us, his sharp gaze glancing down the production lines of the factory our small family business operated. He inhaled slightly and spoke warmly, "Achaar, the smell of home."

Once upon a time, I hated achaar for its pungent acidic smell that had all the kids in elementary school glancing at my lunch in disgust. Ammi always used to pack me a rolled flaky paratha stuffed with tangy pickled vegetables. The lunch inspired my parents to start a condiment business called Sheikh Pickles, where they sold authentic Punjabi achaar and other chutneys in a jar as traditional alternatives to the big brand garbage full of sodium and vegetable oil.

With that, I either had to learn to hate it or accept it. I chose the latter, and now I was on the precipice of taking over that same business when I entered university next year.

"Asalaamualaykum Osama," I began. "Bold of you to enter enemy territory. I'm assuming this is recon, just like the last time you 'visited' our old commercial kitchen. But we Pakistanis are welcoming and hospitable to all, even the unworthy." I smiled and Osama took the insult in stride, which was typical in our routine of verbal sparring.

"This is a new factory?" Osama said by way of a greeting.

"It's with a new co-packer we signed with. We needed a larger facility because of the increase in volume of retail orders," I said, a touch too smugly. At eighteen years old, it was the summer before my senior year of high school—and because of my "vigorous youth" as Baba liked to call it, I was the best person to drive to grocery stores, pitch our product, greet product managers, send late night emails, and help with demoing our product across retailers while my parents handled the production side of Sheikh Pickles. In truth, I didn't hate it.

Inheriting this business was my ticket to the future. And standing in my way were the ambitions of a certain curly-haired boy.

Osama began studying our Sheikh Achaar jars almost clinically, the production staff overseeing the manufacturing. What did Osama think?

In honesty, the Khan family was beating us badly in sales distribution. Getting to claim Afghan and Pakistani cuisine, the Khans had that going for them while still branding themselves as authentic, which eventually led to the opening of two of their Afghan restaurants. If I had a stronger spine, I would have refused to sample their chapli kebobs.

But of course I did, and they were delicious.

Enemy, enemy, my internal radar went off.

I reminded myself of this fact even as my stomach flipped the longer I stared at him, so I lowered my gaze to the . . . less attractive recycling bin in the corner of the room.

Osama shoved his hands in his pocket and smiled at me. "I'm not surprised that you're in a bigger factory. You were always good at sales pitching."

His compliment threw me off. "Credit also goes to Kassim. He's very charming with the store managers." I nudged Kassim who yelped at the sudden attention.

Osama's eyes didn't leave my own. "I doubt he's the only one who was charming."

Enemy, enemy, I chanted again.

"Now you think you can charm me," I said. "I know why you're here. Investigating our new factory. Trying to take a piece of our company back with you." I raised a brow.

Osama only laughed as if my accusations were easy to flick away.

My eyes narrowed. Last month, two different uncles had approached us to buy out our company in cash, but we weren't so oblivious. Baba's friend's brother's son investigated and informed us of their findings. Those uncles had ties to the Khan family. The Khans were trying to acquire our company to eat their competitors and have an achaar monopoly on the market.

In retaliation, my Ammi spread all sorts of rumors that the Khans were jealous of our authentic Punjabi line of achaar— because we had the loyalty of half the Punjabi customers in town.

Switching tactics, I scooped up a packaged jar of Sheikh Achaars from a new flavor line and held it out. "If you're so curious to check us out, take a gift. Give it to Auntie Ruqayyaah, please."

Auntie Ruqayyaah was his mother.

To my surprise, Osama took the jar. "Will do, if you agree to come with me to our house tonight. For dinner. Around Maghrib time."

Kassim gasped beside me like we were in a Pakistani drama. Now I elbowed him hard enough that he wheezed, "Ma'am."

"Dinner," I said coolly. "Where's this invitation coming from?"

At Osama's silence, I realized he wasn't joking. Inviting me for dinner? Not returning my insults in our verbal sparring? This was the first red flag.

Osama nodded to Kassim. "Is there an office where Salama and I can have a private discussion?"

"There's a co-working office bhai," he offered.

"I will not be in a room with Osama alone and let the Devil be present," I protested.

"Fair enough." Osama narrowed his gaze. "I can't tell if you just called me the Devil."

I gestured at my cousin. "Great. Kassim will be in the office with us, Osama bhai."

Oddly enough, Osama stiffened at the usage of the Urdu term for brother even though in Islam it was meant as an honorific more than the platonic implication of blood sibling. That was red flag number two.

Once inside the office, I crossed my arms and leaned against the wall. "Please explain."

Osama raked a hand through his hair. "It's my amma. She's been pressuring me about marriage."

My eyebrows knit together. "But you just turned nineteen. Isn't marriage a little soon?"

He shrugged. "I don't mind it. We're Muslim. A lot of us don't date; it's not halal. My parents brought up the idea of marriage a few weeks ago and I didn't think much of it. I told them I was ready whenever they were."

He was right. My parents were beginning to broach the idea of marriage to me too, but with it, my nerves jittered, unsure if I was ready for such a life-altering step.

He continued, "But then yesterday, Amma brought her friend's daughter . . . as a potential marriage prospect. The girl was great."

For some reason, my heart squeezed. I forced a smile. "Wow, mashallah," I lied with the blandness of stale paratha.

"The girl was great," Osama repeated, and he looked at me intently.

"What does this have to do with me?" I urged.

"She wasn't you."

It took a second for his words to register and when they did, my vision seemed to blur until I realized I forgot to inhale.

Osama frowned. "Are you okay? Usually if I compliment a girl, she doesn't look like she's about to pass out."

"I . . ." My voice trailed off. I instructed myself to breathe slowly. Was I hallucinating? I needed a reality check. My gaze settled on my cousin to see his reaction to all this because this was ridiculous—

"Kassim, put the phone down!" I yelped. "Who are you calling—oh you better not be recording this!"

Though shamefaced, Kassim continued holding up his phone, the camera trained on us. "Salama baji," Kassim protested. "This is a love confession!"

"This is a prank," I realized.

"No!" Osama hurried to clarify. "This isn't a prank. I don't want to marry that girl, or anyone else my amma introduces to me."

"Why? Are you crazy?"

"You're so dense, Salama," he groaned. "We go to the same mosque, we volunteer at the same Islamic halaqas, we organize the same community dinners, and we both manage the same family businesses. You're a religious Muslim, you're smart—especially in business—you're kind, and you're one of the most generous Pakistanis in our community. I've known you for years."

"What are you trying to say? Why are you flattering me?"

"Because I'd rather explore the idea of marrying you."

Silence.

"Salama?" He watched my reaction carefully.

"But we argue all the time," I finally sputtered.

"For fun," he said. "I enjoy our arguments."

"Our families hate each other. That's not for fun."

He half grinned with a look that made it hard to think clearly. "I'm inviting you to dinner with my family. My amma doesn't hate you. In fact, I think she respects you for all the work you've done for your family business."

I snorted.

"I think if we sat down, business misunderstandings aside, this could change everything. Instead of fighting all the time, our families could see past their differences."

"I don't even know if I want this." My voice seemed faraway. The reality of it hadn't set in.

His lips turned down. "I know. I won't pressure you. I only want you to think about it. Pray the istikhara prayer, like I did. But I didn't rush into this decision. For the past year, when I thought about marriage, I imagined asking your family formally about a proposal in a few years. But I also know you. You would never give me a fair shot if you didn't properly meet my family outside business rivalry, because you're always so worried about your parents and what they think. So I don't want you to come to a decision without having dinner with us."

My head was already shaking because his words sounded dangerously sensible and I didn't like that. "You're Pashtun."

"Don't tell me you actually care about racial politics."

"I don't. I would never," I corrected him. "But I know my parents better. And you'd be stupid to ignore that. Racial politics matter to them. They would never let me marry anyone who isn't Punjabi. And I know your parents. They wouldn't let you marry anyone who isn't Pashtun."

He opened his mouth to protest and Ya Allah, he was being too idealistic. I cut him off quickly. "Let me guess, the girl your ammi showed you was Pashtun, wasn't she? She wasn't Punjabi."

Sensing the thickening tension, my cousin put his phone down. "Baji," Kassim interjected nervously. "I think you should give Osama bhai's suggestion some thought."

But my mind was narrowed in on my parents and their reaction and inevitable disappointment if I even considered this proposal. I was all they had left.

"I don't have to. I can't marry you, Osama."

To my displeasure, Osama appeared unsurprised. "You always follow your parents, in everything. Even if it means deciding who you'll marry. I was expecting a rejection for reasons other than racial purity."

"I'm being practical and saving both of us from years of family feuds and heartbreak. I wouldn't do that to my parents; I'm their only child. You have four other siblings. My parents only have me. I have to respect their values," I stated coldly.

After the death of my eldest brother, my parents' hopes and dreams were thrust onto me. That included the future, the business, marriage, everything.

Osama winced. "Values?"

I realized my mistake and tugged self-consciously at my hijab. "Values wasn't the right word. I misspoke—"

"So, I'm below your family because I'm Pashtun?"

"I didn't mean it like that—" I tried to correct my horrible error.

"Salama, I never cared that you were Punjabi. What mattered to me were your values as a person in our deen. It's what our Prophet always preached, that no one has any superiority over the other except based on righteousness. Our religion says to respect our parents but not to blindly follow their flawed belief systems and definitely not their obsession with blood purity. I respect our parents, but I can also stand my ground. That's why I came to you. A union between our families could have made a world's difference."

A sudden image popped in my head. Of a world where our parents got along, where it wasn't about business but instead the deep appreciation of Pashtun and Punjabi culture. Of dinners where it wasn't about racial superiority but a plate of food that reflected Pakistan: a union of cultures cooked with love. I imagined seeing Osama every day and not being caught between our parents' whims; not having to hide our stolen conversations and pretending to not enjoy our banter; being able to grow my business for the pure joy of it instead of having to meaninglessly compete against him for the sake of family pride and bragging rights.

"I—I . . ."

It was a dream for a reason.

Osama waited but I was caught between my own desires and my own fears of the looming future with endless possibilities that I couldn't make sense of.

All I could imagine was our respective mothers accusing each family of setting up a marriage to steal "trade secrets"; the aunties that would gossip and torment our parents for marrying into the enemy's family; his mother and my mother fighting and fighting . . . us caught in the middle of a Pakistani diaspora civil war.

And what would happen to our businesses? I couldn't think about it. I didn't want to. Our families were disjointed pieces from different puzzles.

My parents' grief for my brother who was gone, mixed with their desire to see me as a replacement, meant that their expectations would always take precedence over what I wanted, and I was okay with that.

At my silence, Osama received his answer.

Before leaving, he turned slightly, but I could only see the back of his shoulder, and I deserved that.

"I'm supposed to be leaving in a few weeks for university. We're moving, too, because of the restaurant expansion. I was hoping to change that."

Then he left. My fingers clenched into fists, and I bit my tongue hard because the urge to cry suddenly came over me. My eyes burned but I blinked it away furiously even when on the inside, everything hurt.

That day I lost my oldest rival . . .

And I hadn't seen him since.

PRESENT DAY

My family arrived early at the nikah venue. I was in a simple kurti ensemble beneath a black abayah I'd bought years ago during an umrah pilgrimage from Saudi Arabia.

In the venue's garden, as I awaited the makeup team, I stole the small recess of peace to bask in being alone.

From a distance, I watched the employees lay out the finishing touches of white and blue woven prayer rugs for the nikah ceremony. A smattering of white and dawn-blush roses woven into tapestries lined the outdoor gardens with a row of straw chairs creating a small semicircle. The seat at the center was reserved for the Islamic priest—the imam—during the afternoon ceremony.

Behind me, a cry broke the serenity.

"It's ruined!" I turned around to see Ammi pacing furiously before the frantic venue manager who was trying to placate her. "Everything is ruined!"

"What's ruined?" I strode over to them.

"The food! The food the venue prepared has gone bad!"

"Gone bad?" I repeated. "How is that even possible? Food doesn't just spoil!"

"It was the refrigerators, ma'am," the manager said, panic gleaming in his eyes. I would've pitied him if not for the fact that this was my nikah day. "Our kitchen staff found that all the refrigerators stopped working into the night. We have a technician at work. But in all my years as a manager, this has never happened. Rest assured, we have contacted our partner caterer from our second location to replace the food, ma'am. We are checking the cameras for foul play, ma'am."

"How could this happen?" Ammi was nearly crying. "On my daughter's nikah of all days!"

"Don't let the aunties find out," I told Ammi. Not properly feeding guests at any Pakistani wedding festivity was the ultimate hallmark of shame—we'd be insulted in the gossip circles for years to come. In fact, they'd even think someone had cast the worst of evil eye for this to happen.

"Ma'am, no one will know about this," the manager assured me.

"But how can you replace food to feed over a hundred guests in two hours?"

"That's what I said!" Ammi wailed again.

"Our restaurant partners are the best in the city, ma'am. Your food will arrive on time, ma'am."

Momentarily placated, Ammi grabbed her cell phone to call Baba, who was arriving later with my uncles and cousins.

Inside the dressing rooms, I prayed two nafl prayers to ease my nerves. For my du'a, I asked God to remove any doubts. To take away what will be bad for me by replacing it with something good. Surely, that would mean this nikah ceremony would go smoothly?

Soon, the salon women arrived to dress me for the nikah ritual, with the infamous Auntie Haneen and her army of sisters—they typically did all the makeup for the local Pakistani brides in their garage.

"So how long have you known the groom?" Auntie Haneen asked, as she tucked my hair under a soft blue jeweled headcap to match my nikah outfit.

"I've known Ismail for three years. But after the formal engagement, I've been speaking to him for six months on WhatsApp calls and chats. We've been out to dinner a few times, and I've known his family, since he's a family friend. He's very kind."

"Oh." She pouted. "Is that all? No love story then?"

I laughed, but it was awkward and high-pitched. "It's an arranged setup. The love will come after."

"What do you have in common?"

"We both love Islamic art and history," I answered honestly.

Auntie Haneen appeared unimpressed. "I was expecting more drama, but oh, it seems Allah has blessed you with an easy rishta in this marriage."

Arranged marriages have had a spectrum of meanings in Pakistani culture. By arranged, it was still consensual, but it also meant that our parents had introduced the couple in a halal— Islamically lawful—manner, and if we were compatible after getting to know each other for a period of time, we'd be engaged. That's how I met Ismail Abdullah. His father, Uncle Shevqat Abdullah Malik, was my father's close friend, so naturally, after he'd graduated college and I was about to enter college, our parents had schemed to set us up.

According to my ammi, I had always been a good Pakistani daughter. She even said, "Who else would be suitable for my daughter but the son her parents had picked out and approved?"

A memory sprung in my head of him, but I batted it away. *Please God, not today.*

"My husband and I had a grand love story," a new auntie spoke up as she finished arranging my light blue hijab beneath the traditional gold-jeweled choker set.

"What happened?" I asked.

"In our village—there was a fight between our gangs over my hand in marriage."

I didn't recognize this auntie. Was she a new member of Auntie Haneen's salon team? She had dark brown hair in a bouncy bob cut, deep brown eyes, and a stark mole on the left side of her upper lip. She didn't even look Pakistani.

"A fight? Over you? This isn't Bollywood."

"Oi, do not insult us by comparing us to Bollywood," Auntie Haneen cut in with her seething. "Bollywood does not respect Muslims; they can go to Hell!"

"Enough, baji." Her sister, Baji Hajar, rolled her eyes. "Spare the poor bride on her nikah day!"

The mysterious auntie continued her story: "My husband's family had a long-going feud with my own. It was over a land dispute. His uncle had even been accused of setting up the murder of my uncle!"

All the other aunties gasped, and I was suddenly relieved they were no longer fixated on my nonexistent love affair.

"But my soon-to-be husband was a good boy. He prayed on time. That was enough for me. God-fearing men, those are rare!"

"But what about your parents' wishes?"

The auntie waved her hand around, lipstick between her fingers. "Oh, they came around. They always do. They are family, after all. Sometimes these unions are bigger than marriage between two people—it's a marriage between entire khandans, between lineages. With time, family understands because, well, they're family at the end of the day."

I smiled politely because what else was I supposed to do?

"Beta, did you want your rishta to be a love marriage?" Auntie Haneen patted my blush-powdered cheek affectionately.

My smile disappeared.

"Oho, don't ask her such questions, not on her nikah day. We don't want her to get cold feet." Baji Hajar spoke as if I was not present in the room.

"Why does love even matter? It's not practical," I said quickly, but my traitorous mind cut to a certain someone with light brown eyes.

The mysterious auntie's eyes narrowed as if she knew I was secreting away memories from her prying gaze.

"Hmmm," she hummed aloud. "We will see about that, God willing."

A long maang tikka was pinned to the top of my hijab, with layers of jeweled gold chains laid against the side of my head, attached to the long train of parandi fastened at the end of my hijab, the tassel holding a full bouquet of white and red flowers— a family heirloom. My nose itched from the heavy weight of my ammi's old bridal nose ring. For many Pakistani families, jewelry was passed down to daughters for their wedding. I felt like a chhoti gurhyaa—a little doll—as the aunties preened me for the nikah ceremony. The maroon swirls of my mehndi complemented the pastel pink and blue hues of the sparkling organza gharara bought and designed all the way from Lahore.

As they were doing the finishing touches, a loud commotion disrupted our small talk. It sounded like yelling.

"What was that?" I struggled to stand but the weight of my heavily embroidered gharara weighed me down. The mysterious auntie grabbed my elbows before I hobbled toward the doorway of the dressing room.

Auntie Haneen yanked open the door . . .

And the scene before me was absolute chaos.

My ammi was standing with my baba holding her back from lunging at the banquet hall manager, who held his hands up, frightened. Behind them, two employees were stacking the appetizer trays on the buffet line.

I noticed the food trays labeled with a familiar logo. Khan Foods.

"Oh no," I whispered.

"How dare you bring Khan Foods into my daughter's nikah! This was the caterer you found?" Ammi pointed accusingly at the manager.

Before he could answer, the worst possible voice answered instead. "Why yes, we are the top-rated catering chain for the city's major banquet halls," Auntie Ruqayyaah drawled with a smirk. A woman I hadn't seen in well over a year.

"When the call came about an emergency catering order, we rushed our chefs and personally oversaw this delivery. Allah has blessed me indeed because to my delight, the Sheikh family was our desperate customer." Ruqayyaah's voice dripped in undeniable victory. She'd hold this over my ammi for the next decade to come, I was sure of it.

Already, guests were taking notice of the commotion and bracketed around the hall corridor, some aunties holding their hands to their mouth in shock and in thinly veiled delight, as if this were the set of some Pakistani drama.

"Why you—"

"Enough, Ammi, please not in front of the guests." I hurried over to my parents despite my heavy fabrics. But if I deterred World War III, then my nikah outfit be damned.

It was too late. Ammi pretended as if she hadn't heard me. "I will not feed our guests the enemy's food. How embarrassing that our family, relatives, and closest friends will be eating from the people who've humiliated us over and over again. The ones who tried to tarnish our business!"

Ruqayyaah's features twisted. "Tarnished? We didn't tarnish your name. You and your antics debasing our business began it all! As always, you have been jealous of our success!"

Ammi didn't hear her, carrying on with a tirade. "—don't think I was blind at your attempts to buy us out of our own company! And now this. This is below our standards. I would rather our guests starve than eat by the Khans' hands."

My eyes began blurring, from tears or shock, I was not sure.

"You would starve your own guests? How dishonorable!" Ruqayyaah's sharp laugh cut through the hall.

"You dare speak of honor?" Ammi snapped.

"Of course! Someone must educate you about honor!"

"Oh you——" Ammi lunged.

Auntie Ruqayyaah was ready for it, holding a hand out.

"Ammi!" I threw myself between the quarreling women.

"No!" my baba cried.

"Salama!" a new voice yelled, and a hand grabbed my long train of dupatta as if to pull me back, but it only made me wobble into the employee beside my mother——

Ammi turned around, eyes widening in horror. "Salama, no!"

Splat!

Hot liquid drifted down my back and chest, saturating the heavily beaded fabrics. My shut eyes stung, but I slowly forced them open, my nose assaulted with the scents of garlic, ginger, and spices.

My world was greasy curry and pickled peppers.

Distantly, I heard someone screaming. I think it was Ammi but my vision tilted and my hands trembled as my feet slipped in the pile of curry.

Did this really happen? I wondered. No. Not on my nikah. *Surely ten pounds of curry and pickles hadn't just splattered on me.*

More yelling. They were all screaming my name, but I was too busy trying to keep my balance in a puddle of oil and stewed meat.

Someone gripped my elbow.

"Come, beta. Let's take you to the bathroom," the mysterious auntie from the dressing room whispered into my ear. I couldn't piece together any coherent thoughts through my embarrassment, so I dutifully followed her.

In the background, my closest relatives and guests were stunned. Ammi was wailing again, and my baba was staring in horror. My cousin Kassim was beside him—

Oh, and his phone was out, recording it all. His guilty gaze locked on my own as he slowly put his camera down. And in front of my ammi, sporting a surprised look of her own, was Auntie Ruqayyaah and . . .

Her son.

"Take me away from this," I almost sobbed to the mysterious auntie. It wasn't the fact that all the food had spilled on my dress and hair and clothes—it was seeing him.

"Come now, follow me to the bathroom."

Through the curry, Osama's shocked eyes never left mine. He looked apologetic, and . . . an emotion I couldn't decipher. Probably because the curry made everything so hazy.

I nearly tripped hurrying to the dressing rooms bathroom, but from behind, heavy footsteps pounded after us on the marble-tiled floor.

It had to be Osama, who had grabbed my dupatta, to stop me from bumping into the caterers. But of course, men underestimate how heavy Pakistani clothes are. Because of him, I'd tripped into the catering trays instead.

Why was Auntie Ruqayyaah here? Why was Osama here? Why did they have to rub this catering nonsense in my mother's face on the day of her only daughter's marriage? It was a low blow when our emotions were running high.

Why, why, why—

Inside the bathroom, the mysterious auntie began wiping away the curry with a wet towel.

My fingers itched and suddenly I wished the sturdy counter-top of the kitchen were before me, knife at the ready, fresh curry leaves and green mangoes cut in chunks waiting to be sprinkled with nigella seeds and mustard oil.

"Yes, good. Breathe," the auntie instructed me.

I pictured the calming rhythm of pickling vegetables into achaar and the sticky sensation of green mango drying under the sun, skin and all. I imagined the cooled mustard oil poured on top of the curried vegetables.

Everything will be okay, Salama, I attempted to console myself.

The bathroom door opened and shut with a resounding boom.

My eyes were still shut but I felt the mysterious auntie tense beside me. "This is a women's bathroom."

"I know."

I heard a resounding *click*.

I opened my eyes to see Osama locking the bathroom door.

"I swear I'm here to only talk and apologize." He raised his hands at the auntie. Then he paused and squinted slightly at her. "Auntie, you look familiar."

She deadpanned, "I've been to your restaurants around the city many times. Great chapli kebobs."

I scowled and seemed to find my voice again. "Leave!" I snapped at Osama.

"I can't without apologizing."

My temper rose against my will, and if it were not for the auntie holding my arm, I'd be unsteady from the barrage of emotions inside of me. "You have some nerve and now you want to apologize?" I nearly yelled. "It's my nikah! You made me trip into the catering food and—and your ammi and you had the audacity to show up!"

"Believe me, we had zero clue it was your nikah. This banquet hall is our sister venue. When they called and told us their refrigerators no longer worked, I had to arrange for portable coolers to hold the ordered food. We were worried after the manager informed us about their malfunctioned kitchens. They called in an emergency catering order from the other side of the city. This was supposed to be a routine check-in for me, so imagine my surprise to see the girl I'd asked to marry me over a year ago, marrying someone else!"

The auntie gasped.

"That's beside the point! You made me fall into a tray of curry!" I cried.

"How is your marriage not relevant to this conversation?"

I was shocked into silence. My mouth opened and closed but couldn't form words.

"How long have you been engaged to him?"

"I . . ."

"Were your parents setting up this rishta when I asked you a year ago?" he pressed.

"You don't have a right to ask those questions!"

"Why not?"

"It's too late!"

That silenced him. To my surprise, he thumped his head against the door, eyes upturned to the ceiling.

"Look at me! I can't yell at you if you're not looking at me! It's like beating a puppy!"

"I can't," he said.

Rivulets of oil ran down my neck and my tears along with it. "Why are you here?" I hiccupped.

"You're getting married. I dropped curry on you. And I feel terrible."

"Then why aren't you apologizing?"

"Because if I do, then I'll have to leave. And all of this will be over."

His admission hung in the air. The raw honesty of it was too much. Maybe it was my emotions running high from the stress of the morning, or maybe it was because I finally owed him a shred of honesty, too, but I made an admission of my own.

"I can't look at you because it hurts. Please." My voice hitched. "I need you to leave."

He hesitated, a small, sad smile playing on his face. "I think you were right. About our families."

His light brown eyes skimmed over the mustard oil doused on my kameez, the slosh of it ringing across the room each time I shifted.

He emitted a low laugh. "We're a recipe for disaster."

Why did this make me feel so much worse? And why did I have an urge to laugh, too?

"Did you know, I prayed before all of this happened." I gestured around us. "I prayed that if this nikah was good for me, to give it to me, but if it was bad, then to take it away from me."

Now, he looked at me properly. "Do you think your prayer was answered?"

"I don't know."

He nodded before quietly unlocking the door and departing. It wasn't lost on me that he hadn't actually apologized.

I barely had time to gather my bearings as the auntie wiped my face with a damp cloth, before the door banged open again.

"There you are," my fiancé breathed.

My stomach dropped. "Ismail," I said quietly.

He closed the gap in two quick strides but didn't touch me. "What happened? I just heard! I was on the groom's side in the dressing rooms. I heard yelling and saw the spill, but you were gone. What, why—how are you feeling?"

"I . . ." I couldn't answer. Just seeing him made it hard to speak, and not in a head-over-heels flustered way. I couldn't even muster the energy to be embarrassed or angry about the whole ordeal anymore.

"Can I help with anything? Here." Ismail pulled out his hand-kerchief from his kameez's breast pocket, handing the gold fabric to me.

The auntie took it even though we had a pile of towels to work through. He watched her wipe down my arms. He didn't speak. The silence felt more suffocating. I wanted him to say something, but he paced, as if he were nervous. I suddenly wished Osama was back in the room—at least with him, I could yell and laugh mor-bidly; I could do something other than drown in my own worries.

As if picking up on this, the auntie paused in wiping my skin and released a drawn-out, heavy sigh. "Oh, beta. Salama needs space. Give her some space. Your pacing isn't helping her." Then she trained her ominous black eyes on me. "And you . . . you need to get a grip on yourself."

"Right." Ismail paused his fidgeting and forced a shaky smile. "I'll be outside with our parents. Find me when you're ready. Take your time, Salama."

After he left, the auntie quickly locked the door again before other guests deduced that we were hiding in the bathroom. Then she laughed. "My mother told me on my wedding day that it is not a proper wedding without big fights, big love, and big feelings."

"I could do without the big fights. We need to finish cleaning up." I thrust my left arm under the faucet, using my other hand to rub the dispenser soap over the film of grease, but the stark turmeric of the curry had already stained my henna and skin into a sickly yellow, as if to mock me.

"Beta, stop that."

"What do you mean?" I muttered, as I watched the soap suds form under the water.

The auntie shook her head. "Beta, I said stop."

I turned frantically. "Why have you stopped?"

She approached me slowly. "You're so young. You are so blind to what fate is making happen around you."

"I may be young," I said. "But I am getting married."

The auntie grunted in disbelief. "Tell me, how do you truly feel about this marriage?"

"What kind of question is this? We're wasting time, I have to clean up."

"It's an easy question, beta. And if the answer was clear, you would have no trouble answering it."

"Please don't make me answer this," I nearly begged.

At my silence, she placed her fist against her hip, leg propped out. I recognized this stance: It was the lecture pose.

"Remember the story of my village and my marriage? The one about our rival families?" she asked, and I nodded. "My situation was not so far off from yours, except mine involved murder plots, gangs, and all sorts of nonsense antics. But my husband and I made it through. We did because we believed that through all our respective families' pushback, deep, deep, deep, I mean truly deep down, it was from a place of tough love. They cared about my happiness, but they assumed what they were doing was my way to happiness. Sometimes, parents think they know better when they don't. And when they are wrong, you are allowed to respectfully push back."

"You aren't speaking about my fiancé." I jabbed a finger accusingly.

The auntie rolled her eyes. "Oh, it's so clear that you care about Osama. You had more chemistry with him than Ismail. Watching you and your fiancé was like watching someone eat unstuffed paratha with no chai or yogurt—it has no spice, no taste, and frankly, it never works! Why in the world aren't you pushing for an engagement with Osama?"

"What are you saying?" I gaped at her as if her ideas were heresy.

"In fact, I think we need to slow down. You're young, barely nineteen, and confused about your feelings. This marriage shouldn't be happening. You should be engaged to Osama and be married much later!"

"Excuse me, are we just skipping over the massive fight our mothers had!"

"Fights exist in every family. You, my dear, are scared about pushing back against your family's wishes. You haven't thought about what you want."

"My parents didn't force this marriage on me," I snapped. "I know I could push back, but who else would I marry? Osama's family—they aren't just any family!"

"Have you even tried broaching the subject? I would believe you if you told me that you tried."

Shame rose so suddenly that it took me aback. I hated wise aunties because they were too good at reading me. It was like a sport for them to practice their nosiness and unsolicited advice.

"No, I haven't tried," I admitted.

"And why is that?"

I didn't know how to articulate all the complicated answers tumbling inside of me like leaves in a harsh gust of wind. My fingers began twisting the hem of my kameez, knowing the real answer was right there, ready for the taking, but I couldn't quite reach out.

"Don't make me say it," I whispered.

"Look past your pride, beta."

With eyes shut, I swallowed hard. My pride—what always kept me from saying the truth aloud. Astaghfirullah to this pride.

I blurted, "Because I was a coward."

"There it is," she said, and *hmphed*. "If you expect marriage to be so easy, without all this drama, then my beti, you are not ready for marriage."

Another dose of heavy truth. I tried not to wince.

"Marriage isn't just between two people; it's between entire families and it requires sacrifice."

Sacrifice. Osama had considered all the barriers and he'd come to me twice now, with honesty, to give us a chance. He'd embraced the sacrifices and compromises, but had I?

Suddenly, I wanted to speak to him. Now.

The auntie folded her arms. "With that done, let's try this again. How did you feel after the curry fell on you?"

"I can't answer that nicely."

"Why?"

"Because the truth is I felt relieved," I said quietly. "I feel relieved about this fight ruining the nikah and it makes me terrible. I know."

"Finally, some honesty. And yes, you should feel terrible for going along with this ridiculous engagement, only realizing you were wrong to agree to it because the worst possible curry disaster befell you."

"But I can't call off a wedding. Not when everyone is here! And my ammi, she'll be horrified."

"I know you agreed to this wedding, but you are letting your parents' pressure influence your actions," the auntie said. "Doting Pakistani mothers are normal, but there are limits to it. You are so young, you are being swayed by your mother, and later you'll come to regret it."

"How do I call off the wedding, then? What reasoning do I use?"

The auntie took my chin and pointed it at the bathroom mirror. "What wedding, my dear beta? We have no food. And the soon-to-be-bride is covered in mustard oil so thick, you will need a minimum of three showers. Didn't you say you prayed? And then the fight happened. Look at the fate God's given you."

"I'm not getting married," I realized.

"You are not getting married," she agreed.

"I'm not getting married," I repeated.

Unlocking the door, the auntie looped arms with me, and together we marched out of the bathroom and back into the venue hall, leaving a trail of curry and pickles in our wake. I knew what I had to do—what I should have done a long time ago.

The corridor was a flurry of guests, employees, and managers, cleaning up the mess of food.

"There she is!" Kassim shouted across the hall.

"Oh beti." Ammi threw herself at me before stopping short from the state of my gharara. Her eyes were bloodshot from her incessant sobbing. "Look at my poor daughter!" she said aloud. "My poor beti!"

"I'm okay, Ammi. In fact, I feel good."

Amma's sobs stopped short. "What?"

The rest of the guests had taken notice and a thick crowd was forming, imam included. I spotted Ismail elbowing his way toward me, his parents in tow. My nerves rose to the surface but this time, I swallowed it down.

"Salama," Ismail said, eyes wide in concern. "How are you feeling now?"

He reached out but I stepped back. "I have an announcement to make."

"I know. We can reschedule the date. We'll take you home—"

"No." Then I raised my voice. "I'm calling off this wedding."

He froze, as did the rest of the guests. Behind him, Osama and his mother looked confused. I avoided his gaze, focusing on Ismail.

"Salama!" Ammi yanked at my arm. "What are you saying?" She turned to my baba. "She's gone mad!"

"No, Ammi. I'm sorry. I've been praying so much istikhara, asking God to show me if this wedding was right for me. But then one after the other, these mysterious incidents of the refrigerators, the food, the catering—it all occurred."

"Mishaps happen all the time!"

"No. I feel this in my gut. I trust it. I know this marriage is not meant to be. This is not a simple evil eye," I said extra loudly.

The guests in the crowd nodded slowly. If there was one thing that Pakistanis held dear to their hearts, it was their istikhara prayers, but also superstitions. Not that I believed in superstitions, but to save my parents from embarrassment, I would pull every excuse to make calling off the wedding seem like the most logical outcome of this entire mess.

"Do you know, on the day of the engagement, how many terrible nightmares I had for my Ismail?" Auntie Noshi said before turning to me. "But beta, this is only the evil eye."

"Ammi!" Ismail protested. "Nightmares don't mean anything."

"They do," I insisted.

Auntie Noshi's features twisted. "You are blaming us for this evil eye?"

"N-no," I stuttered, but the auntie was already shaking her head.

"Look at the embarrassment you've already put my family through. Calling off a wedding in front of the entire hall? If your prayers made you feel that this marriage would not be right, why drag our family along!"

I'm sorry, I wanted to say, but the apology clogged in my throat would never be enough.

Ismail looked at me pleadingly. "Salama, you're in shock. You can't call off our entire rishta!"

"I have to, Ismail, Uncle Malik, and Auntie Noshi. I really am sorry. But surely you would not want to marry me when such prayers are answered in such ways," I said. "This marriage is not meant to be. Not for me at least. It took me a long time to realize it, and I'm sorry that I realized it at the last minute."

Auntie Noshi looked angry. "With this mess, I must pray more before we consider moving forward with your family," she said.

"No!" my ammi yelled.

Uncle Malik looked between us. "This is an embarrassment to our family. We will discuss this after. For now, let's take our leave," Uncle Malik said to his son and wife.

Auntie Noshi squeezed Ammi's shoulder. "We will call you tonight, baji."

With the marriage called off for now, the guests began trailing out of the venue hall. My eyes dragged on Ismail—at a future that could've been but I'd let spill from my fingertips like the curry splattered around me.

Despite the unusual circumstances, my shoulders felt lighter. I'd never wanted that future. I'd only forced myself to believe I did.

"Wait! Please!" Ammi said, but Baba held her back. Ammi's eyes darkened at me. "Salama!"

"I'm sorry, Ammi. I am so sorry, but this marriage, I don't want it."

"That boy was perfect for you!"

"No. He was perfect for you, but not me." I paused before the words spilled out. "I want to marry Osama. Not right now. I'm not ready. I have university soon, and the business to grow, and my own feelings to work through. But I want us to think about an engagement with someone that I prefer, too."

Now Ammi looked ready to pass out. "My beti has betrayed me. She is possessed. What nonsense is coming from her mouth!"

"Enough," Baba said before glaring at me. "What's gotten into you!"

"Tell me, truthfully, what Osama lacks? The only thing that stops you from considering him is your ridiculous rivalry with his family."

"My daughter is crazy!" Ammi refused to address me, facing my baba instead, and my heart sank.

Auntie Ruqayyaah interrupted from behind us. "No need to worry yourselves. I would never let your daughter near my son."

Osama pulled her back. "Please, Amma."

My skin prickled at Auntie Ruqayyaah's glare, but I didn't expect any of this to be easy. It would take time to explain our decision to our families, but I was ready for the work.

"I understand this is shocking," I said. "But when I think of who I would marry, it's someone who understands me. I've known Osama my entire life. He's dedicated to the deen, we're at the same mosque together, he understands my family, he understands all the work we do, and he cares. We're Muslim and that comes before all the politics of Punjabi and Pashtun. We're siblings in this ummah—all of us, and that makes us family already more than anything. All families fight, and I imagine that'll always be the case for our situation, but I think a union between us is also a way forward past our differences. I don't need to marry someone Punjabi just because of racial politics." Then I faced Osama. "And I owe you an apology. It was me who should've been apologizing to you from the start. You came to me a year ago and I stomped all over your feelings. You deserved better."

His lips tugged up. "You can make it up to me then."

My eyes narrowed. "This sounds like a dangerous deal."

"I suggest we amalgamate and rename our companies to Khan-Sheikh Foods. What do you think? Two companies joined together. I like the sound of it," he mused.

"Sheikh-Khan foods," I pushed back. "Our name put before yours."

For once, my mother and his mother agreed on one thing as they both yelled: "No!"

"Absolutely not. No marriage, no merging." Ruqayyaah crossed her arms.

"Of course, not with the ridiculous name your son suggested. *Khan-Sheikh Foods*," Ammi mimicked.

"Oi, excuse me! Ridiculous? Your daughter suggested Sheikh-Khan, how more ridiculous!" Auntie Ruqayyaah scoffed.

"Sheikh-Khan is a first-class name over your third-class Khan-Sheikh!"

"Third-class? I'll show you third-class!" Ruqayyaah yelled.

Osama began laughing before tugging me away from our bickering mothers.

"See? Progress? We've managed to trick them into agreeing to a shared company," he said into my ear.

"This is going to be a Pakistani civil war," I groaned.

"Oh beta, when I asked for drama, I did not mean calling off an entire wedding," Auntie Haneen broke in as the salon team joined our entourage. "But promise me for your real wedding, you'll be calling Auntie Haneen for all your makeup needs."

"Of course." I glanced behind her. "Where is the other auntie, the one who was with me in the bathroom?"

Auntie Haneen shrugged. "I don't know. Maybe she left. She was an emergency replacement, after all."

"What was her name?"

"Oh, I don't know. She called herself Baji Lovely."

My jaw dropped.

Auntie Haneen continued, "I don't know her name. We don't check for such things." Then with an air-kiss to my cheeks and a chorus of salaams, the salon aunties departed with their cases of makeup.

Osama shook his head at their receding figures. "If I knew it would take a curry accident and a team of aunties to get us this far, you only had to say so, Salama."

I shoved him with an elbow, making sure the mustard oil stained his crisp button-down. "Oh, what's that? You'll be footing the bill of the venue's food disaster, cancellation fees included? That's so generous. Consider it the beginning of my mahr."

Osama blanched before grinning. "Nicely done. Cold in business and cold in the heart. We're already negotiating the dowry I'll pay you. Does this mean you've officially accepted my proposal, even before I've formally proposed?"

Now it was my turn to blanch. "Negotiations first. Baby steps."

He let out a laugh. "Negotiations I could do."

A reluctant smile creeped on my face and finally, I allowed myself to feel all the feelings I'd been ignoring.

Behind us, it went silent. Osama's laughter had momentarily broken our mothers' argument. They were staring at us, shocked, and I realized why. They had never seen Osama and me together like this, smiling at each other.

"Khan-Sheikh Foods," Auntie Ruqayyaah reluctantly muttered, unable to look at my ammi or me. "We'll discuss this later. Let's go, Osama. We must prepare for negotiations."

Ammi hooked her elbow through my own as she stared down Osama and his mother. "Sheikh-Khan Foods and that's final. I'll be expecting a large amount of payment for the mahr."

"Astaghfirullah," Ruqayyaah said, her chin jutted out. "How greedy of you."

Osama winked at me before pulling away. "I'll see you at the negotiating table."

A Very Bloody Kalyanam

ANAHITA KARTHIK

*T*here is blood on my kurta and it's not mine.

I scrape away at the dried flakes under my nails, painfully averting every set of eyes boring into my skull. There is a hushed chatter in Tamil floating across the room, and for once, everyone's talking about the same incident. The thing about being part of a joint family, especially when you're from the South, is that you could be in the same room with a dozen other groups, each having their own conversation, and you'd eventually learn to tune them out. But here, in the opulent hall of the Iyer household, it's difficult to ignore them when they're talking about *me*.

About my massive screw-up.

Amma gets me a davara and tumbler of steaming filter coffee, blood bubbles frothing at the top. It's the peak of April summer here in Wellington, Ooty—nestled among low-hanging clouds and green hills—which means it's colder here than in the rest of the country. I'm shivering, and the coffee scalds my tongue, but I haven't felt this comforted in well, a few hours.

"Get her a shawl," Paati tells Amma. "She's shivering."

"No," I say through my gritted teeth. I don't want to get his blood on more of my clothes.

"Are you okay?" Periamma asks.

"Do you want more coffee?" Chithi asks.

"Someone should get her cleaned up," Athai says.

"*Enough!*" Appa barks, and the dozen conversations subside immediately. I flinch at the sharp tone of his voice.

Appa is seated on the red leather chair by the fireplace, legs crossed and fingers fiddling with his thick mustache. I used to do that to him when I was a kid, tying the ends with rubber bands of all colors, sitting on his lap on the same chair by the same fireplace.

Amma and I are the only ones who have seen the gentle side of him—or at least, we used to, before he took over as the leader of our cult after Thatha's passing. For the rest of our relatives and the other families of our cult, he's their தலைவைர்[1], someone to be enamored by and frightened of.

It's that glint, Paati tells me, that glint in those lethal black eyes, that could make humans and vampires alike cower. It's what keeps those who are aware of our existence in check and helps cover up the blunders of the blood hunt. And since the hunt happens every Purnima, the possibility of a misstep is more common than one would think.

Things might've been easier if I'd been caught, forgotten to use Witch's Gold to seal up the bite wounds, or even accidentally killed a human. Seriously, anything but this. But I had to go and imprint myself to another vampire.

And not just any vampire, the notorious voice in my head says, *but Kritik Nathan, the heir of a rival cult.*

"How could you let this happen?" Appa says, his eyes glinting in the light of the red chandelier, depthless and cold.

---

1. Thalaivar (leader of cult).

"I don't know," I croak.

"You ran all the way to Coonoor," Appa snaps, getting to his feet. "You broke into the Nathans' bungalow, into that boy's room, and you're telling me you don't know?"

"I can't explain it. Something took me over. One moment, I was on the forest path by the tea estate, and the next, I blacked out. When I woke up, my fangs were in his throat and there was blood dripping down my front."

Periamma places a hand over her heart. "It's a miracle they didn't kill you."

Appa's face is lined with rage. "It's not a bloody miracle. Shloka is imprinted to the boy. If they'd killed her, he would've died as well."

Silence falls over the room. My heart drops to my stomach like a heavy anchor.

I open my mouth to speak but am interrupted by an urgent knock on the door of the living room. It swings open to reveal one of our servants, Shankar, standing outside. His left hand rests on his knee while the other holds the cordless landline. He's wheezing like he just flew up ten flights of stairs.

"What?" Appa says impatiently.

"It's—" Shankar pants, rushing over to hand him the cordless. "It's the Nathans from Coonoor."

Paati starts muttering a string of prayers, her thumb counting the rosary beads clasped in her right hand. Appa puts the cordless to his ear and glares at all of us before retreating to a corner of the room to talk. None of us utter a word, and it's silent save for Paati's chanting. My coffee sits long forgotten on the side table. I'm shivering again, but no one's looking at me this time. Their worried gazes are set on Appa, whose face divulges nothing as he speaks in a low, gruff tone.

He lowers the cordless after a few minutes. Amma sets her hand on my shoulder, eyes wide. "What did they say?" she asks.

"They're coming over tomorrow, for the பெ·ரண்ண பார்க்கல்²."

"What does that mean?" I blurt, dread pooling in my stomach. Amma's hand tightens on my shoulder.

"You two are to be married. You and Kritik Nathan."

That has me jumping straight to my feet. A sudden vertigo threatens to send me sailing back, but I hold my ground. "What the hell?"

"Shloka!" Amma cries. "Mind your language!"

"He can't be serious, Amma," I exclaim, whirling toward her. "I'm not going to get married to Kritik Nathan!"

"You're imprinted to him, and two vampires who are imprinted must get married."

"I just turned a hundred twenty last month. I can't be married so young!"

"You don't have a choice," Appa says, terrifyingly calm. He's like the sea before an incoming storm, quiet and motionless, fore-warning of the destruction to come. "You imprinted yourself to the boy."

"I didn't *choose* to do it."

"Then it is not in your hand. The Gods have willed it."

"And what if I don't get married to him? I have listened to you all my life, but nothing I ever do seems to make you happy."

"Stop," Amma pleads. Nobody else has opened their mouth. Usually, they always have something to say. "Shloka——"

"If you cared about me, you wouldn't marry me to a Nathan.

2 . Girl-seeing (a ritual in Iyer weddings where, if both the boy's and girl's families approve, the former visit the girl's home on a decided day. After this, their marriage is fixed. Usually, this happens after their horoscopes have been matched, but in the rare case of an imprint—a blood connection between two vampires that is willed by the Gods—their horoscopes aren't read. Their fates are predestined, and they're bound to each other for the rest of their lives).

You almost *died* because of them."

Appa's fangs pop out, digging into his lower lip so sharply they send a smattering of blood flying outward. I stumble back as his eyes flame red, the color of tempered metal. A collective gasp echoes through the room—everyone watching his wrath unleashed.

"It is *because* I care about you that I'm getting you married to that boy!" Appa snaps. "Do you have any idea what will happen if you don't?"

I stare back at him, my words lodging in my throat.

"You'll die." Appa takes a step toward me, fangs tipped with blood. "If you stay a moon away from him, you'll die."

"I know that," I say, and my voice is barely a whisper. "But I don't need to be married to him to sustain myself. There are other ways."

"Neither of which abide by our பாரம்பரியம்[3]. And in this house, tradition is law. Your duty to your cult comes before self. Have I not taught you anything?"

"Amma, you can't let him do this to me. Tell him—"

"*Not another word,*" Appa roars, making everyone flinch. "The Nathans are coming over tomorrow. They're willing to forgive us for what Shloka did, and they're being respectful enough to see the marriage rituals through in an orderly manner." He turns to Amma, who looks like she's trying hard to contain her tears. "Archana, make sure we give them a grand welcome."

Amma nods, refusing to meet my eyes. There's a pinch in my heart, as I'm once again reminded of all those times she picked Appa's side, all those times she didn't have the courage to stand up to him for me. Why do I keep hoping she'll change one day and grow a spine? Why do I keep hoping that the icicles frozen over Appa's heart will someday melt?

---

3. Tradition.

Appa orders everyone to disperse from the living room and retire to their chambers, and they carefully avoid looking at me as they walk away. I catch Amma's gaze, her eyes welling up with tears, and ignore the apology hanging in the air between us.

Because it doesn't matter anymore.

The Gods wove Kritik into my fate, and they'll kill me if I stray.

I scowl at my reflection as Amma, Periamma, and Chithi fuss over me, rushing to and from the dressing table. It takes everything in me to not swat them away and to continue to ignore Amma's intermittent pleading glances in the mirror.

It's always been like this. Amma refuses to stand up to Appa for me, the guilt racks her, she apologizes. And I ignore her until I convince myself that *it's okay, it's just this time.*

But now I've had it with her. I'm done expecting. Last night was all it took for me to realize something that never hit my disillusioned self before—it is always going to be tradition for the cult. Above their own daughter. Above their own lives.

Or maybe it wasn't disillusionment. Maybe it was adamance that made me keep forgiving all of them and hoping I'd one day be reunited with who Appa was before he became the leader.

By the time my two hours crammed in front of the dressing table are up, Amma and her sisters have dolled me up to look like a proper Tamil bride. But since it's just the பெ·ண்ணு பார்க்கல்[4], they've donned me in simple attire and muted temple jewelry.

I'm wearing a brand-new kanjivaram saree that Amma had her handmaiden bring in from her favorite boutique just this morning.

---

4. Girl-seeing.

The silk is threaded in sunset ombre, gradating from soft yellow to cotton-candy pink. The borders are spun in gold, which matches my necklace and the jimikkis hanging from my ears. A bindi dots the space between my freshly threaded eyebrows.

"Such beautiful eyes," Chithi says, spitting on me lightly to protect me from the evil eye. "Look how the kajal makes them bigger."

"If only she weren't scowling," Periamma says disapprovingly. "You must smile, ma. I remember when your periappa first came to see me. I couldn't stop smiling and blushing." Her face suddenly breaks into a wistful smile. "When I went to serve him tea, he looked up at me through those long lashes of his, and in that moment, I just knew he was who I wanted to spend my life with."

"You nearly spilled the tea all over him," Amma says, and Chithi bursts into giggles.

"Ayyo, must you remind me?" Periamma says, lightly smacking the two of them.

Normally, I would smile, but I can't. It might've even been better if it had been an arranged marriage, if I hadn't known Kritik the way they think I do. For me, he isn't just the heir to a rival cult that used to be part of ours before his father split ways for more power.

Kritik was my first love, the first of many that transpired unbeknownst to my parents. Especially Appa, who would've killed me if he'd known about any of them—I can't imagine what he might've done if he'd ever found out some of them weren't even boys.

I was ridiculously in love with Kritik. We were together for nearly twenty years, forming a connection both in the presence of and away from the elders. The former involved silly grins and stolen glances, unseen by the rest of our cult when we were all gathered at the temple during Amavasya. The latter involved sneaking out of our houses at night back when Kritik used to live in Wellington, exchanging shy kisses as we sat on the rocky cliff at the edge of the forest.

It used to be our spot.

I haven't been there in forty years, not since his father betrayed Appa, leaving him bleeding on the altar. Appa nearly died that day, all because of the Nathans and *Kritik*—I grit my teeth—who hadn't told me about his father's plan.

The Nathans had disappeared along with their allies from our cult, and as we had later found out, revived the powers of the centuries-old temple in Coonoor. Despite my anger, I'd hoped and yearned for Kritik to return, or send over some sort of message. I couldn't possibly move on from the relationship we'd shared for twenty years, even as it seemed to crumble away beneath my fingers.

And then, after a month of waiting, his bat Mukhut had flown to my window and perched himself upside down on the sill. My heart had nearly stopped when he'd dropped the note in my hand. I'd opened it with shaking fingers, and skimmed the contents:

Dear Shloka,

I'm sorry. I'm sorry for lying, disappearing, and shattering our future together. I know nothing else I say at this point will help undo what Appa did. All I can hope is that uncle is okay.

I wish it didn't have to end like this. But know that I loved you, and know that I always cared, even if it didn't matter in the end.

I hope you one day have the wedding of your dreams.

—Kritik

Loved. Cared. End.

It was those three words that had stuck with me, long after, through my sobbing and heartbreak that seemed to last decades—and maybe it had, I don't know. And it's the same three words that echo right back in my head, murmured in Kritik's soft voice.

I never stopped feeling anything for him. It was only that, with time, the love morphed into desperation, then heartache, and finally, hate. Over the course of forty years, I had moved on, even though it had taken unnecessarily longer than I'd hoped, and I honestly believed I'd never have to hear his name uttered again. I'd known Kritik and I had always shared something special, something innocent and painful, something only a first love could mimic.

I never thought this *hate* I'd finally come to peace with would morph again—and form an imprint.

I shudder as Amma and her sisters lead me out of the room when a handmaiden rushes in, hastily whispering, "They're here!" as if they might hear her three floors down if she talks too loudly.

The blurry memories of last night play before my eyes. I'd only read and heard myths of how an imprint could form with anyone, at any point in a vampire's life, and how it eliminated the one thing every living being in the world seems to fight for: choice.

Younger me had had Cinderella dreams, hoping an imprint would one day form between Kritik and me, believing he was my forever.

And now, I'd manifested it.

We descend the spiraling stairs, past pictures of my Iyer ancestors and sconces eternally aflame in red. The Witch's Strontium fire burns brighter than ever, reflecting off the surfaces of the lacquered wood.

We're joined by the other ladies of the house as we pass each floor, all of them glittering in grand kanjivaram sarees and jewelry. I need to grip something to steady myself as I'm met with a shower of compliments, but my hand refuses to reach out for the banister.

Three floors down, and I'm led through the dimly lit corridor that forks two ways, the right leading to the hall of our household, and the left to the sanctum, where we welcome only our most revered guests. We take the left turn, and the ladies whisper eagerly. What the Nathans did to us has already been forgotten, drowning in the heady rush of festivities.

Tamil weddings are like that, so very elaborate they almost consume you whole. God knows every wedding in our cult has made me feel like that. Only this time, I haven't yet stomached the fact that it's already my turn.

I don't know if it's nervousness or the effects of the imprint setting in, but my heart pounds faster as we draw closer to the sanctum. I can sense him from here, and while my mind begs to differ, my body moves forward with urgency, wanting to be close to him. The ladies notice this, because Athai points out, "Look at her, already excited to see our young groom."

Amma apprehensively meets my eyes as we push through the doors and into the sanctum. I can't ignore her this time; I want to throw up and cry and bury myself in her arms. Even though she's never stood up for me, she's still my mom, and I've never needed her more.

A hush settles in the sanctum. The twenty-foot-tall chandelier shimmers above our heads, an intricate matrix constructed from stained red glass: glowing pockets of light emanating from the heart of the bloodstones. The ceiling is patterned in ancient Tamil script so complex I can't read it, and it holds secrets passed on through generations of vampires. Life-sized pictures in bronze frames hang on the wooden wall.

And right under the chandelier, at the center of the sanctum, sit the Nathans, on olive-green sofas opposite Appa and the other members of the household.

My blood pulses against my wrists and throat, urging me in his direction, but I refuse to look at him. Appa's brothers, seated on either side of him, get up to make way for me and Amma. The other ladies join our family members gathered behind the sofas. Everyone exchanges cordial greetings, but there is a tension hanging above us like a Damocles sword. Amma guides me to sit between her and Appa, directly opposite the Nathans.

I train my gaze on the glass table, where davaras of filter coffee, plates of bhaji, and a huge thali with sweet mango kesari have been arranged on the surface, all untouched.

"You remember my daughter," Appa says, as Amma places her hand on my shoulder.

"Yes. Shloka. It's wonderful to meet you again."

My cheeks get hot with rage at the sound of Balaswamy Nathan's voice. I nearly spit something nasty at him, but Amma squeezes my shoulder. Her eyes implore me through the corner of my vision, and I swallow my words.

"You've grown into a beautiful young woman," Asha, his wife, says.

I can't begin to imagine the toll it must be taking on my parents to sit before the *asshole* who tore our cult apart and nearly killed Appa. For them to have to cage their emotions in the hopes of cordially closing the knot between our families.

Tradition. Law. Both once again holding Appa back from leaping across the table and wrapping his hands around Balaswamy's throat.

Even if I am not solely responsible for it, I imprinted myself to Kritik and I need to find my way out of this mess without bringing my parents down with me. And that needs to start with being polite, so the morning doesn't end with fangs being bared.

"Thank you," I say, eyes staunchly set on the table. I can't look up yet. Every inch of me knows he's right there, a sole glass table separating us. Hopefully, they'll just assume I'm the vision of a shy Tamil bride.

"You remember Kritik, don't you?" Asha says. I can sense the smile in her voice. "The two of you used to play together as kids."

I purse my lips together, his presence making my body itch. I can't say it. I can't say we used to just know each other, because it was so much more than that.

Amma smiles nervously. "She's just shy."

Do it, I think. *Look at him. Rip it off like a Band-Aid.*

I look up.

Balaswamy is seated on the right, dressed in a white shirt and veshti, vibhuti drawn on his forehead in three horizontal and parallel lines. Asha sits on the left, adorned in a gorgeous green madisar saree, which, unlike the six yards worn by unmarried women, is nine yards long. The rest of the Nathans stand behind their sofa.

And in the middle of the sofa, seated right opposite me, is Kritik.

"Would the two of you like to talk to each other in private?"

I snap my head up, looking at Asha, who just spoke. I don't know how long it's been since I went into switch-off mode, the way I usually do during large gatherings and conversations I wish to be no part of. A skin of bloody malai has formed on the surface of my filter coffee, so I guess it has been long enough.

"Shloka?" Amma asks tenderly. "Would you like to talk to Kritik in private?"

Before either Kritik or I can open our mouths, Balaswamy speaks up. "It'll be good for the future bride and groom to get to know each other. Would you ladies accompany the two of them to a spare room?"

I have never wanted anyone more dead the way I do the absolute pig of a man that Balaswamy Nathan is.

Amma turns to glance at Appa, who hasn't said much throughout the exchange, her eyes wide with question. Appa waves his hand stonily, hatred burning in his eyes. For once, I relate to what he's feeling more than anyone else in this room.

"The guest rooms on the first floor have been cleared out, Akka," Chithi says to Amma. "They can spend as much time as they'd like."

One of my younger cousins giggles, and Athai quickly shushes her, covering up for the girl's misstep. "I suppose we could set out the lunch for the guests until then?"

Amma nods, awkwardly turning to Asha, who gets to her feet, smiling. I avoid looking in Kritik's direction entirely as we're led outside the sanctum. Asha converses with Amma, and I try to plummet back into switch-off mode but Kritik's gaze on me burns a hole through my cheek. I am annoyingly hyper aware of his presence, down to every little movement.

Before I know it, we're ushered into one of the guest rooms on the first floor. There's a king-sized bed within, headboard against the wall, canopy curtains gleaming in the light of the fire sconces. Amma throws me a last glance before shutting the door behind her.

And then it's just Kritik and me. Alone.

At first, there's dead silence in the room, and I stubbornly look at the wall, finding the engravings on it remarkably interesting. Kritik moves to the bed, and it creaks as he sits down. We're quiet for a whole minute, and I feel like my skin will fall off because of how jittery I am. It's crazy how arranged marriages work this way, how any parent could believe locking their daughter in a room with a man they know little of is a good idea.

Kritik clears his throat. "This room's nice."

I stay silent, crossing my arms over my chest and tucking my palms into the crooks to stop the blood underneath from pulsing so hard.

"I know you have every reason to ignore me," he continues. "But we're going to be in here awhile."

I shut my eyes, annoyed.

"You don't have to look at me, but I don't want you to have to stand there the whole time." There's a long pause, and I nearly let out a breath of relief in the hopes that he's shut up for good. Alas. "We could switch places, I guess. You could stay like that for ten minutes, and then I could stand, so you get your turn with the bed as well—"

That's it.

I march over to the door and grab the handle. I cannot spend a moment more with him in here, and I frankly don't care about what anyone thinks of our early return.

I pull, but the door doesn't budge.

Kritik sighs. "They've locked us in from the outside."

I pull again, and the door strains on the hinges.

"Let it be, Shloka." The bed creaks as he settles back. I don't know how I am able to trace every movement of his without looking at him, but I do.

A frustrated growl escapes my throat. I wonder if I should remain here, facing the door, but realize there's no point. Knowing Kritik, he's going to keep talking until we're let out of here, whether I respond or not.

I turn, my back against the wood, and slide down until I'm sitting on the floor, knees pulled up to my chest. And again, I look at him. The glow from the bloodstones outlines the sharp edges of his face. His wild hair waves above his head and covers his small forehead, brushing his eyebrows. I'm horrified, disgusted, *and* annoyed that I still remember the way it used to tangle in between my fingers. He looks different, and yet he looks the same—only taller, broader, and sharper.

Unlike what the myths say, vampires don't live forever. Instead, we age very slowly (and can reproduce much less, so there aren't too many of us alive at the same time). One vampire year is about six human years, which means I look like I'm twenty, when I've lived six times that amount.

But regardless of how my appearance might be perceived by a human, time doesn't slow down for us. In my cult, I'm treated the same way a twenty-year-old might be treated in a human family, but that doesn't negate the fact that I've lived for more than a century. So, forty years? Time like that doesn't just fly by.

Forty years is a long, long time.

I thought it was long enough to brew all my love into hate, but looking at him now, unaged when compared to the rest of the world, I feel a sense of longing. It's like the feeling is an entity separate from me, existing on its own.

The imprint.

"You feel it, too, don't you?" Kritik says suddenly.

"The imprint?" It's the first thing I've said to him in years.

"Yes. It's like this hyper-awareness, like I can—"

"Trace my every movement without looking at me?"

"It's unnerving."

"Unnerving?" I scoff. "Is it 'unnerving' because we were together for twenty years and you ended the relationship by letter?

Or is it because you were too much of a coward to say all that shit to my face?"

I didn't want to act like this. Last night, I promised myself I wouldn't expose how bitter I truly felt toward him. But I didn't anticipate that pig Balaswamy forcing us into a room together.

Kritik grips the bedsheet in both his fists. "I know it was wrong of me to end things like that, so suddenly, without any reason or explanation—"

"No, don't give me that." I glare daggers at him. "There *is* a reason. You're just like your father."

Kritik flinches. I stare at him as his eyes drop to his lap, my heart twisting with a sort of dark satisfaction because I know exactly how to pinch his nerve and hurt him most. Just like he did, when he flung my fantasies of the perfect wedding in my face—*I hope you have the wedding of your dreams*—and mocked me for it.

"It probably doesn't matter right now," Kritik says softly. "But I didn't break things off willingly."

"No, you did. You had a choice. You just chose to be a coward."

"Sending that note to you—that broke me. I haven't moved on. I could never move on."

"I don't give a damn about what you felt, Kritik. In fact, I'm quite glad for it. Because the sort of prick who wouldn't tell his girl-friend of twenty years that his father was going to attempt murder on her father is someone I wouldn't want to ever see again."

"I didn't know."

"Didn't know *what*?"

"I didn't know Appa was going to do what he did."

"I swear to God, Kritik, if you have any self-respect left, don't hit me with that bullshit."

"I didn't!" Kritik gets to his feet. My nerves spark, feeling the hurt rushing through his blood, and I jerk back. "I didn't know what Appa was planning. The night he confronted your father at the temple, I was asleep. I was awoken by Amma when the fight broke out between our cults and our house went up in flames. Next thing I knew, I was being absconded out of Wellington with no clue of what was going on. I only remember wanting to break off and look for you, save you, or at least get a chance to say goodbye because I couldn't help feeling I'd somehow lost you forever."

My heart is beating in my mouth. Kritik brings his hands up to his hair, eyes shut tightly.

"And I was right. I had lost you forever. Even my blood connection to the temple had broken. Only once we got to Coonoor did my family tell me everything."

"Give me one reason to believe this elaborate lie of yours. Why would they keep the truth from you when half the cult knew of Balaswamy's plans for years?"

"Appa thought I knew. Everyone thought I knew because that's what Amma told them. But she'd kept the truth from me. She knew if I came to know, I would tell you."

"Your mother didn't even know if we knew each other."

"She did. In fact, she knew what we . . . were."

Oh God.

"You told her?"

"No. She found out. Apparently, she'd known for years. And she never told me."

The whole time, Asha Balaswamy had known about Kritik and me and she'd kept the truth of her asshole husband's plans from him.

Oh God.

"She used it to threaten me," Kritik says, his face scrunched up with pent-up anger. "She told me that if I dared to see you or associate with you in any way ever again, she would tell the whole cult about what had been going on between us. And she'd make sure that word of our intimacy was known: that Krishnamurthy Iyer's daughter was . . ." His voice trails off.

I shake my head, shock pricking me everywhere, like sharp pins. "Impure? Tainted?"

Kritik cringes. "I couldn't let that happen to you. I couldn't let my desperation to see you and be with you again cost you your cult's already dwindling reputation that *my* father had ruined. And I knew Amma would keep her word, because her devotion to that bastard comes above all else."

Just like my mother.

"I had no choice. I begged her to let me write you one last note, a goodbye note, so you could at least gain some sort of closure. She read it, and then had Mukhut fly over to you. Deep down, even if the thought of you reading it hurt me, I wanted you to move on."

"Move on?" There are tears stinging my eyes, and I push them back with all the strength I have left within me. "You ripped my heart into a million pieces. People don't just move on from things like that. I grew to hate you."

"And I'd take that any day, rather than have your reputation suffer because of me."

"You're not the hero here. You didn't *do* anything to me. What happened between us was consensual. Sure, I'd have become Krishnamurthy Iyer's damaged, impure daughter, but I would take that any day over recovering from the state you left me in. You didn't have the right to make that choice for me."

"I'm not asking you to forgive me, Slo," Kritik says, and I don't think he's realized that he's just called me what he used to. "But I'm sorry."

The words hang in the air between us for a silent minute. I'm reeling from everything he said, all the truth that could've erased these forty years of believing a lie.

Then a hysterical laugh burbles out of my throat. Kritik looks at me from where he's standing, and the expression on his face makes me keel over, laughing breathlessly.

"The look on your face . . ." I wheeze, shoulders shaking violently with mirth. I guess I've finally snapped. It was bound to happen at some point, with all the mental damage I've endured.

"Shloka—"

"No, wait." I wipe the tears from my eyes, and although I'm laughing, I've never felt regret and pain of this sort. "You know what's the best part? If we'd been imprinted when we were together, literally none of this would've happened."

Kritik falls to his knees, as if the truth of it is finally sinking its teeth into him. "Why didn't we get imprinted then? Why now?"

"I don't know. All I know is it's unfair."

Kritik stares at me. We're physically five feet apart, but mentally mere inches away.

I settle back, head leaning against the wood. My emotions have frozen over and now I'm just numb. Cold does that; it numbs you after a point. Until you stop feeling.

"What happened yesterday was crazy," Kritik says, funneling out a heavy breath.

"I don't remember any of it."

"Neither do I. I was blacked out through most of it, but I remember waking up with you on top of me, my blood dripping out of your mouth."

I nod, seeing flashes of the memory.

"At least it was like the old times," Kritik says, with a small grin.

My face turns hot. "Don't do that."

"What?"

"Flirt with me."

"Why?"

"Do you not realize how unhinged all of this is? We were apart for nearly half a century and now we're imprinted; I find out we were thoroughly screwed over by your parents; and we're going to be *married*. That is not normal."

"Yeah, being married wasn't exactly in my cards right now." Kritik leans forward, staring at the floor vacantly. I watch him, the way I used to before, when he wasn't looking. "Or at all."

"Why not?" I don't know why I dread asking the next question, but I swallow the feeling and blurt it out. "Don't you have a 'someone' in your life?"

"No. I didn't . . . date anyone after you."

My mouth falls open. "What—"

Just then, a knock shudders through the door behind me. Amma's voice sounds through: "Shloka? Kritik? May we come in?"

I glance at Kritik. He's avoiding my gaze and looks a bit flustered, but I don't have time to dwell on it as I say, "Yes."

The lock slides open as I leap to my feet, rushing to the bed where Kritik's seated himself. We must at least look like we've been making conversation civilly. An awkward silence hangs between us before the door opens and both our mothers walk in, eyes questioning.

I paste a cold smile on my face in reply to the one Asha shoots me.

As Kritik and I are led out of the room, the distance between us grows, both physically and mentally. And with it, so does the anger at Asha and Balaswamy, who single-handedly destroyed what we could've had. Some of it is also directed at my parents, who never gave me a choice from the very beginning of it all.

It was never Kritik who was the coward. It was all four of them.

And they're pretending everything's okay, acting like the horrendous past can be signed off by a marital contract. It's disgusting, how Appa's down there right now, entertaining the family that nearly killed ours. And how Balaswamy is sucking up to him so he can marry his son off to me and save face before the society.

Because as usual, the question of honor arises for both. For it, they will do anything, even if it means destroying their children's lives. Brahmins are like that: Our entire existence is based on a casteist hierarchy that believes anyone who acts out of line, anyone non-Brahmin, is "beneath" them.

The நிச்சயதார்த்தம்[5] is three days later.

I'm swathed in a pink-and-green kanjivaram saree that used to be Amma's, the one she wore during her engagement ceremony to Appa, with emerald and pink sapphire jewelry to match. Once I'm ready, Amma and her sisters accompany me down the spiraling stairs to the hallway below, where our relatives greet me with loud gasps and compliments.

Among the chaos, I find Appa looking at me with an impassive face, completely devoid of any feeling. A surge of anger rushes through me, not just at how wrong this is all turning out to be but also because my own father is seeing me get married and chooses to feel—or rather, show—no emotion.

He said he's forcing all of this on me for my protection, but

---

5. Engagement (in Iyer tradition, the parents and relatives from the girl's side go to the boy's house, taking with them trays of gifts—new clothes, delicacies, flowers, fruits, betel leaf, areca nut, and slaked lime. In vampire tradition, the girl's family also bring offerings of precious bloodstones, and the number they bring along is often indicative of the power they hold among the cults. After the arrival, the priest sets the date and time of the marriage between the boy and girl).

if he genuinely cared, he wouldn't have listened to Balaswamy Nathan's suggestion of locking his son up in a room with me.

I'm lucky it was Kritik. But all these other girls in my family, who got married in an ostensibly grand way . . . who knows what bastards they were married off to? Who knows what they gave up on the night of their wedding?

My body seethes and shakes. My fangs nudge the bottom of my lips. I tamp the anger down as I'm led to the shaded limousine waiting in front of our estate, and the fangs slowly inch back. It's unusual for fangs to appear on any day that isn't the day of the hunt, but colossal rage can often bare them, the way they did for Appa when I imprinted myself to Kritik. I have been angrier in my life, but as the daughter of the leader, I've learned to mask it. I don't slip up with my fangs.

Or at least I thought.

The driver starts the limousine, packed with the ladies of our family. Amma is seated next to me, and she shoots me a nervous smile. Ignoring is what I usually do. But today, with everything I know now, I'm losing control, bit by bit.

"Why did you lock me up with Kritik, Amma?" I say through gritted teeth, lowering my voice so only she can hear me. Luckily, the boisterous chatter of the ladies manages to drown everything else.

"What?" Amma whispers, startled.

"You locked me in that room. With Kritik. A man you barely know."

"I-I didn't. Asha said—"

"And you just chose to listen to Asha? Did you, for even a second, pause to consider the weight of the situation?"

"Kritik is a good boy. He has good morals, he is Brahmin . . ."

There it was.

God, this was all the same, fucked-up, casteism I'd been seeing all my life.

"STOP!" I spit, louder than I expected. The rest of the ladies turn toward us, eyes wide, conversation suddenly hushed. I don't care that they're listening. For once, I don't give a shit about any of it. I know that this anger is misdirected, I know that this is everything I've wanted to say to Appa all these years, but Amma has been a part of it as well, and that makes her equally at fault.

I'm reminded of the epic *Mahabharata*, which Paati used to narrate to me when I was little. She used to tell me the *Mahabharata* was the only one that stood out among other epics, because it showed us that the world wasn't all black and white, but varying shades of gray.

And that although Duryodhana had been the one to humiliate Draupadi by stripping off her saree in front of the entire Kaurava court, her five husbands—yes, *five* husbands—had just stood and watched. They'd watched as Draupadi had been manhandled, had her hair yanked, and then proceeded to be disrobed.

All because her husbands were more concerned with abiding by their dharma than protecting their wife from being dishonored and assaulted.

Because those who witness oppression happening and don't do anything to stop it are just as vile as the actual oppressors. But fear holds us all back, just like it did me, when I never showed my real, true self to anyone except Kritik. I was constantly terrified and anxious in every relationship after him, if one could even call them relationships, because I never let them last.

"You and Appa cannot assume someone is good because he has been raised in a Brahmin household. Would you have said the same thing if I'd been imprinted to a non-Brahmin boy? Or, get this, a *girl?*"

Gasps resound, and before any of them can shush me, I continue, "The only reason Appa is going along with all of this is because he wants to save face. As for you, Amma . . . I honestly haven't expected much from you all my life, given how you always wither under Appa's shadow, but yesterday, you made me realize I wasn't just unsupported around you but also unsafe."

Only once the words have escaped my mouth do I realize that I've done irreparable damage. Something I wouldn't have done if it wasn't for the damned loss of grip I have over myself.

Amma's eyes pool with tears, and it takes a few seconds for the other ladies to take control of the situation. I glare at all of them, expecting them to scold me as they console Amma, but surprisingly, they don't.

Instead, they stare at my mouth, where my two fangs jut out, leaking blood.

When the driver pulls the limousine up the driveway of the Nathan estate, I glance out the window, taken by how massive it is. The driveway forks into two and winds around a fountain lined with sparkling sand.

Nobody helps me out of the limousine this time, not even Amma. Her eyes are swollen and red, and I can predict the whispers and rumors the ladies will soon spread to the rest of the society. Up the sweeping stairway to the grand entrance, and we're welcomed by Balaswamy, Asha, and a few other elders. I scan the crowd for Kritik but can't see him anywhere.

We're led into a magnificent hall, where the furniture has been cleared out for the engagement. A floral-patterned cloth has been spread out at the center of the carpeted floor, and it is covered with delicacies and prasad. Everything from mountains of vada, dosas shaped like tepees, silver-embossed boxes of sweets, ladoos, coconuts, milk, betel leaves, flower garlands, fruits, vegetables, kumkumam, chandanam, vibhuti, and a valakku, which is a prayer lamp.

A priest sits among it all, dressed in a veshti and mundu, a poonal tied diagonally across his torso. The rest of the hall is packed with vampires from the Coonoor cult, people I recognize from many years ago, those who chose to betray Appa. I glance at him sideways as our relatives join the crowd—seating themselves cross-legged on the floor—finding him stiff-faced with his jaw jutting out. Our servants set out the trays of offerings we brought along on the cloth, joining the rest of the pile.

I don't see Kritik at first, but as we weave through the crowd, I spot him sitting with his back facing me, opposite the priest. He's wearing a veshti and a baby-blue shirt that makes his shoulders look broader than usual. My heart skips a beat as Asha gently ushers me to seat myself next to him, feeling the knot of the imprint connecting us.

Kritik turns to look at me as I sit, and his eyes widen.

"Hi," he says throatily, and the rest of the room drowns away. It's like we're cocooned together, unaffected by our surroundings.

"Hey."

"You look really beautiful." Kritik's brown skin flushes. Or maybe it's just because the hall's lit up in red. "I always loved it when you used to wear jasmines in your hair."

"I remember," I say, my heart feeling all soft and fluttery. Forty years apart, and he continues to have this effect on me. "You used to buy them for me every time you went to the market."

"I would always insist on pinning them to your hair."

I'm hit by a flash of memory. Kritik and I, meeting at our

spot at the edge of the cliff, the mist curling around our feet as he stepped closer to me and pinned the flowers to my hair. His breath gushing over my shoulders, making goose bumps pop up all over my skin.

I shake myself out of the sudden dizziness, only to find him still looking at me.

"Why are you looking at me like that?" I focus my gaze on the patterns on the cloth. Anything but him and his deep eyes.

"I told you. You look beautiful."

"Kritik."

"Shloka."

I finally gather the courage to look at him. An urgency builds in my gut, the longing to close the space between us, the imprint thrumming under my skin. "Why didn't you date anyone all these years?"

"I was hoping you wouldn't ask me that."

"Forty years is a long time to go without . . . you know." At this point I'm rambling, my heart beating faster every minute. "Unless you hooked up with people."

Kritik laughs softly. "It has never been about the sex for me, Shloka. I mean, sex is great, but I never wanted to do it in the absence of love."

"And you didn't ever fall in love again?"

"I couldn't bring myself to love anyone after you." Kritik turns to look at the loud, chattering crowd around us, eyes vacant. "Trust me, I tried, because I knew there was no way we'd ever see each other again. But I guess a tiny part of me kept hoping, as the wars died down, and a sort of peaceful rivalry set in between our cults. I hoped I might get to see you one day, even if it was far, far in the future." Kritik smiles. "And here we are."

My heart is overflowing with emotion, unable to believe we're here, after so many decades, together again.

"You were waiting for me," I whisper, unable to believe it. "This whole time."

"I wasn't waiting. I couldn't afford to wait for something uncertain. But I hoped, and it kept me going."

"I don't know what to say."

"You don't have to. It's embarrassing, really. I've revealed myself to be someone who pines."

"You always used to pine."

"Maybe. Not as much as you, though."

"Oh, *please*."

"Did you? Date anyone?"

I look away, ashamed.

Kritik leans closer to me. "You don't have to feel guilty, Shloka. Both of us know how things ended between us."

"You waited for me for forty years. I can't say the same." I bite my lip. "I'm currently single, though."

"Not that you have much of a choice."

"This is actually happening, huh?" I say, mostly to myself, looking around at the crowd that hushes down as the priest prepares to start the ritual. The valakku is lined with Witch's Strontium powder and lit, brass gleaming. The rest of the lights in the hall are dimmed, until everyone's just dark outlines and silhouettes.

Before Kritik has a chance to reply, the priest starts speaking in Tamil. "Today, we all have gathered here for the engagement ceremony of Shloka Iyer, daughter of Krishnamurthy Iyer from the Wellington cult, and Kritik Nathan, son of Balaswamy Nathan from the Coonoor cult."

He performs a prayer to our Gods, murmuring mantras in Tamil and Sanskrit, making the flames in the valakku leap and sputter. I close my eyes, joining my hands in a namaskar, and the guests become silent, the hall filling entirely with the priest's intonation.

"Open your eyes."

When I do so, I feel a pull in my gut, as if a thread is gently being tugged within, in Kritik's direction. He turns to look at me at the exact same moment I turn to him. "You felt that too?"

I nod, and my body shudders with the urge to stay here, beside him, forever, as if he's the star I'm meant to orbit around.

"First," the priest says. "The bride's father and his brothers will present the offering to the groom's side. Following which the groom's parents will present the chandanam kumkumam to the bride's parents. Then, one female each from both sides will proceed to gift the bride and groom new clothes, and one male each from both sides will welcome the bride and groom with flower garlands. Finally, the couple will seek blessings from their elders."

Our families proceed with the gifting, and my knee violently bobs up and down. Kritik places his hand on my knee, urging me to stop. He always used to calm me down when I got anxious. It hits me then that I've missed it. So, so much.

He only moves his hand away when his athai walks up and hands me a gorgeous pink kanjivaram saree. I settle my palms on the soft, expensive silk. My athai does the same, handing Kritik a matching pink kurta and white pajama. We're bestowed with the flower garlands, and then we take our blessings from the elders.

As we return to our places, my legs wobbly under my saree, the priest speaks again. "Shloka Iyer and Kritik Nathan will be married a week from now, on the fifteenth of July." He reads out both our parents' names, grandparents' names, the venue, and the மூஹூர்த்தம்[6] when Kritik will tie the thali around my neck and officially become my husband.

My husband.

---

6. Auspicious time.

I stare at the valakku, vision blurring, the two words echoing repeatedly in my head.

In a week's time, I will be his wife.

The சுமங்கலி பிரார்த்தனை[7] is conducted one day before the wedding date.

Amma and I haven't talked since the day of the engagement. Even during the ritual, we're quiet, focused solely on the task at hand. By the time the Sumangali prayers are over, I'm exhausted. Although everyone continues to celebrate downstairs, I retire to my bedroom early, and nobody bothers me.

I seat myself on the cushioned stool in front of the mirror, desperate to undress, clean up, and get into bed. I've barely slept the past week, the imprint and my anxiety keeping me up late at night. It's not like I can speak to anyone about it either. I am part of a joint family, but I'm more alone than one can imagine.

I've only just unpinned my hair when there's the sound of flapping wings outside my window. My heart almost stops as I spot a bat outside the glass, perched upside down above the sill.

I stumble over to the window, sliding it open for it to fly inside. It lands on my bed, drops a note onto the quilt, and zips out before I've had a chance to thank it. The cool night air rushes in, and shivering, I pick up the note.

I know it's from Kritik before I've even opened it, but I'm dead scared because the last time I received a note from him, he ended our relationship.

---

7. Sumangali prayer (a function conducted every year—or before any auspicious occasion, such as a marriage, in which the function is treated as an official send-off for the bride—by Brahmins to honor the women in the family who have passed away. Though all the women in the family attend the ceremony, only Sumangalis—women who are married and live with their husbands—and young girls who haven't attained puberty yet are allowed to sit for the actual ritual).

You're literally getting married to him, I think, *what could he possibly want to say? That he wants to break it off?*

I snort at the stupidity of the thought because that's the last thing either of our parents would allow, or we wouldn't have even been engaged. And breaking off a wedding post-engagement is a stain to reputation neither Appa nor Balaswamy can take. I take a deep breath, open it, and read the contents in his awfully familiar handwriting:

Dear Shloka,

I know we're getting married the day after tomorrow, but I need to see you before. There's so much I couldn't say after our engagement because there were too many people, and I can't write all of it down.

If you can, meet me at our spot at midnight. I'll be waiting for you.

—Kritik

Sneaking out of my house is easy; there's a hundred-year-old tree outside that's as tall as our mansion, and one of its branches winds right past my window. I scale it downward to our back garden, comfortable in the cotton kurta and tights I've changed into. Then it's across the grass and over the fence, and I'm in the forest. My fangs are out and bared in case I run into danger, and my now-red vision helps me see clearly in the dark.

It takes ten minutes to get to our spot from there. The trees clear a few feet ahead, and through the mist, I see Kritik's outline. I pull my fangs back in and my vision clears, getting rid of the reddish hue. Then I comb my fingers through my hair as I step out, leaving it wind-blown and waving down my back.

The fog parts to reveal a small, rocky space that gradually drops into the forest below. A hundred memories and emotions hit me at once. Kritik's sitting on the rock where we had our first kiss, dressed in a long-sleeved gray sweatshirt and black pants. His hair dances in the wind, pushed away from his forehead. I dodge the craggy path to him, and he turns to me as I draw closer, a smile spreading across his face.

"Hey," he says, holding his hand out.

"Hi," I say, taking it. An electric current rushes through my palm and up my arm as he hoists me up onto the rock. I sit next to him, brushing my hair away from my face. There's a pile of blood-stones on the mossy floor behind the rock, which provides a faint light so we can see each other despite the moonless night.

"You look gorgeous," Kritik says. "As always."

"Thank you."

"I haven't been here since the last century."

"Same. But it doesn't feel like it's been that long, does it?"

"No," Kritik says, and gazes intensely into my eyes. "The memories are as fresh as ever."

My face turns hot as a memory dribbles in. The mossy floor behind us was where we first made love, on a frayed picnic blanket, drunk on wine. It's been ages, but it feels like just yesterday that we were lying here, side by side, staring up at the star-studded sky.

"What did you want to tell me?" I ask, trying to stop the ache in my stomach from building.

"I need to give you something first." Kritik puts his hand in his pocket and pulls out a package wrapped in newspaper. Before he even opens it, the strong scent reveals the jasmine garland within.

This guy, I swear.

"Where did you even get this from?" I say, concealing how truly touched I am.

"I stole it from the puja room," he says with a lopsided grin.

"Seriously?"

He nods, and then holds the garland up. "May I?"

"Yes."

There are two hairpins attached to the end of the garland. He leans toward me, breath caressing my cheek and ear, hands looping around my neck to pin the flowers to my hair. This is the closest I've been to him in forever, and my eyes automatically shut. A kinetic charge builds between us, and I know Kritik feels it, too, because his hands tremble ever so slightly. He fumbles for a few seconds and moves back once he's done.

Our faces are so, so close.

My eyes are half shut, and I'm looking at him through my lashes. Kritik's palms cup the sides of my face, and my stomach does cartwheels. "Slo," he whispers, using his thumb to stroke my cheek. "What are we doing?"

"I don't know," I say breathlessly. "I just know that I need to kiss you right now or I'll hurl myself off the cliff."

"Me too," he says, brushing his mouth against the corner of mine, making my lips tingle.

I start to turn my face so I can capture his lips fully, but he moves away. His palms tighten on my cheeks.

"We need to pause for a moment and consider what we're doing."

"Does it matter?" I cannot remember the last time I was this desperate to kiss someone. "We're going to be married tomorrow. We're imprinted."

"Yes, but those are things that were forced upon us. By our tradition. By our Gods. The yearning we have—to be around each other—is real, but we've been reunited after decades of being apart. We're both hurt and we're healing."

"What do you mean?"

"I want to know if you see a future with me." Kritik's eyes brim with fierce emotion. "I want to know if you think you can fall in love with me again. I want to know if we can have a relationship outside of our blood bond and marital contract. The way we used to."

I gaze up at him, overwhelmed. Desire might've been a temporary respite, but what Kritik's saying parts the clouds shadowing my mind. I thought I had no say when it came to any of this, but Kritik's offering me a chance to see beyond what the fates have decided for me.

"I don't know." I shake my head. "At this point, the only thing drawing me to you is the imprint." A part of me knows that's not entirely true, but I'm not ready to come to terms with my emotions. Yet. "I—unloved you all those years ago, Kritik."

"Do you think those emotions can come back?"

"It'll take time."

"I'm willing to wait as long as it takes for you to fall for me again." Kritik places his forehead against mine. "I never stopped loving you, Shloka. I need you to know that. Because I see a future with you. I always have. And someday, I hope you can, too."

Iyer weddings are a two-day-long affair. We go through the rituals in the grand banquet hall in our residence, which our servants have been decorating and prepping for ever since the date was announced.

As the guests from Wellington and Coonoor arrive, our driveway fills up with shaded cars. The Nadaswaram players pipe out tunes in varying octaves, accompanied by the chatter of ladies resplendent in kanjivaram sarees. There are technicolor flower garlands decorating every nook and corner, and at the very center of the raised platform, the sacral fire burns merrily. Long buffet tables have been set out along the far corners of the wall, on either side of the stage, displaying a lavish feast—everything from a live dosa counter, three types of payasam, six types of chutneys, idlis, vadas, rice, sambhar, rasam, appams, uthappams, avial, kesari, and curd rice.

Vrutham and Kaapu are conducted on the first day, followed by Paligai and Januvasam, all of which are rituals mostly centered around the groom. Brahmins believe that men live their lives in four stages. Until now, Kritik was in the Brahmacharya (student) stage, and since he is to be married, he must go through the rituals to make a switch to the next stage, Grihastha (householder). It has always been the way grooms in our family have been inducted into the next stage, so Kritik's occupied the full day, clad in the traditional white mundu and veshti. I sit through them all, but actively participate only during the repeat of the நிச்சயதார்த்தம்[8] ritual.

The first day ends with a makeshift reception for the guests, after which we have performances scheduled by Carnatic singers and Bharatanatyam dancers. I barely sleep that night.

But if I thought the first day was tiring, the morning of the actual wedding is one full of chaos.

After I've bathed, shaved, and exfoliated thoroughly (for the fourth time in the past month), Amma and her sisters sit me down in front of the dressing table at four in the morning despite my protests. They take a huge leap up from what they did the last few times, even calling my athais to help.

They drape me in six yards of blood-red kanjivaram silk, with a border and blouse sewn from real gold. My makeup is darker, and jasmine garlands are clipped to my hair, which is half up and half down. Bloodstones and gold glitter on my ears, throat, and forehead, the heaviest temple jewelry I've ever worn. I swear if

---

8. Engagement.

someone sliced my head off and ran away with it, they wouldn't have to work another day in their lives.

This is the grandeur of South Indian weddings, and they most certainly are a notch above those ridiculous white royal weddings that seem to keep happening every decade.

The ladies work tirelessly, and I doze off through most of it. Younger me used to dream of these moments, as I watched every girl in my family get married in a glorious way. But Kritik—or, as I now know, his parents—crushed that dream.

And they came right back to taunt me for it.

When Amma finally helps me up, I nearly topple backward because my legs have fallen asleep. My body prickles as blood rushes back into its thirsty crevices and corners. But I barely feel the pain, because my attention is fixated on my reflection in the mirror. Everyone's is. Amma is crying, and Periamma rubs her shoulder up and down in comfort, whispering soothing words.

"You look like an அப்சரா[9]!" Athai says, pecking me softly on my cheek.

No, I think to myself, my throat hitching, *I look like a bride.*

I turn to Amma, who is sobbing into Periamma's shoulder. "Could you give me a few moments alone with her?"

Periamma nods, and slowly lifts Amma's head. I take Amma's hands as the other ladies leave the room, door shutting behind them. There's a long moment of silence between us. I reach my mehndi-patterned hands out and wipe the tears streaking her cheeks.

"அழாதே அம்மா[10]. If you cry, how am I going to get through today?"

"I'm sorry," she says, burying her face in our clasped hands. "For everything." She's too choked up to say the rest of it, but I

---

9. Apsara (celestial nymph).
10. Don't cry, Mom.

know what she means.

"It's okay." I tenderly kiss her forehead, pulling her into my arms. I know her apology can't undo everything, but if I'm going to say goodbye to my family, to her, I don't want to leave unspoken words hanging in the air.

"I've been a horrible mother to you. Now you're getting married, and you look so beautiful, and I can't even say everything I want to—"

"You don't have to. I get it. And it's *okay*."

"Will you call me?" Amma looks up at me, her eyes wide and moist. "After you move there?"

"I will. You know that. And I will come home every weekend. I'm barely fifteen minutes away."

"I love you so much."

I smile wistfully down at her.

"I love you too, Amma."

I am taken before Kritik only once the Kasi Yathra ritual is over.

I've always loved that little bit about Iyer marriages, where the groom, now in the second stage of his life, suddenly pretends to get cold feet and goes off to continue pursuing his education in the hopes of escaping from worldly clutches and duties. And that's when the bride's father steps in, convincing the groom to stay by offering his daughter's hand in marriage.

As the groom relents, both families continue pleading with him, and they offer him toiletries, slippers, and new clothes, all in the hopes of ridding him of the grime he's collected in his time as a student because he's been unbothered by his appearance. Then the groom takes a bath, cleansing himself for the next stage, and that's when the bride is brought in front of him.

All of this is performed like a play, and I remember exploding with laughter once as a kid when one of the grooms refused to come back until they brought him a box of motichoor ladoos. Which they eventually did.

How delightful that I'm missing the one part of my wedding I'd always looked forward to.

My stomach churns with anxiety as I'm led into the marriage hall. I didn't feel like this yesterday because the actual marriage wasn't happening then. But now, flanked by Amma, Periamma, Chithi, and my athais, it hits me that once I walk into the hall, I will exit only once I've become a wife.

Fuck, I need to throw up.

I swallow the squeamish feeling as we enter the hall, and everyone turns to look at me. There are "oohs" and "aahs" and gasps and compliments showered generously upon me by the guests, and it's the one thing that offers me respite. Because I've realized that when you look good, you also feel good. And God knows I need a reason to feel good right now.

The crowd's huge, but even through it all, I can sense him, my blood surging as I draw closer to him. The sea of people splits, and I'm led through it toward the platform, where the sacral fire burns.

Where Kritik is seated.

He's looking at me as if I just dropped from the moon. I join him on the stage, puckering my heavy saree in my hands so I can find a comfortable way to be seated. The mundu only covers part of his torso, revealing his smooth, toned back and stomach. I blush: not just because I've seen him way more undressed before, but also because he looks . . . broader, somehow. As if he could whisk me away with one arm. Or thrust me up against a wall.

"Why are you blushing?" Kritik whispers, as the priest greets the guests and introduces the rituals to be followed today.

"Why are you staring?"

"Because you're more gorgeous than anything I've ever set my gaze on."

I don't know if it's the proximity to the fire or his compliment but heat rushes to my cheeks. "Thank you."

"Stop thanking me. And get used to me saying it, because you're going to hear it for the next few centuries." Kritik gives my thigh a brief and discreet squeeze, and I feel his touch through all the layers. It nearly makes me gasp out loud.

Get yourself together, Shloka!

"You look good, too. You're . . . muscular."

Kritik chuckles. "Yeah, I used to be really skinny."

That's when the priest turns to us. "Shloka Iyer and Kritik Nathan, I request you to make your way down the platform for the Maalai Mathral. In the meantime, I request the maternal uncles of the couple to step forward."

Kritik gets to his feet immediately, stretching a hand out to me. I take it, and I swear I hear girly giggles in the back of the marriage hall. We get off the platform slowly and walk toward our uncles, all of whom pretend to crack their knuckles and stretch their bodies to ready themselves. The Nadaswaram in the background loudens; Kritik and I are handed the garlands; and before I know it, my mama has lifted me up.

I squeal as I'm raised above the crowd, and my other mamas rush forward to help carry me. Kritik lets out a loud laugh as his uncles struggle to hoist him up, but then his cousin comes forward to help, and somehow, he's up as well.

Our eyes lock in this space above everyone else, smiles lighting up our faces. The Maalai Mathral involves the exchange of flower garlands exactly three times, with one being above the other each time. It signifies that if we ever feel above our partner during the marriage, expecting them to give in, then we must be ready to give in at times as well.

As Kritik and I are carried forward, I reach out to loop the garland around his neck, but he dodges me, grinning, making everyone burst into laughter. I mock glare at him and have to try two more times before finally managing to get the garland on. Cheers explode around the room, and the Nadaswaram pipes louder, filling the hall with its happy, melodic tunes.

Kritik hoops the garland around me on the very first try, and he gets so close for a moment I can almost reach out and touch him. My eyes sting with tears as we exchange the second set of garlands, and then the third—one step closer to being wed.

This is what I dreamed of. And the person looking at me right now, all smiles—is *who* I dreamed of.

Once the Maalai Mathral has been done, we're carried to the corner of the room where the Oonjal swing has been set up. Kritik and I sit side by side on the wooden swing, lit up by lights and flowers. As it rocks gently back and forth, our relatives sing songs, bless us, and ward off evil eyes. Kritik and I steal intermittent glances as we swing, catching each other laughing, both feeling unnaturally surreal.

Among the swarm of ladies blessing us, one lady approaches the swing, her brown eyes twinkling as she smiles warmly at me. Her dark hair is cropped in a bob, and she has a cute mole above the left corner of her mouth.

"What a lovely couple," she says in broken Tamil with an accent that indicates she isn't from here. She bends down, dazzling in her cornflower-blue saree that doesn't look to be kanjivaram silk, hands smearing milk and sandalwood paste on my feet. "May you have the strength to find each other even among the rocky times."

"Thank you so much . . . Auntie? I'm sorry, I can't seem to place you right now." I smile sheepishly. She isn't from our cult, and I can't recall having seen her in any of my relatives' weddings before—although she certainly acts like she knows me. Maybe she's from Kritik's side? I can't confirm it with him right now, though, because he's occupied with another relative.

Auntie leans forward and places a kiss on my forehead. "That's all right, love. My own wedding was a big, fat desi one, and I didn't know ninety percent of the people present there. And trust me when I tell you a *lot* of people attended it."

I laugh softly. "Are you here from Kritik's side?"

She flaps her hand, chuckling. "Oh, here and there."

What is that supposed to mean?

Before I have a chance to ask her, she strokes my head, saying, "I must leave now, but before I go, I want you to know he's a lovely one, Shloka. Keep him close to your heart, even if it takes you time to let him touch it."

I stare up at her, surprised. I turn to Kritik, placing my hand on his shoulder, and he looks at me, eyebrows raised in question. "Before you leave," I say to the auntie, turning back. "I thought you might like to speak to Kritik as well . . ."

My voice trails off.

"Who're you speaking to?" Kritik asks, frowning at the empty space where the auntie stood just seconds ago, warmth and famil- iarity oozing from those warm brown eyes.

"She was right here," I splutter. "A relative of yours."

"What did she look like?"

"Bob cut, mole in the left corner of her mouth. She knew my name as well."

"Weird."

Especially considering that she'd (sort of) indicated she was from Kritik's side. But if she was, why would she not bless Kritik and leave? Before I can dwell on the thought of the auntie for too long, we're approached by another set of chattering guests.

After the Oonjal ritual, we head back to the platform, our hands clasped, and the priest announces that Amma and Appa must come forward for the Kanya Daanam.

Appa steps up to the platform and seats himself cross-legged on the floor. I avoid his gaze as I walk up to him and seat myself on his lap, as the ritual will soon involve him "giving me away" to Kritik.

Appa is stiff behind me. I shut my eyes as the sudden memories of sitting on his lap in my childhood trickle in. I miss those days, when not a day went by without us spending time together. He used to be so different, so jolly, so loving.

Leadership changed him.

The priest gives me a betel leaf, areca nut, and a gold coin to hold in my palms. Appa circles his arms around me to cradle my hands. His hands are big, calloused, and warm, and they give me a sense of comfort I haven't felt in a long while. I have to blink rapidly to stop my tears, and Kritik glances at me worriedly as he places his hand underneath the cradle of our hands.

Amma pours water from a pot in a steady stream, onto all our hands, and as the water cascades, Appa slowly places my hands in Kritik's. This is a sign that he's giving me away to him, passing on the responsibility of taking care of me and protecting me. I don't break eye contact with Kritik when this is happening because I feel like I'll burst into tears if I look away for even a second.

Everything's getting all too real.

The water stops pouring. Amma straightens, her eyes shining with tears. My hands are now in Kritik's, who holds them tightly. I turn to look back at Appa one last time before the priest says I can get off his lap.

I'm shocked to find he's crying.

Amma nearly gasps when she notices it, mere seconds after I do, and for a fraction, it's like the four of us are alone in this room, with no one around. Appa's cheeks are streaked with tears and his shoulders tremble as he cries. I am completely immobile on his lap, overcome with too many emotions at the same time.

I have never, ever seen him like this.

"Slo," Kritik mouths, loosening his grip on my hand. "Hug him."

I stare up at him, and then down at our hands. Then I hand him the areca nut, betel leaf, and coin, and turn toward Appa. He looks up at me, his eyes speaking volumes too vast for words. And I see it all. The regret, the sadness, the apology.

I wrap my arms around him.

The crowd hushes. Even the Nadaswaram players stop playing as I hug Appa, who hugs me back, tight, sobbing quietly into my shoulder. He is more vulnerable than he's ever been around me, around anyone. That ice in his heart is melting.

"என் அன்பே[11]," he says. "I'm so sorry."

"It's okay, Appa," I whisper back.

---

11. My dear.

The Season Ends

A layer of snow dusted the cottage roof. The vibrant greens and bright pinks and violets of summer had dulled as the season passed. Stomach full of gulab jamun and garlic naan, the invitee entered her home. The rich aroma of freshly brewed chai stirred the air. Her home knew just how to make her feel welcome. Taking off her bangles and dupatta, she headed for the kitchen. The invitations on the table were long cleared, a steaming cup taking their place. Another successful wedding season had come to a close. A season full of beautiful brides, handsome grooms, and loving, and at times overwhelming, family members.

Tempted by the chai, she grabbed the cup waiting for her and thought of all the magic and love she witnessed, and how much more she would the following season. Yes, next season would be just as enchanting as this one, and she couldn't wait for it to begin. But for now, she was content and satiated and ready to hunker down until wedding season returned.

As she sat back in her chair, the mail bell chimed. She leaned forward and caught sight of a thick white envelope slipping through the slot in the doorway.

Then again, it was never too early for another wedding season.

Acknowledgments

NOREEN

Bismillah hir rahman nir rahim.

Thank you, Prerna, first and foremost for including me in this anthology, and being so patient with me as I fought numerous deadlines writing and otherwise. Sarah, for inviting me to be part of this collaboration. Lauren and Page Street, for letting us tell brown and happy stories. All my fellow authors, for writing these wonderful stories. My family, for putting up with my absences and supporting me in this dream.

ANAHITA

I would like to extend my heartfelt gratitude to Mrs. Anuradha Harish, whose blog was the best resource I stumbled upon as I was researching Iyer weddings and rituals for A VERY BLOODY KALYANAM. Her posts hold a gold mine of information with detailed explanations and writing that creates gorgeous imagery. Without her, I would've not been able to do justice to my depiction and critique of Tamil Brahmin culture, and I'm so honoured she's my writing mutual now. Additionally, I am beyond grateful to Prerna for having given me this opportunity (she truly made my desi wedding dreams come true) and my wonderful beta readers Srishti Yadava, Mansi Rao, Varija Nateshkumar, and Megan Fletcher for reading an early version of this story. Lastly, I would like to thank my mother, Dr. Nithya Karthik, for reading this story with a hawk's eye and making sure I submitted not just a clean, proofed draft, but also one that balanced the culture and myth well.

AAMNA

Thank you so much to Prerna Pickett for arranging this anthology and to our lovely editor, Lauren Knowles. Thank you to my agent, Emily Keyes. Thank you to my wonderful family, especially to my sister, Zaineb, and my cousins, Noor, Mahum, Hamnah, and Umaymah. Thank you to my amazing friends, especially to Arusa, Isra, Sara, and Justine. And thank you to all the readers!

IASHIE

Thank you to all of my loved ones, but a special thank you to Maheen, Nabil, Naveed, Nivali, Raisa, Sheehan, Tahsin, Tiana, and Zareen. I named y'all alphabetically, so no complaining about who comes first!

SYED

My thanks to Prerna Pickett for inviting me to be part of this project and her hard work of getting this anthology together. I'd also like to thank Lauren Knowles, Alexandra Murphy, Shannon Dolley, Hayley Gundlach, and the entire Page Street Kids team for their hard work on this project. Also, as always, I'm grateful to and for my agent, Melissa Edwards, for everything she does.

PAYAL

One of the most enjoyable parts about writing "A Confluence of Fates" was drawing inspiration from my own Gujarati-Zoroastrian wedding. The story pays homage to the blending of two beautiful cultures and I'm grateful to have had the chance to relive it! The details about Zoroastrian wedding customs, especially the lavish wedding feast, wouldn't have been possible without my mother-in-law Kamal Moradian's meticulous input as she guided me in creating an authentic Zoroastrian wedding setting. I'm ever so grateful to her, Sangeeta Ramakrishnan, Mary Anne Williams, and Feroza Mehta who (always) on very short notice read my many drafts and offered their invaluable insights. I couldn't write this story or any book if it wasn't for my ride-or-die husband, who isn't a fiction reader but reads all my drafts and finds the most creative ways to entertain our daughter so Mummy can get her writing time. I'm indebted to Olivia Chadha for thinking of me for this anthology and to Prerna Prickett, Lauren Knowles, and Page Street Publishing for trusting me to lend my voice to this delicious mélange of culturally rich and fun-filled stories. Lastly, I would be remiss not to mention the Hilton in Bloomington, Minnesota where I checked in for a night and speed-wrote the first draft with a (un) healthy supply of coffee and barbecue Lays!

PRERNA

I want to start off by thanking my amazing family for always supporting my dream and encouraging me to pursue my passions. Cam, I love you so much, thank you for always being my biggest fan. To my kids: Thank you for inspiring me every day, I love you all (equally). To all the incredibly talented authors who agreed to be in this anthology you have no idea how much it means to me—thank you for trusting me with your stories. A big shout-out to my former agent Veronica Park for believing in me and this anthology. To Lauren Knowles: Thank you for being the absolute best champion for MBFDW, I couldn't have done this without you. To the team at Page Street: Alexandra Murphy, Shannon Dolley, Hayley Gundlach, Lauren Cepero and Lizzy Mason—you have been a dream to work with. Thank you, Rosie Stewart, for your amazing cover design and Azra Hirji for bringing it to life. Finally, thank you to all the readers for choosing this anthology. I hope it brought a smile to your face.

About
the Authors

SARAH MUGHAL RANA is an author and student. Her contemporary debut *Hope Ablaze* releases 2024 from Wednesday Books and Macmillan. She completed her bachelor's at the University of Toronto and is now at Oxford University specializing in Asian studies. She works at the intersection of human rights and policy. She is a BookTok personality and the co-host of *On the Write Track* podcast. Outside of school, she falls down history rabbit holes and trains in traditional martial arts.

NOREEN MUGHEES loves hugging trees, people, and cute kittens when she's not daydreaming about HEAs for brown people like her. A desi food addict, she loves cooking and having a mug of garam chai (hot tea) next to her. When not writing she can be found traveling to places—real and imaginary.

ANAHITA KARTHIK (she/her) is the Indian, queer author of *Better Catch Up, Krishna Kumar*, her debut YA road-trip rom-com slated to release in 2025 with HarperTeen. She is a soon-to-be postgraduate student at the University of Cambridge, author of the Amazon bestselling short story *All I Have Left* and a contributor for *My Big, Fat, Desi Wedding* anthology. When she's not reading or writing, she takes commissions for social media graphics and mentors querying authors. You can find her @ana_scribe everywhere, or check out her website at anahitakarthik.com.

AAMNA QURESHI is a Pakistani, Muslim American who adores words. She grew up on Long Island, New York in a very loud household, surrounded by English (for school), Urdu (for conversation), and Punjabi (for emotion). When she's not writing, she loves to travel to new places where she can explore different cultures or to Pakistan where she can revitalize her roots. She also loves baking complicated desserts, drinking fancy teas and coffees, watching sappy rom-coms, and going for walks about the estate (her backyard). She currently lives in New York. Look for her on IG @aamna_qureshi and Twitter @aamnaqureshi_.

TASHIE BHUIYAN is the author of *Counting Down with You* and *A Show for Two*. She recently graduated with a bachelor's degree in Public Relations, and hopes to change the world, one book at a time. She loves writing stories about girls with wild hearts, boys who wear rings, and gaining agency through growth. When she's not doing that, she can be found in a Chipotle or bookstore, insisting 2010 is the best year in cinematic history. (Read: Tangled and Inception.)

SYED M. MASOOD grew up in Karachi, Pakistan. A first-generation immigrant twice over, he has been a citizen of three different countries and nine different cities. He is the author of two YA novels, *More than Just a Pretty Face* and *Sway with Me*.

PAYAL DOSHI (she/her) loves to write about fantasy adventures set in her home country of India that celebrate her South Asian heritage. Her debut middle grade fantasy novel, *Rea and the Blood of the Nectar*, was the recipient of the IPPY Gold Award. She graduated from The New School in New York with a master's in creative writing. Raised in Mumbai, she currently lives in Minneapolis, Minnesota with her husband and precocious five-year-old daughter, and can be found daydreaming about fantasy realms to send her characters into. This is her first foray into the world of YA contemporary and romance short stories! Her favorite smell is that of old, yellowed books. And coffee, of course.

PRERNA PICKETT was born in India and raised in Northern Virginia. She has seen many places and loved most of them. Being a writer has always been Prerna's dream and she quite enjoys living that particular dream. Her debut, *If You Only Knew*, was released with Macmillan in February of 2020. She currently resides in the Pacific Northwest with her one husband and many children. You can find more up to date information by visiting her website www.prernapickett.com.